MW01505801

NINA LAURIN

The Last Thing She Saw

"This book was suspenseful, propulsive and not to be missed!"

—TheBookishLibrarian.com

"I think this one would make an excellent TV series, something along the lines of *Sharp Objects*. This may be the author's best yet."

—CravenWild.com

A Woman Alone

"Laurin crafts a *Rebecca* for a new generation, tapping into the old fears of domestic security, predecessor anxiety, and adding in a dash of high-tech paranoia. This is domestic suspense taken to a logical, terrifying extreme." —CrimeReads.com

"[A] chilling novel of psychological suspense.... Readers will keep turning the pages as the secrets of Venture's residents come out, along with potential motives for murder. Laurin is an accomplished storyteller." —*Publishers Weekly*

The Starter Wife

"This addicting thriller rachets up the suspense until the very last page."　　　　　　　　　　　　　　　　　　*—Woman's World*

"Laurin, with her knack for psychological suspense, here portrays the effects of obsession in chilling detail as the facts of Claire's life are revealed. A spine-tingler."　　　　*—Booklist*

What My Sister Knew

"Nina Laurin's psychological suspense thrill ride will have you ripping through its pages at warp speed as you dig for the truth about a fateful event that drove two twin siblings apart."

—PopSugar.com

"A twisty, mind-bending thriller that will keep you on the edge of your seat as she probes the bond and secrets between twins."

—USAToday.com

"There are an abundance of suspense/thriller writers, but none is better than Nina Laurin at fooling the reader as her plotline takes numerous 90 degree turns, while she builds suspense one red herring at a time."　　　　*—NYJournalofBooks.com*

Girl Last Seen

"Every good thriller has a shocking plot twist. *Girl Last Seen* has many. Author Nina Laurin's eerie novel will stay with you for days, months, even years to come."   —HelloGiggles.com

"*Girl Last Seen* by Nina Laurin is a chilling suspense about two missing girls whose stories intertwine—perfect for Paula Hawkins fans."   —EliteDaily.com

"From the very first page, *Girl Last Seen* jettisons the reader into the life of a crime victim trying to outrun her past. Fast-paced and hard-edged, it is a heart-stopping thriller that had me guessing to the very end."

—Heather Gudenkauf, *New York Times* bestselling author

THE SHADOW GIRLS

NINA LAURIN

GRAND
CENTRAL

New York Boston

This book is a work of fiction. Names, characters, places, and incidents are the product of the author's imagination or are used fictitiously. Any resemblance to actual events, locales, or persons, living or dead, is coincidental.

Copyright © 2024 by Ioulia Zaitchik

Cover design by Shreya Gupta
Cover images: Snake © Claire Rosen; bouquet and hand from Shutterstock.
Cover copyright © 2025 by Hachette Book Group, Inc.

Hachette Book Group supports the right to free expression and the value of copyright. The purpose of copyright is to encourage writers and artists to produce the creative works that enrich our culture.

The scanning, uploading, and distribution of this book without permission is a theft of the author's intellectual property. If you would like permission to use material from the book (other than for review purposes), please contact permissions@hbgusa.com. Thank you for your support of the author's rights.

Grand Central Publishing
Hachette Book Group
1290 Avenue of the Americas, New York, NY 10104
grandcentralpublishing.com
@grandcentralpub

First Edition: April 2025

Grand Central Publishing is a division of Hachette Book Group, Inc.
The Grand Central Publishing name and logo is a registered trademark of Hachette Book Group, Inc.

The publisher is not responsible for websites (or their content) that are not owned by the publisher.

The Hachette Speakers Bureau provides a wide range of authors for speaking events. To find out more, go to hachettespeakersbureau.com or email HachetteSpeakers@hbgusa.com.

Grand Central Publishing books may be purchased in bulk for business, educational, or promotional use. For information, please contact your local bookseller or the Hachette Book Group Special Markets Department at special.markets@hbgusa.com.

Print book interior design by Jeff Stiefel.

Library of Congress Cataloging-in-Publication Data
Names: Laurin, Nina, author.
Title: The shadow girls / Nina Laurin.
Description: New York ; Boston : GCP, 2025.
Identifiers: LCCN 2024047917 | ISBN 9781538707272 (trade paperback) |
    ISBN 9781538707289 (ebook)
Subjects: LCGFT: Detective and mystery fiction. | Novels.
Classification: LCC PR9199.4.L38415 S53 2025 | DDC 813/.6—dc23/eng/20241021
LC record available at https://lccn.loc.gov/2024047917

ISBN: 9781538707272 (trade paperback), 9781538707289 (ebook)

Printed in the United States of America

LSC-C

Printing 1, 2025

PRELUDE

March

THIS SIMPLY CAN'T be happening. Georgina can't wrap her head around it. She sits in the kitchen, a cup of herbal tea cooling in front of her, its plume of steam thinning until it disappears completely. She wishes she had something stronger. The kitchen's clean, modern lines, once familiar, now seem hostile and unknowable. Outside the window of the small but comfortable condo where she's lived with her daughter for over a decade, the darkness is complete. She can't bring herself to get up and turn on the light above the table.

A part of her wants to spring to her feet, her once-legendary legs eager to move. Not to perform a grand jeté but to run somewhere and scream in someone's face. Or maybe fall to her knees and beg—she's not above that. Anything to end this nightmare.

If only it were that simple.

Just this morning, everything was as it should be, everything

1

in its place. She made Anna a poached egg on spelt toast, filled her water bottle from the filter, and checked her duffel bag to make sure she had everything: the pointe shoe kit, leg warmers, toe tape. That afternoon was the first full rehearsal. Georgina dressed up for it, did her makeup extra festive, and now she sits here in her Valentino sheath, which is too tight now because the diets don't help, and with pearl studs in her ears that she loathes because of their origins, but they do look good against her skin. She sits here with six shades of taupe on her eyelids and mauve lipstick she's sure has smudged.

Just this morning, everything was right. Now her world has split apart as suddenly and irreparably as Anna's metatarsal.

It all happened because she didn't attend the rehearsal. The first time ever—she never missed a rehearsal until now. She was supposed to meet Anna later to celebrate, but just as she finished getting ready, she got the call.

An unfamiliar number. "Hello?"

She'd expected anything but this. As soon as the unfamiliar voice crackled in her ear, distorted by the bad connection, Georgina began to spiral into unreality. The words *fracture, break*—then all those medical terms she didn't really understand—seemed to fracture and break her instead. Crack, crack, crack, like blows of a baseball bat.

How could this have happened? How did it happen?

No one has any answers. Least of all Anna. Georgina went to pick her up at the hospital, and by the time she arrived, it was a done deal. A huge, clunky brace encased Anna's elegant foot—a perfect foot with a high arch and flexibility for fine footwork but with enough stability for hops and other moves that required endurance. The result of good genes, something no amount of money can buy. Anna sat there, blank-faced, and Georgina assumed she was in shock; they'd probably given her painkillers. The doctor had no answers either. He repeated words like a robot: *six to eight weeks, six to eight weeks. Don't you think I fucking know that?* she wanted to scream. *I danced ballet for two decades. How long once that hideous thing comes off?*

No one gave her an answer, but that, in itself, was the answer. Too long. Too long for Anna to dance in the end-of-year performance in front of recruiters from New York and San Francisco and everywhere else that mattered.

And Anna just kept repeating, like one of those dolls that say *Mama* when tipped over: *I just want to go home, please, Mom, let's just go home.*

Georgina took her home. But once the drugs wore off, Anna shuffled to her room, her crutches clacking down the hall before her door slammed. And that was it. She didn't say a word beyond *I fell,* delivered with a shrug. A shrug like she'd spilled a glass of milk, not destroyed her entire future.

How had it happened? Georgina had no idea. Where had it happened? Anna had been at school since before seven that morning. So it must have happened at school.

At last, this is the thought that clicks into place in Georgina's mind. It happened at school.

How could they have let this happen? To Anna. To their star. It's impossible. Unthinkable. *I fell*, she said, and everything they've worked for is in shambles.

Georgina wraps her hands around the ice-cold mug of tea and raises her head with painful slowness. No, it wasn't those two words. Everything had been falling apart for a while. She knew everything was about to go to hell all the way back then. Back when that new choreographer showed up...

ACT
ONE

1

August

GEORGINA HASN'T MISSED a single meeting since enrolling Anna at the school. Five years has been long enough for everyone to forget the supposed conflict of interest. No one would dare accuse Georgina Prescott of trying to curry favor—not after all the money and time she's invested. Every fundraiser, midyear concert, graduation gala, and final performance, Georgina was there. Her name might not mean much outside the shrinking world of ballet, but within its confines, it still holds weight. Eyes widen and eyebrows lift as much as Botox allows. "Georgina Mironoff," they say. "I loved you in *Swan Lake* in ninety-six!" Georgina smiles, clinks glasses, and the school can afford the fancy costumes, decorations, or new light equipment. What will they do without her?

Her last name isn't Mironoff anymore since she got married, and besides, Anna doesn't need anyone advocating for her.

Anna's dancing speaks for itself. It always has, ever since she first donned a tutu at age five.

On her way to the conference room, a windowless, soulless space with suspended ceilings and neon lamps, she catches a glimpse of her reflection in a glass door. The janitor just passed through, leaving smears on the glass; her face is distorted, her red-lipsticked mouth a blur. She stops cold. Her heart thrums, desperate to escape from under her rib cage, from under the tight embrace of her corset. She wants a cigarette, though she quit ages ago—mostly quit, at least when on school grounds.

"G!" A voice startles her. She hadn't noticed Fabienne sneaking up on her. "There you are. They haven't started, but the new AD is here. Come, I'll introduce you."

Right. The new AD—she hasn't forgotten. She organized the farewell party for the last one when Edith retired last spring. Edith assured her the replacement was someone worthy, experienced—a former dancer, then choreographer at a prominent European company. Someone with the right ideas to steer the school in the right direction, as Edith put it. Then Edith herself smiled magnanimously through the farewell party, accepted the giant bouquet of white roses Georgina had paid for, shed a single tear that didn't smudge her perfect makeup, and decamped to Florida.

"Georgina?"

She looks up to see Fabienne holding the door for her.

"Coming," she says, hurrying over, her heels clacking on the tile floor.

Fabienne teaches here, and the students love her. A little too much, in Georgina's opinion. A ballet teacher shouldn't be loved—she should inspire reverence and fear. A god who holds your future as a dancer between her manicured hands. But Fabienne prefers to be more Lilac Fairy than Carabosse, always gushing praise even when it's not deserved. But she loves Anna and feels almost as invested in her ballet future as Georgina herself.

The conference room door swings shut, locking with a soft, ominous click. Three of the other dance teachers and the vice principal are already seated in their usual spots, dictated by the unspoken hierarchy of the school. Perhaps that's why Georgina feels such cognitive dissonance: One of these things isn't like the others.

"Walter, meet Georgina. She helps with fundraising and organizes events. I don't know what we'd do without her."

Walter doesn't take Georgina's proffered hand. He doesn't even get up from his chair at the head of the table—where the school principal should be sitting. Walter measures Georgina with a look. She does the same, hovering awkwardly. Walter has a silver ring in his right nostril and several more in his ears. He drums his tattooed knuckles idly on the table.

"Georgina Mironoff," she says at last when the silence becomes untenable.

"Nice to meet you, Georgina." If she didn't know better, she'd swear the name meant nothing to him. And he has a pretentious accent—not British, but the kind of American who wants others to think he's British. She wants to ask why he's in Alexandra's seat, but when Alexandra breezes in, she doesn't notice—or pretends not to. On the contrary, she's beaming. Again, if Georgina didn't know better—

Alexandra launches into exuberant introductions: Walter Graf, here from Boston by way of New York and London. So that explains the accent. Georgina's apprehension turns to real alarm: The ice queen who rules the De Vere Academy with an iron fist is fawning like a schoolgirl.

"And of course, the all-important subject we're here to discuss: the ballet for our graduating class this year."

Finally, Georgina catches Alexandra's eye, like the woman only now notices she's there. She acknowledges Georgina with a nod and a smile.

"The class that includes, of course, Georgina's lovely Anna."

"*Sleeping Beauty*," Georgina says, surprised at the roughness of her voice. She clears her throat. "*Sleeping Beauty*. We all agreed it should be *Sleeping Beauty* this year."

"A classic," Alexandra says, her usual composure returning. The unbecoming grin slides off her face, replaced by her well-worn half frown. "We're lucky this year. Many promising graduates, and we need something to showcase their talents to the recruiters."

Georgina catches Fabienne's eye, and Fabienne nods in encouragement. *And such a beautiful part for our Anna*, Fabienne said last week.

The vice principal speaks up. "A beautiful ballet. Youthful. Perfect for springtime. Last year, we did a lovely production of *Romeo and Juliet*, but the cast..."

Alexandra winces. "Fifty graduating students, and we could barely find a half-decent Juliet. Not all years are equal."

"I thought it was nice," Fabienne chimes in, failing to read the room. "Melanie did a good job."

"Yes, and now she's probably serving French fries somewhere. With that skill level, we can forget about *Sleeping Beauty*."

Georgina zones out. There's nothing to fear. Anna can dance Juliet—she could have danced Juliet at twelve. More importantly, Anna can dance Aurora, and the role of Aurora is pretty much guaranteed for her. The other girls will be fighting for the remaining parts. Anna's place is secure. They talked about it at home, and Georgina had time to help her rehearse the more complicated moves, like the Rose Adagio with its impossible balances.

"The sets will be expensive," someone points out. "And the costumes—we might tailor the ones from last time."

"Perhaps I can help," Georgina says. "We'll figure it out."

"You all seem to have decided before I got here," Walter cuts in, his tone noncommittal, setting Georgina on edge.

"We pretty much have," Alexandra says. "It suits the class perfectly."

"And I'll bet you already have someone in mind for the principal roles."

Alexandra exchanges a glance with a dance teacher. "Of course. No point holding auditions when we already know the outcome."

"I like auditions," he says with an infuriating grin. "Good to see the students perform under pressure. Really shows who can handle stress. It's a skill they'll need in the future."

Georgina's blood boils. Who does this prick think he is?

"I, for one, am not so stoked about *Sleeping Beauty*."

It isn't up to you to decide, Georgina thinks, seething.

"If you had something else in mind—" Alexandra stammers.

"I gave it some thought. Last year, I saw the end-of-year performances—and Alexandra, I agree, half of those students shouldn't have graduated. But we need the checks from the parents. Although I digress. Forget the subpar *Romeo and Juliet*—I took special care to pay attention to the junior class."

Georgina momentarily feels better. Anna sparkled in the junior class performance, a scene from the White Act of *Giselle*.

"But I also snuck into a couple of rehearsals—"

What? No one told her. No one warned her. Her furious gaze travels across the faces at the table; even Fabienne looks away. She should have been told. She should have warned Anna.

"—and it gave me a better idea of who I'm dealing with than a polished final performance. The more I thought about it, the more I realized the best ballet to play to everyone's strengths—and weaknesses—will be *La Bayadère*."

Georgina's heart drops. *The Temple Dancer*, with Nikiya as

the principal role. Anna as Nikiya? They haven't prepared for that.

She, Georgina, hasn't prepared for that.

"That's ridiculous," she hears herself say. The room falls silent. Walter turns to her as if just remembering she's there—even though she sits directly across from him.

"And why is that?"

"It's just—" She stammers. "—It's so . . . sordid."

"It's no more sordid than *Swan Lake*. And God knows that's been done to death. Including here at the academy. Every other year it's *Swan Lake* or *Sleeping Beauty* or some other diabetes-inducing Tchaikovsky-Petipa creation."

"We haven't done *Sleeping Beauty* in—"

"You know perfectly well what I mean."

"And so do you." Georgina puts her hands firmly on the table. Her rings look dull in the neon light, emphasizing how clawlike her hands have become. To think she once had the best hands in ballet school . . . But—enough is enough. Someone has to stand up to him, and why not her? Anna will never forgive her if she springs a new role on her like this. "All that backstabbing and seducing. You want fifteen-year-olds to dance that? They could never dance those parts with any conviction. It's not a ballet for children."

At first, his face shows stunned incomprehension, and Georgina dares to think she got through to him. But then his eyes narrow, and his mouth stretches into a grotesque grin.

"Yes, I want fifteen-year-olds to dance that. Because no one will do it better."

"Georgina has a point," Alexandra chimes in. Georgina feels vindicated. Alexandra will put him in his place. "*La Bayadère* is a little too..."

"It's exactly what we need. But we'll make it simpler, more raw. The Russians' version, two acts only. And lose those problematic costumes. Save some money at the same time."

"Walter, with all due respect. Listen to yourself. You can't insult the ballets that made this school's reputation. You're insulting all of us."

He mirrors Georgina's stance, putting his hands down as well. Intentional, no doubt. Defying her overtly.

"It's still classical enough not to ruffle your more...senior... donors, and to uphold your precious reputation for pastel tutus. And I'm sorry, Georgina, but...with all due respect, as you say. When was the last time you danced? Your final ballet, what was it?"

Blood rushes to her face. Oh, if it weren't for Anna, she'd tell this prick exactly what she thinks. She'd tell him where and when she danced. She's sure he was in kindergarten when she was promoted to principal.

"Well, things have changed since then."

"Walter, please." Alexandra speaks up. "There's something to discuss for sure. But we're not going to change everything on a whim without talking it through."

"There isn't anything to discuss," Georgina says. "They'll be dancing *Sleeping Beauty*. That's final."

She immediately understands her misstep. He goaded her, and she fell into the trap. The frown on Alexandra's face tells her it's too late. "Alexandra, you've been running this school for how long? You know what's best. Don't you?"

Alexandra stays silent, avoiding Georgina's gaze.

Walter stands up.

"You know why I'm here? Because Alexandra wanted something new. Alexandra wanted a change of image. That's why Edith Spencer reached out to me. Because every year it's harder to gather the recruiters, or at least the good ones the students expect from this school. The donors are following suit. And the parents of all the little ballet prodigies, the next big things—everyone needs a little extra motivation to get out here, in the sticks. The academy is falling behind. Outdated. Musty. That's because your graduates aren't what the recruiters are looking for these days. Which is not *Sleeping Beauty* or *La Fille Mal Gardée* or some saccharine retread of *Romeo and Juliet*."

"Let me remind you we specialize in classical ballet. Which is alive and well. And before you break the rules, you must first master them—"

"And you wonder why recruiters from New York are taking a pass. This. This way of thinking." He jabs his tattooed finger in her direction. "Why are you here? Are you an employee of the school?"

15

"Georgina is an invaluable member of our collective," Alexandra pipes up, her face scarlet.

"Unless she's on the payroll, she doesn't belong here. So if nobody minds, we'll be holding our meetings without Ms. Mironoff in the future."

The late-August afternoon is a shock to Georgina's system. She checks her gold watch: four o'clock. She's not usually outside at this time. During the school year, this is when Anna gets home and Georgina prepares dinner. Even though Anna eats like a sparrow, it takes time to chop, slice, and steam everything. During summer break, this is when she supervises Anna's home rehearsal at the barre, set up in a crisply air-conditioned room.

Just as Georgina succumbs to the siren song of the pack of Benson & Hedges buried at the bottom of her purse, the door bangs open behind her. It's the emergency exit, but classes haven't started, so the alarm isn't connected yet. She looks up from rummaging through her Chanel tote, old but well preserved like an impoverished aristocrat. Fabienne holds out a cigarette to her, and Georgina doesn't like the pity in her eyes. Georgina danced Giselle and the Swan Queen to sold-out venues—people like Fabienne don't get to look at her with pity.

"How the hell did this happen?" Georgina asks, taking a grateful puff of the freshly lit cigarette. Fabienne's brand isn't to her taste, but now's not the time to complain. "How could Edith do this to me?"

"Edith didn't do anything," Fabienne says somberly.

"Well, she must have known who she was hiring!"

Again, that look of pity. It lasts only a second before Fabienne's gaze slides away to the toes of her cream-colored shoes.

"Sorry," Georgina mutters, fighting the urge to tap the ashes from the cigarette onto those satin shoes. That's a few hundred dollars down the drain.

"It wasn't Edith," Fabienne says. "It was Alexandra."

"No. Alexandra—this academy is her baby. She wouldn't wreck it like this."

"Everything he said was true, G. Enrollment's been at record lows for the last three years—"

"And I'm only hearing about this now?"

Fabienne says nothing. Georgina understands. That prick was right—she's not an employee of the school.

"There are other things we could've done. Galas. Advertising, for heaven's sake. If Alexandra wanted to bring the school into the present, she should've started an Instagram campaign. Not brought in that human wrecking ball."

"And the recruiters?"

"What about them? We had the artistic directors of the top companies last year—"

"And they left with nothing."

"That has nothing to do with the choreography. And this

year, they won't leave with nothing. Well, they might, if Alexandra lets him have his way. Did you see how she was staring at him? I thought they might start undressing each other right there on the conference room table."

Fabienne tactfully ignores the remark. "Our Anna will shine regardless. She's our star. And the rest of the class is pretty strong too—"

Georgina wants to scream, *I don't care about the rest of the class.* She's not supposed to say that—she's supposed to keep up the pretense that there's no conflict of interest. But here, alone with Fabienne, she can be herself. Anyway, no point worrying about conflict of interest now that she's been thrown out by that tattooed freak. "I care about the fact that my daughter's graduation role is a freaking belly dancer. *La Bayadère.* That's just a glorified stripper, isn't it?"

Fabienne sputters. "It's still a lovely part. In a classic ballet. And the Kingdom of the Shades scene is beautiful."

Georgina simmers down. "If he doesn't butcher it."

"Anna will make a great Nikiya. Naomi could do Gamzatti."

Georgina blinks. Right, Naomi—Anna's friend. She'd forgotten about Naomi. Now a new layer of dread gathers on top of the existing one. "That prick wants to hold auditions. Auditions! What the hell?"

"I'm not worried. He may hold all the auditions he wants, but he's not the only one who decides. We'll outvote him."

Georgina exhales a big puff of smoke. She already regrets

the cigarette: She hasn't eaten today, and the spoonful of sugar in her coffee doesn't count. The nicotine makes her hands shake. She stubs the cigarette out underfoot with unnecessary force. "How am I going to tell Anna? We've been preparing for Aurora all summer. She was so excited. She's loved this ballet since she was a little girl."

Fabienne puts her hand on Georgina's sleeve, a gesture meant to be calming, but it only puts her on edge. "No matter the role, Anna will shine. That's not what I'm worried about."

Georgina watches warily as Fabienne puts out her own cigarette, crushing it with three aggressive staccato stomps of those satin shoes that somehow remain impeccable, and then heads back indoors.

Alone once more, Georgina takes out her phone and looks dejectedly at the notifications on the screen. She left a message for Colter Prescott, her ex-husband, but he has yet to get back to her. She jolts unpleasantly when she spots the number of the one missed call; it's the second time in a week. She ignored the previous message, the polite, tentative voicemail the caller left her, but apparently avoidance wasn't enough to get her point across. Some people choose to be obtuse. Well, she supposes she'll have to call back and make it crystal clear.

The phone rings as she taps her foot. With every tone in her ear, her anger at such insolence grows. They agreed on this years ago, didn't they? A clean break, a fresh start. So why call her now?

Luckily—or not, depending on perspective—the call goes unanswered, so all of Georgina's pent-up fury is for nothing. She waits for the beep and then records a message:

"Listen, I don't know how you even got this number, but whatever it is you want, I'm not interested. You need to let it go. Don't call me again."

And stay away from Anna, she almost adds, but before she can do that, she ends the call, and the phone screen goes blank once more.

And then Georgina puts it out of her mind. There are more pressing matters at hand. She'll have to somehow find a way to break the news to Anna, to prepare for this new curveball, to help her learn and rehearse for her new role.

Anna deserves a chance to shine. That's all that matters. And Georgina won't let anyone take that away from her.

So she forgets about the phone call and the message, just like she forgets to ask what exactly it is that worries Fabienne.

2

NAOMI

IN BALLET FICTION, there's always that trope: the outsider who rises to the top against all odds. To be fair, it's not just in ballet fiction—it's in most fiction because the audience is supposed to identify with her. She's the girl without the natural advantages her nasty rival has, like perfect arches and obliging parents paying for ballet school. But she works harder than anyone. She overcomes obstacles, family strife, personal drama, biscuit feet, big boobs, you name it. In the end, she always dethrones the other girl, who is cast as the villain, the living obstacle to our intrepid heroine, like a human version of a big toe that keeps popping out of joint.

The truth, of course, would disappoint moviegoers and binge readers everywhere. In ballet, there's no such thing as working harder. Everyone in that studio, every girl in her leotard and pointe shoes, works at 100 percent of her capacity—or she wouldn't last a month in ballet school. And since everyone is giving their best, the girl with the natural advantages always wins. The girl who works 100 percent *and* has the right metatarsals. And the right build. And the right look.

At the De Vere Ballet Academy, that girl isn't me. It's Anna Prescott.

This is unfair to Anna because, besides being a natural-born ballerina, she's one of the nicest people I've ever met. In ballet, that sets a different standard. When you're that talented, you don't have to stoop to backstage drama. You don't fight tooth and nail for parts because your teachers are happy to lavish them on you. You never have to demean yourself, put glass in anyone's shoes or slip laxatives into someone's water bottle (which happens more often than the glass in the shoes). You can afford to be nice.

But that's not the only reason it's hard—nearly impossible— to resent Anna Prescott. Watching her dance the same adagio I just sweated through with ease and perfect grace, like she could hop on a real-life stage any second, I remember, for a brief moment, why I love ballet in the first place. Watching other students, I can't help but compare myself, mentally listing my weaknesses: Her jump is higher, her fouetté steadier. But watching Anna dance, I become a spectator. I can't compare myself because I could never dance like that in a million years.

Anna is perfectly positioned to be the villain of the story. She has a pretentious old-money last name. She has the mother who was a principal at the Massachusetts Ballet. And her dad has his own law firm in Boston. All these perks for someone who doesn't need them. What a waste.

But Anna being Anna, the competition in our class isn't for the principal role—that's always hers—but for the second best. The Lilac Fairy, Myrtha, Lady Capulet. Every once in a while, I get it, and I tell myself I'm satisfied.

But then, on any given morning, I stride into the studio, my pointe shoes slapping the floor, full of determination, and there, in the front-and-center spot at the barre right next to me, is Anna. That angelic face, blue eyes, porcelain limbs, vertebrae on display above the low-cut back of her leotard, and I feel stupid for even thinking it.

"Naomi!" Madame Fabienne, our morning class instructor, barks the moment I walk in. "Where have you been? We're not going to wait for you!"

I'm not even late. There's still a minute until seven. But I shut up and stand at the barre, second position, and get ready for another day. Another beautiful day in the shadow of Anna Prescott, my best friend.

The first day of classes usually starts with endless warm-ups with Fabienne, who never fails to stop by every single student to tell her how she's lost her form during the break, her arabesques look weak, her spine is stiff, her stomach sticks out, and that she should sign up for tap dancing at the community center. A great morale booster, Fabienne. But today, she's oddly quiet. She watches us wearily with those sunken eyes of hers. Some aging ballerinas blob out, and others do the opposite, flesh shrinking away beneath the skin. She's one of those. She looks like a crow in all black, with obligatory French-girl red lipstick, even though Fabienne hasn't lived in France in four decades.

Then the doors open, and the principal strides in, as usual, in high heels and with a dizzying veil of perfume that follows her like a vengeful spirit. She's not alone. There's a man with her.

"Class," she says, clapping her hands. She talks in a loud, grade-school-teacher voice that the room's acoustics amplify. "I'd like to welcome you all to the new school year. The year many of you will graduate."

Many of us—meaning some will get kicked out. Subtle as usual.

"At the same time next year, some of you will be starting your first season at ballet companies all over the world. It's an exciting time, but also a very important time. This is when all your hard work pays off. This is when everything is decided."

She pauses, the pause calculated and rehearsed, yet everyone drinks it up. Every pair of eyes in the room is on her, and I can tell she loves it.

"At our annual end-of-year performance, as you know, recruiters from top companies will be in attendance. Not to put the pressure on you or anything."

The remark gets the nervous laugh it was meant to. Alexandra waits as it dies down.

"This performance represents not just you—each and every one of you—but also the school. And, as I like to say, we at the De Vere Academy deal in dreams, in beauty, in magic, and all that still holds true! But—what many may not know—we are also at the forefront, on the razor's edge of technique and innovation in the world of dance. We blend the modern and the classic, the past and the future. We do the impossible. And to help us with that daunting task, I'd like to introduce you to our new artistic director and your choreographer for the end-of-year performance—Walter Graf."

The applause is thin at first but then picks up as they realize she's not kidding. This is probably the first time in the history of this room that someone has walked in wearing jeans. It's so tempting to sneak a peek at all the others' faces that I think I'm going to explode. But I manage to stay still, my gaze trained on Walter Graf. He looks self-satisfied, and no wonder. Probably anticipating lording it over a bunch of teenagers. There isn't a person over thirty who isn't secretly dreaming of putting us in our place, is there? Because their time was the real golden age of ballet or music or art or whatever, and we missed it. But at the same time, we magically have it too good and too easy, and that's why we expect everything to fall into our laps.

Walter Graf's gaze glides across all his new subordinates—pardon, students—as he takes in the wealth of smooth, young faces. It slows down when it reaches me. I can practically hear the screech of invisible brakes in the air. And then it slips away, to the next girl and the next.

I can't help but notice that in his hurry to look away from me, he slipped right past Anna without a second glance.

"Hello, students," he says. That accent—something about it takes me by surprise. Is it fake? It's got to be. He then runs his hand over his hair, a gesture fifteen years younger than he is, just like his outfit. He's got an undercut, and the top part is overgrown, flopping conveniently over his hairline, which, when he pulls the hair back, is revealed to be rather V-shaped. "You know what, I had a whole speech for you, but to hell with it. We're not here to talk. Everybody, take second position."

Anna and I exchange a glance, and she stifles a giggle. No one sees it except me, just like she intended. Outwardly, she's like one of those porcelain ballerinas in music boxes, turning and turning to a tinny waltz, delicate, blond, and blue-eyed. Like every good ballet dancer, she's a skilled illusionist. Everyone thinks she's the embodiment of perfect, dainty femininity, but they don't know her like I do.

So right now, everyone who looks at her sees what I'm seeing: perfectly turned-out feet encased in freshly broken-in pointe shoes, endless legs in silver-gray tights, the half moon of bare back exposed by a low-cut leotard, a chain of vertebrae like a perfect line of desert hills because Anna doesn't even need to starve herself to weigh under ninety pounds. Hair in a braided bun, not a strand out of place. The elegant curve of an arm, a hand as gentle as a feather. Even in a room full of other girls with long legs and straight backs and elegant arms, she stands out. Parked next to her at the barre day after day, I know I don't compare favorably, but I don't have much of a choice. Not because we're besties—no one here cares. We stand next to each other because we're supposed to be the two best dancers in this year's class.

And I wonder if I've only been delaying the inevitable because when Walter sees Anna—really sees her, and he will—he'll see perfection.

Then the music starts, and Fabienne barks orders like a drill sergeant, and we all do our plié/relevé over and over while Walter paces back and forth. Is this it, then? All this fuss, for nothing?

The music concludes, and we all go back to second position without being told. What now?

"I hope they're all just out of shape from summer holiday," Walter remarks—supposedly to Fabienne, but loud enough so we all can hear. Which, I suppose, was the point. But you should see Fabienne's saggy mug light up like Christmas came early.

Did he really just say *holiday* instead of *break* or *vacation*? What a colossal douche. I wish I could glance at Anna because I know she's thinking the same thing.

"You're all going to have to do a lot better than that," Walter says, "because *La Bayadère* is not a ballet for amateurs. Yes, I know—sorry some of you are disappointed—"

Is it just me, or does he glance at Anna when he says that?

"—but we're not doing *Sleeping Beauty*. *Sleeping Beauty* is sweet, sure, but if we want those recruiters to be interested, we have to give them something other than diabetes." Another look in Anna's direction. I risk a sideways glance, and her porcelain skin all but becomes transparent. I can practically see her heartbeat thrumming in her blue veins, like she's a dissected frog in biology class.

"So forget all your preconceived notions. The primas better pay attention because it's time to stop resting on your laurels. Those who have been wanting to prove yourselves—this is your big chance. I'll be doing the casting from scratch. So after warm-up, I want to see all of you in the main ballroom. The door will close at exactly eight thirty, and it won't open again until the audition is over, so don't be late."

"Shithead," Anna mutters. She's filling her pink water bottle at the drinking fountain, and she says it so quietly I'm the only one who hears. The girls behind me tap their pointe shoes on the floor. "Mom warned me. He's going to tank me on purpose, I just know it."

"It's so unfair." The squeaky little voice takes me by surprise. I spin around, and sure enough, there's Sarah. I never noticed how she snuck up on us, but here she is. Sarah sucks up to Anna because Anna comes from a ballet family and is everything

Sarah isn't and never will be. There's such a gulf between them that any competition would be pointless, so I guess it's the only strategy for someone like her. "You'd make such a beautiful Aurora."

And Anna, the angel that she is, gives her little sidekick a shit-eating grin. Then, as Sarah plods away (even though she's five foot two, her shoes are at least a seven and a half, poor thing), I watch as the grin slides off her face. Raw hatred glints in Anna's blue irises. "Yeah, beautiful Aurora. See? Nobody thinks I can do a dramatic role. Others are doing daring, original things, and I'll float through my whole career in a dusty white tutu. Or at least, until I'm, like, twenty-five and too old to be the ingenue."

"Nobody thinks that."

"This Walter does."

"Walter is a wannabe-British twat."

She fishes her phone out of her bag's side pocket. The flawless, uncracked screen of the latest iPhone lights up, revealing her wallpaper: Svetlana Zakharova as Odette, caught midleap against a powder-blue background. "Come on. Ten minutes left."

"Did he text you?" I ask sotto voce as we're about to merge with the stream of students headed for the main ballroom.

"Who?"

"Come on. You know who."

Anna grunts, which I take to mean no.

The main ballroom is a bit of a misnomer—it's a classroom like the others, with mirrored walls and barres all around, only much bigger. It's where all the main rehearsals take place. Here, the entire class fits along one wall, but even then, the hierarchy remains. Anna and I take our places in the center without thinking about it. There's Sarah, not too far off. Gemma, who's a decent dancer but has an anxious nature that makes her fail the easiest moves at the worst times. Samantha, tons of determination but the wrong proportions. Brianna, who stays because her uber-rich parents donate to the school. All the other ones, good but not great for a plethora of reasons. The guys aren't here, just the girls. Suppose Walter wants us all to himself.

"What's *La Bayadère* about?" Here in the main ballroom, the ceiling is high, and his voice carries. "Anyone?"

We've all been in ballet school since before we can remember, so yeah, everyone knows what *La Bayadère* is about. But maybe they're all intimidated by Walter because no one speaks or raises her hand.

I feel the pull of an irresistible temptation. What can he do to me? Knowing this is probably a bad idea, I speak up:

"The same as all the other great ballets. Everyone dies because some guy can't decide what he wants."

An uneasy laugh ripples through the class before fizzling out under Walter's pointed look. But if I didn't know better, I'd think that was a smirk lurking in the corner of his mouth.

"And who might you be?"

"Naomi Thompson."

"Naomi," he says, as if tasting the name. "I'm pretty sure I've heard that before."

Really now, you asshole.

"Someone mentioned you at the teachers' meeting. It wasn't all good but not all bad either. They said you lack subtlety. Can't imagine why they'd think that."

The class feels emboldened to giggle, now that it's at my expense.

"Well, you're not entirely wrong, Naomi Thompson. But let's look into the core of the thing. *La Bayadère* is . . ."

"A tragedy," Sarah pipes up.

"Thank you, Captain Obvious. Yes, a tragedy. We have our tragic heroine, Nikiya, aka the holy grail of roles, and her beloved Solor, but the princess Gamzatti wants him for herself, and tragedy ensues. *La Bayadère* is, at its core, a love triangle. But not like any love triangle you know. Not like your *Twilight* nonsense."

"Nobody reads *Twilight* anymore, you prick," Anna mutters next to me.

"There's no happily ever after. No peaceful resolution. And there never could be. The stakes here are life and death. Mostly death. Keep that in mind when you try out. You're dancing to the death."

He rattles off a sequence of moves, a complicated sequence. And it's not Nikiya's act one variation. Next to me, Anna looks panic-stricken. No wonder. She probably spent the last three days rehearsing every step of Nikiya's role under her mom's supervision.

"Go ahead. Surprise me."

Without being asked, Anna steps forward. Her spine is straight, her chin at just the right angle, her high bun emphasizing her doll-like profile. Her calves are somehow sinewy yet slim, her feet perfectly turned out, and the mirrors on all sides reflect it all back at her—back at all of us, Anna within Anna within Anna, a daisy chain of a hundred perfect little Annas.

Goddammit. This time next year, when I'm apprenticing in New York and she is—wherever she ends up—I'm going to miss the bitch.

3

Now

GEORGINA GETS READY to leave in a hurry. She doesn't bother with makeup, apart from a swipe of red lipstick—just enough to convey authority. You never get what you want by being a hysterical scarecrow.

But before she leaves, she can't resist peeking into Anna's room. She hovers at the door, where a welcome plaque features a ballerina in arabesque with the text DANCING IS DREAMING WITH YOUR FEET. Georgina made it herself when Anna started her first ballet class. This shade of purple was popular back then, but all the glitter has fallen off by now. Georgina considers knocking but then decisively turns the handle.

Anna is on the bed, her foot propped up on a pillow, leafing through an old issue of *Pointe* magazine. She seems reluctant to look up. "Mom?"

"I'm going out," Georgina says, unable to keep the cold out

of her voice. The guilt she feels for being angry with her sick child doesn't outweigh the anger itself.

"Do you think you could pick up some yogurt?" Anna asks innocently, stoking Georgina's fury. Is she doing this on purpose? "The usual, zero percent, strawberry, with stevia."

"I'm going shopping tomorrow," Georgina says. Anna shrugs. Even though she's already put on her outdoor shoes, Georgina steps into the room, tiptoeing on the carpet. Anna looks unkempt—her hair is in a fraying ponytail, greasy strands clinging to her forehead. Her skin has broken out, a rash of tiny red pimples along her hairline and jaw. Without wanting to, Georgina thinks of the incident months ago. Maybe she shouldn't have flown off the handle—the girl clearly needs more than Clearasil.

Indeed, a lot of things that used to get her worked up now seem...insignificant.

But what unsettles her isn't the acne, the dirty hair, or the whiff of BO she detects as she sits on the edge of Anna's bed. It's the look of complacency on Anna's face, the dullness in her eyes. She's never seen her daughter like this. She doesn't seem to mind being a mess.

"I don't understand how you can be so calm," she says, knowing she's about to lose her own calm.

Anna winces. "Mom, please..."

Georgina jabs her finger into the magazine cover. This issue features a soloist newly promoted to principal dancer at a major

New York company. "You know, at this rate, that'll never be you. Doesn't that bother you at all?"

"Mom, I'm still graduating. You know I am—Fabienne said so. Next year, I can go audition—"

"You bet you're going to audition," Georgina grumbles. "But all this hard work...Instead of auditioning, you could have signed with ABT or the San Francisco Ballet right after the show. It just kills me—"

"Mama." Anna lowers the magazine and puts her hand on Georgina's arm, a soft butterfly touch. Ever since she was a little girl, her every move overflowed with ballerina grace without her trying. You can't buy these things; you can't even work for them. You only get that from good breeding. And she doesn't understand. "I'll work all summer, and then I'll audition. I'll get in, one way or another."

And Georgina almost gives in, almost lets herself be mollified by those big eyes and that earnest face. But then she thinks of everything that's already happened this cursed year, everything she learned about her daughter, and reality snaps back like an elastic band stretched too far. "Anna, tell me what happened."

Her daughter's face hardens. She pulls back. "I already told you. I don't know."

"You do know. How can you not know? You fell. And you just happened to break your metatarsal? How stupid do you think I am?"

"I don't think you're stupid, Mama."

"Was it that boy? Did he have something to do with it? That's it, isn't it?"

Her daughter's face darkens. "James is back home in New York," she says. "He's been there for weeks now. This has nothing to do with him."

"Then why won't you tell me?"

She grips Anna's slim shoulders, feeling every bone. Anna's jaw clacks. She stares blankly at her mother.

"I'm sorry, okay?" Georgina mutters. She's never been good at this. There's nothing to be sorry for. Anna may have the natural advantages, but Georgina took them and made her into what she is—a future prima. "I just don't understand why—"

Her mind does what it does best, clicks over and finds a problem to solve, something she has control over. "There's still more than two months before the show," she says brightly, shooting to her feet. She should have eaten—the sudden movement makes her dizzy. "Six to eight weeks is enough. If we get you PT, then you can still make the show."

Anna gives her a blank look.

"Don't play dumb, Anna. We rehearsed it. We rehearsed it all, and I know you remember every move by heart. You always do."

The hospital is uncrowded at this hour. Winter is over, so the tide of ski injuries has receded. Georgina finds Dr. Huang's office by memory alone. The trick is to walk past reception, triage, and the nurses like you belong there, like maybe you're here to visit someone—though visiting hours have likely ended.

She gives two delicate knocks on the door with the silver plaque spelling out his name, waits for a response, then enters without wasting time.

"Lucky me," she says, "you're still here."

Luck wasn't involved—she called the hospital and lied to the receptionist to find out when he'd be there. But Dr. Huang doesn't need to know that. She barely noticed the first time, but he's young, early thirties maybe—can't be long out of med school.

From the looks of it, though, he recognizes Georgina instantly. His otherwise handsome face becomes drawn. "Mrs. Prescott."

"Ms. Mironoff," she corrects. "I'm so happy to have caught you. I wanted to apologize for my behavior the other day. I don't normally act like this, it's just—this is so stressful, both for Anna and myself. Anna's whole ballet future—"

"I'm aware of your daughter's ballet future," he says, "and believe me, it's not in jeopardy. Anna will absolutely make a full recovery. Now, if you don't mind—"

Georgina reaches into her purse and takes out the present. It's a bottle of champagne. A nice bottle, one she was saving for a special occasion. Well, the occasion isn't what she hoped for, to say the least, but it's as special as can be.

"Please accept this," she says, "as my apology."

He measures her with a look. "Mrs. Prescott, I understand you're not just here to apologize. But I've told you this already, and I'm telling you again. I can't share anything more about Anna's injury with you."

"What do you mean, you can't? I'm her mother. Of course you can. It's your duty as a—"

"Actually, Anna is sixteen. Correct? She turned sixteen last November. And as per the laws of this state, she's now entitled to patient confidentiality."

"Confidentiality." Georgina sputters, mispronouncing the word twice before she gets it right. That hasn't happened in years. She's spent almost two-thirds of her life in the United States. "Confidentiality. From her own mother? That's ridiculous."

"This is what Anna requested, and I must respect it. I'm really sorry."

He doesn't sound sorry. Georgina feels the anger rising in her chest like hot steam. It takes a titanic effort to stamp it down. "She doesn't tell me anything anymore," she says, her voice softer, plaintive. "Something terrible has happened to my little girl, and she won't even tell me what. And you don't want to help me. Okay, I understand you can't talk about the details of Anna's injury. Can't you at least tell me how it happened? She must have—"

But his expression remains impassive. "I believe it was a fall."

That's all she's going to get? A fall. *I knew it was a fucking fall, you idiot*, she wants to scream.

"How could she have fallen? Where?"

"At school, as logic would have it. Down some stairs, perhaps? There are so many ways to fall."

Georgina gulps. She can tell by his dismissive look that he's just making it up as he goes. Either Anna didn't tell him, or he's keeping the secret.

A secret. From her.

"Thank you," she forces herself to say, and proffers the bottle of champagne. "If you could just—"

"I can't accept that, I'm afraid. I don't drink. On the job or otherwise." And he gives her that flat shit-eating smile that's like a glass mask. She knows it. She's given it a number of times, but back when she was young and limber and a principal dancer at a prestigious ballet company, no one saw it for the fakery it was, or at least nobody cared. But now, her work is gone, her art is gone, and her power is gone. Wasted on all those ungrateful people who forgot her the moment she stepped off the stage. And the only lasting thing she has to show for it is Anna, but now even that is slipping away.

She puts away the bottle, turns on her heel, and walks out of the office. Before she's even made it to the lobby, she snatches her phone out of her purse.

Her hands are shaking, and she accidentally snaps off the tip of her fingernail in the purse's zipper. She scrolls through the contacts, marveling at how her extensive list has magically shrunk overnight. All the names are still there, sure, but now that she truly needs something, there's nobody to call.

She scrolls past Alexandra's number, seething. Everything she's done for her—for their school—only to be thanked like this. She gave her time, energy, and yes, money when she had it, for free, expecting nothing in return.

Finally, her jagged fingernail hovers over the right name. Before she can hesitate, she lets the rage course through her and jams her finger into the name as if wanting to punish the person on the other end.

It rings once, twice, three times, and then goes to voicemail. Which means one thing—he saw who was calling and hit DECLINE. Fucker. All the best years of her life—

She can't think about it now. "Colter," she says to the voicemail. "It's me. I know you don't give a shit about anybody or anything"—when she's angry, her accent comes through strong, her consonants sharp enough to cut glass—"but I thought you'd want to know your daughter is injured. Yes, she injured her foot, and we could really use a second opinion at a real clinic, not full of blundering idiots who'll turn her into an invalid for life. To say nothing of a physical therapist, and do I need to remind you that somehow, for some reason, we are no longer on your insurance? I know you don't care about me anymore, but maybe you can muster a shred of interest in your daughter. Anyway, when you're done screwing whatever nubile paralegal you've dragged into bed, give me a call."

She hits the red button to end the call and throws the phone into her purse. It's getting late, but she doesn't have sleep in one eye. There has to be a bar in this shitty town somewhere. So she drives along the main street, and despite the tourist season drawing to its end, there are places that look open. She winds up at a pretentious hipster wine bar, where she orders the cheapest whiskey without really looking at the rest of the menu.

When it arrives, she upends it into her mouth, trying not to think about how she's going to get home once she's drunk—and oh yes, she's planning on getting drunk.

That doctor, with his offhand dismissal, hit closer to home than he realized.

There are so many ways to fall. Georgina grimaces, and it's not because of the vile taste of the whiskey. How could she have told that smiling jerk that it was her metatarsal too that had obliterated the only life she knew, the only life where she actually felt alive?

She takes out her phone and scrolls through the photos. They're mostly of Anna—recent ones of Anna at the barre at home, in costume and makeup, stretching. There's a twenty-second video she made of Anna's fouettés to show her where her balance was off. She watches it without sound, over and over until it swims in her vision, Anna within Anna within Anna.

At school, she thinks dully. *He said it happened at school.* It had to—that's where she was all day. But now Georgina is looking at it from a different angle. *School.* She opens an app and pulls up the academy's Instagram account.

The last photos are from the costume fitting. Here's the corps de ballet, all of Anna's inconsequential classmates, whose names and faces blur together in Georgina's mind, dressed as the Shades for the Kingdom of the Shades sequence. Just looking at it brings back those faraway corps days, in another life and country, torturously repeating hops and arabesques. Here's the new boy who now dances Solor, caught midjump. He'll do a good job of it—she's noticed him at rehearsals before. Then she's almost taken by surprise by the photo of Anna being zipped into her costume by a seamstress. Her daughter looks so beautiful. Her face is half-turned away from the camera, but her angelic smile beams from the photo nonetheless. Georgina brings the phone closer to her eyes. It's not the seamstress she's inspecting. It's the girl standing behind her, half-cropped out of the photo. Georgina recognizes the costume before she recognizes the face.

Anxiety starts to thrum in her chest, dulled by the weak whiskey buzz. She scrolls to another photo. This one is a group shot. The stars, the dancers in the principal roles, are front and center. Anna, of course. The boy who dances Solor, his arm cautiously around Anna's shoulders. And the girl in the Gamzatti costume—Anna's friend Naomi. She's tagged in the photo, and one more tap takes Georgina to her Instagram account.

Naomi posts many times a day. Selfies, selfies, selfies, of course. But also photos of her rehearsing. An artistic shot of her at the barre, forehead pressed against her shin, the camera near the tip of her pointe shoe. Then a picture of her doing a nicely extended developpé. Who took that? There are videos too, of her doing simple moves, bits of variations, just showing off. Georgina clicks and recognizes the music at once, even through the din of techno thrumming under the bar's ceiling. That music is probably branded onto her brain by now. She watches Naomi turn fouettés one after another, and the anxiety grows.

With Anna out of commission, who gets Anna's part? The show must go on. So somebody is going to get Anna's part. And who better than the girl who currently dances the second-biggest role?

The girl in the Gamzatti costume.

Naomi.

That's why Anna wouldn't say anything. Because Naomi had something to do with it. And Anna is too softhearted. She loves that girl like a sister. Ever since she was a child, she hasn't had many friends because the ballet lifestyle doesn't allow for friendships with outsiders. Outsiders want to stay up late and eat french fries, and they get mad when you can't hang out after school because you have to do pliés at the barre. In some ways, Georgina is grateful for Naomi. She feels bad for her, with her struggling mom, her cheap leotards, her always-tattered pointe shoes. Moreover, Naomi had a purpose in their lives: to keep

Anna company through the lonely years of ballet school, and then to...disappear...to wherever the Naomis of the world went afterward.

Except maybe Naomi had other plans.

Dr. Huang's words resonate hollowly in her head.

There are so many ways to fall.

4

September

Dawn Thompson turns the key in the front door just as the sun finishes rising. She squints in the bright light, trying to ignore the hum of exhaustion in her bones. The front lawn needs TLC, and the little house's once-white vinyl paneling could use a pressure wash. The neighbor is starting to give her that look when she says hello. But who has the time? Or the energy? Certainly not her. And asking Naomi is futile.

Speak of the Devil. As Dawn's day ends, her daughter's begins, and from the sound of it, Naomi has been up for some time. The house smells like fresh coffee, and classical music plays in the background, accompanied by the thunderous claps of pointe shoes against the floor. No wonder she wears them out so fast. The thought of paying for another year's worth of pointe shoes makes Dawn a little dizzy.

She makes her way down the narrow hall, stepping over

scattered shoes, Naomi's coat and backpack, and all the other junk no one's bothered to put away. She pauses at the entrance to what was once the living room. It started with a barre Dawn installed for Naomi when she began at the De Vere Academy, but the ballet zone gradually took over, like a bulldozer razing a forest until there's nothing left. Now there's the barre and three mirrors positioned so Naomi can check her form from any angle, and all the furniture has been pushed to the farthest corner.

In the center, Naomi is performing a sequence of delicate moves that look so easy to anyone who's not in the know. Turns and hops, turns and hops.

"Good morning, sweetie," Dawn calls out.

Naomi stumbles halfway through a turn and lands on the soles of her feet with a thunderous slap. "Mom!" she says. "You ruined my take."

That's when Dawn notices the phone Naomi has mounted on a tripod. This is for Naomi's Instagram, no doubt. She posts all these photos and videos, and Dawn knows she should probably monitor like the other moms. But no one is more conscious of Naomi's image than Naomi herself. Dawn once surprised her doing take after endless take of a gracefully failed move. When Dawn asked why she'd want to post a video of herself failing, Naomi shrugged and laughed. "It's to make me look down-to-earth, Mom."

Now she just plods over to the phone, stops the recording,

erases it, and starts over. Her movements look jittery to Dawn, almost manic. Her joints look big, knobby elbows and knees marooned in the middle of her long, sticklike limbs. When Naomi turned twelve, Dawn first became unsettled by her daughter's protruding clavicles and refusal to eat pasta at dinner. Foolishly, she sought advice from the other moms while they were all waiting to pick up their kids after class and was assured that Naomi was doing everything right. *Nothing at all like mine,* one mom grumbled. *Sneaks chocolate every chance she gets, and the worst part is, her grandparents enable it.*

"School isn't for another hour," Dawn says. "Why don't you sleep in a little?"

"Sleep in?" Naomi barely pauses between pirouettes—or whatever they're called. "Are you out of your mind? They're posting the cast list today."

"I don't see how not getting any rest will change what's already decided."

Naomi stops completely, stretches her shoulders, and walks past her mother, rolling her eyes. "Sure, of course it won't. It'd be nice to have someone around here who actually gave a shit."

Dawn feels guilt, then a sneaking suspicion this is exactly what her daughter wanted her to feel. "Oh, honey, that's not fair. You know I—"

But the bathroom door closes—more like slams—behind Naomi, and then Dawn hears the shower roar to life with a rattle of pipes. Great.

Dawn has no choice but to wash her face in the kitchen sink, over the pile of dishes that's been untouched since she last saw it. She supposes she'll brush her teeth when she gets up. But on the way to her bedroom, she notices that the door to Naomi's room is open and can't resist peeking in.

Naomi doesn't bother with decorating, except for the ballet posters on the wall that she uses as a backdrop for her selfies. Not that there's much room for decor in a place this tiny. But the bed is made, every wrinkle on the faded lilac bedspread smoothed out—by Dawn, the evening before. Naomi hardly ever makes her own bed.

The sound of wet feet slapping on the linoleum makes her jump. Naomi is standing behind her with a quizzical look on her face. There's a towel around her hair, but dark strands escape and cling to her pale forehead.

"Um, let me through? I'm going to be late."

With that, she pushes past Dawn into her room and, without waiting for her mother to leave, starts rummaging through her dresser drawers for clean leggings and a leotard.

"Sleep at Anna's again?" Dawn tries to sound casual.

"What? Yeah." Naomi doesn't even turn around.

"That's how many times this week?"

"Why? It's not a problem—"

"I don't want you to be a burden on Ms. Prescott, that's all. Don't wear out your welcome."

The truth is, Dawn finds Ms. Prescott kind of terrifying,

even though they've known each other for years and she insists Dawn call her Georgina.

Naomi shrugs. She pulls a T-shirt over her head without bothering with a bra. "You know I hate sleeping alone in the house."

Dawn can only marvel at how expertly she turned it around. Now it's Dawn's fault if her daughter's friends' parents think Naomi is some kind of nomad. But it's true. As a little girl, Naomi was terribly afraid of the dark. She had night terrors. And Dawn only took the night shift at the hospital because it pays better—because someone has to foot the bill for the school's tuition, to say nothing of all these pointe shoes that never end.

Dawn is proud of Naomi, of course she is. What mother wouldn't be? But sometimes, as she lies awake in her room, which is too bright despite the drawn curtains, waiting for the sleeping pills to work, she lets her mind wander. And in the split second before the pills pull her into restless, dreamless sleep, she catches herself imagining Naomi as a regular teenager who goes to a regular, free public high school, and goes on dates, and pulls shifts at the local McDonald's or one of the souvenir shops in town, and Dawn's biggest worries are about her daughter staying out too late and lacking ambition for her college applications.

She knows she should be glad, and proud, and happy. But in times like these, she finds herself wishing it would all just end.

Georgina has been jumping at small noises, tripping over her own feet, and bumping into furniture so much that Anna notices and asks if she's okay.

But then her phone rings—well, vibrates, since she set it to vibrate so Anna wouldn't hear—at just past seven in the morning. Too early for anyone else, so it has to be the call she was expecting. She answers, and the woman on the other end gives her the information she's been waiting for.

Georgina composes herself and thanks her. Then she stands still, listening to the familiar sounds of the apartment: the shower splashing in the bathroom as Anna washes her hair, and the hissing of the big, expensive espresso machine—an indulgence she has never once regretted. Right now, though, she realizes she's too wired even for decaf. She opens the window to let in some fresh air, even though early September is still summer-hot. Then she collapses onto the nearest chair and covers her eyes with the heels of her hands.

"Mom?"

How long has she been sitting there? Georgina startles to see Anna at the kitchen counter, fully dressed, hair dry and up in a ponytail.

Georgina leaps to her feet. "Breakfast," she stammers, gesturing at the plate of poached eggs and whole wheat toast that has probably had time to grow cold. Anna obediently sits down and eats the eggs without complaint.

"I hope you got a good night's sleep," Georgina fusses.

"Like a baby," Anna deadpans.

"You have circles under your eyes."

"Gee, thanks." Anna rolls her eyes ever so slightly, and Georgina realizes she's rambling. But she has to keep talking about nothing so she doesn't blurt out what she knows.

"I don't mean it in a hurtful way, Anna. You're always so touchy, even when it's constructive feedback. Why don't you put on some concealer?"

Anna eats and doesn't answer. To keep herself busy, Georgina goes to the hallway and rifles through Anna's duffel bag, which sits by the door, ready to be slung over her daughter's frail shoulder. Ballet shoes, pointe shoes, spare pointe shoes, the pointe shoe kit, the water bottle, foot powder, tape, Tiger Balm—everything carefully compartmentalized in the duffel bag's various pockets. Just making sure she doesn't forget anything, Georgina tells herself.

In a little mesh pocket, she spots Anna's phone. She bought the latest iPhone for her after the end-of-year recital last year. Anna is responsible; you can buy her expensive things and not worry that the screen will crack in a week. She bought her a case for the phone at the same time, at another kiosk at the mall where the Apple Store is. She was in a good mood, and it caught her eye: pink lace over a glitter background. So vibrant, so youthful, so pretty. When she was Anna's age, they didn't have things like that. Especially where Georgina grew up. But now she notices that Anna has changed the case to a plain one, no glitter, no lace, just blank white plastic.

After a quick glance over her shoulder, Georgina presses the phone's side button, only to get another surprise. The background, which used to be a picture of Anna's favorite ballerina (hashtag goals, as they laughed together when Anna set up her gift), is now blank as well—a generic iPhone background. In the split second before she hears approaching steps, Georgina has time to notice that at the top left corner, it says in tiny white letters, NO NETWORK.

Before Anna can see her, she shoves the phone back in the pocket and zips the duffel closed. When she straightens, her daughter is in the hall, winding her diaphanous scarf around her neck. It's got to be eighty degrees outside.

"Are you sure you don't want me to come with you?"

Anna nods. "It's fine, Mom. I can handle myself."

Georgina moves to put her hands on Anna's shoulders, but Anna dodges at the last second, diving down seemingly to tie the laces of her immaculate white sneakers.

"Do you want me to drive you?"

"It's a ten-minute walk. And I figure everyone else will get the bright idea to get there early for the cast list, so—"

"I know you've been working very hard. You've been up late all week preparing for the audition…" Or rather, Georgina kept her up late. "And I know you're grumpy, but I just want you to know that I'm proud of you. No matter what role you get, you'll still be the prima to me."

Anna slings the duffel strap over her shoulder. "Bye, Mom. See you tonight. Oh, is it okay if I bring Naomi for dinner?"

"Of course. You deserve a little girls' night."

Anna shuts the door behind her just as Georgina's awkward "Love you!" bounces off it like a pebble off glass. Georgina has never been good at the lovey-dovey stuff. But one day, Anna will understand.

She places her hand on the door and stands still, pretending she's not listening for Anna's featherlight steps as they pitter-patter across the landing and down the stairs to disappear in the distance. For whose benefit? She can't answer. But once she's sure Anna isn't coming back, she directs her steps to the bedroom door with the plaque on it. DANCING IS DREAMING WITH YOUR FEET. Georgina was the one who made it, but she can't help but scoff at it.

Nothing could be further from the truth.

The door opens without a creak, and Georgina finds herself in Anna's realm. This room was meant to be the master bedroom, complete with an en suite bathroom and the electric fireplace attached to the far wall. The first thing Georgina did was get rid of the fireplace and install a barre along the wall, as well as several full-length mirrors. The rest of the room is strictly utilitarian: Anna's single bed with its ergonomic, therapeutic mattress, a dresser, a desk and chair, a bookshelf—all part of the same IKEA set. The ballet-themed knickknacks Anna has collected over the years still sit on every flat surface: figurines, plushies, glass pointe shoes, music boxes.

Or at least they used to. As Georgina closes the door behind her, she notices that the posters are missing and the figurines have been shoved unceremoniously to the corner of the highest shelf. Anna's clothes, which she usually leaves all over the place, have been put away. She's tidied her desk too. The computer on which she does her homework sits alone on the melamine IKEA desktop. Georgina approaches and jiggles the computer mouse. The screen blinks awake, but a box pops up and demands a password.

She slides open one of the desk's drawers and sighs: The impression of a freshly cleaned room was just that—an impression. Anna simply swept all the junk into the drawer, and now it's practically spilling out. When Georgina tries to close it, it gets stuck.

Georgina mutters under her breath. She tugs on the drawer's handle, but it won't budge, so she kneels in front of the desk and tries to see where it got stuck. It seems there's a little sewing kit in a plastic box, one of the several Anna owns, that got wedged in the back of the drawer. She tries to loosen it, jiggling the drawer—only to have it pop loose, go flying off its rails, and upend, scattering its contents all over the floor and Georgina's lap.

Cursing, she collects the minutiae of Anna's desk drawer: pencils, sticker sheets, several tubes of old lip balm, packets of chewing gum, key chains. She picks up the drawer to slide it back into place only to notice something taped to the underside.

Georgina frowns. It's a piece of brown paper, the kind used in art class for sketching, folded over several times and secured with clear Scotch tape. Catching the corner of the tape with the tip of her fingernail, she gently pries it away, then carefully unfolds the paper until its contents drop into the palm of her hand.

She looks at it, blinking, overwhelmed at first with surprise, then with a sort of giddy relief—and here she thought it would be something worse! She turns the object around in her hands, and with each second that ticks away overhead on Anna's ballerina-themed clock, a wholly different feeling emerges, one not nearly as rosy.

She's keeping secrets from me.

NAOMI

Even though I left early, I'm somehow the last one to arrive. The cast list hangs on the billboard by the double doors leading to the grand auditorium, and as usual, the entire school gathers to see who got what, who didn't, who won bets, and who will be sewing her friends' ribbons for the rest of the semester.

I gotta admit, it was a lot more fun when it wasn't my class up there on that piece of paper, my fate sealed by that tacky laminate. Is it just me, or is the crowd bigger than in all previous years combined? I swear I see some fourth graders in pink leg warmers.

The hallway from the front entrance to the auditorium is lined with glass displays of awards, photos of graduating classes, and framed cutouts from *Pointe* and other publications featuring the academy's graduates. This way, the recruiters here to see our final performance know they're not dealing with some backwater dance school in a church basement. There's a photo of our class from the eighth-grade performance and one of Anna from a competition in Boston last year, right next to the silver medal she won. Some girl from California took gold.

But that's not why I can't bring myself to walk down that hall. The crowd in front of the billboard becomes a malignant, faceless mass. Their loud conversations, punctuated by random laughs and yelps, blur into a rumble that fills my head. My legs, steady through pas de bourrée and piqué turns, my ankles that never let me down in a developpé, feel like they might collapse under the weight of all my hopes and dreams, sinew unraveling like a ribbon.

"Come on," says a voice over my ear. I snap back to reality, and once again my legs are my legs, steady and reliable, holding up all ninety-two pounds of me (as of this morning's weigh-in on my mom's bathroom scale), invisible hopes notwithstanding. It's Anna, looking, as always, like she just splashed some fresh Evian on her face. My own face itches under the concealer caked over my undereye circles. "We can't avoid it forever."

Yeah, as if she has anything to avoid. I laugh to keep from

crying or killing someone in a fit of rage. "Maybe we just say fuck it? Hop on a bus and be auditioning in New York this afternoon."

"Ha. Funny." Anna swings her duffel over her shoulder.

"I wasn't kidding. I'm sixteen, you'll be sixteen in a month and a half. We don't need parental consent—"

"Yes, and we'll sleep under the Brooklyn Bridge. Let's go, Naomi. What's the worst it could be?"

Oh, bitch, you don't really want me to answer that. But she's already grabbing my arm and pulling me through the crowd. As usual, the crowd parts for Anna Prescott. Even the fifth graders in their glitter shoes know who she is.

Yet as she drags me along, her refined ballerina hand like a vise grip on my forearm, I notice how damp her palm is. She's nervous. Anna is nervous?

Oh God, does she know something?

I make myself look up at the laminated paper. It says LA BAYADERE, SENIOR CLASS at the top in plain caps. Below, all the roles are listed in order of importance.

NIKIYA: ANNA PRESCOTT
SOLOR: JAMES RAWLEY
GAMZATTI: NAOMI THOMPSON

And there you have it. Not knowing what to do with all the adrenaline, my body sublimates it into jitters. I crack my knuckles and the joints in my toes in demi-pointe, hopping from one foot to the other.

"Hey, bitch, you got Gamzatti!" Anna whispers excitedly in my ear, her pointy elbow in my ribs. Right. I'm supposed to be excited. Instead, my gaze races across the rest of the cast: the Golden Idol, the three soloist Shades, the rest of the Shades in the corps. Interesting that they picked James to be the male lead rather than Everett. Sarah got a solo part—good for her.

"We'll be rehearsing together!" Anna whispers.

Yeah, yeah. Very cool. Can't wait.

The students start to disperse, having gotten their high for the day and their gossip fuel for the rest of the year. "Congratulations, Anna," a girl says, and the others echo. No one sounds or looks particularly surprised. I know for sure Anna isn't. Even if she were, she'd never show it. A true prima isn't surprised to get the main part. That's just…the way things are supposed to be. The opposite—now that would be a shock.

But not today. Not today.

"I guess you'll be busy with this new role," I say. "I won't be able to cover for you sneaking off to Boston, even for a day."

I turn and start in the direction of our first class but notice she's not following. I glance over my shoulder. Her gaze is lowered to her immaculate white sneakers; her hands grip the strap of her duffel bag so hard her knuckles are white.

"Not here," she says in a low voice. "Can we—go for a smoke first?"

Anna not rushing off to class to make sure she isn't even a second late—now there's something new. All the more reason to find out what this is about. So I grab her hand (still damp, now also ice cold) and we head off to our secret spot.

The school itself isn't our town's only claim to fame. The building it's in counts too. Dating back to the late nineteenth century, it used to be a convent built in that over-the-top Gothic Revival style, with turrets, tall, pointed windows, high ceilings, and arches everywhere. The insides have been gutted several times since, especially when it was refurbished as a hospital in the 1930s, but many of the walls are still the original stone. At least half the school's tuition must be sunk into the cost of heating the place in winter, and even then it's never very effective. We don't just wear leg warmers for the look. The radiators rattle day and night, but the heat they generate floats up toward those faraway ceilings before we have a chance to warm our toes. This might be why the hospital didn't last long and the building sat vacant for more than a decade until a socialite and former dancer turned it into a ballet school. The part that could be salvaged, at least. Ten-plus years of alternately sweltering and freezing in this climate hadn't done the place any favors, and now it's roughly half the size it once was. I wonder why they didn't just build a new building, a nice one without leaking roofs or mildew. The part that used to be the chapel is now our auditorium.

When I first met Anna, we were both ten, and she was convinced the place was haunted. Especially the dormitory, where she lived as one of the boarding school students. Back then, living in the dorms with other girls seemed like the height of aspirations to me, but my mom didn't want to hear it—I later found out it was mostly because the dorms cost extra. A lot extra.

But there was Anna, the shortest and skinniest girl in the class of forty short, skinny girls, always getting shoved to the back of the line at the cafeteria and pushed around at the lockers. We didn't have the same hierarchy we have now, but it was almost like we could all sense who the competition would be and begin forming our alliances.

Maybe I understood on some level that pushing her around wouldn't eliminate her as my biggest competitor, so I decided instead to kill her with kindness. But I think I just felt bad for her, all alone and friendless. A girl tipped over her tray at lunch one day, and as Anna watched, I went and upended the little bully's skim milk on her head. I got in trouble for that, but I guess it doesn't matter anymore, because a couple of years later she got fat, couldn't jump anymore, and dropped out.

Back then, we started sneaking away to our hidden corner of the school, the remnant of the demolished wing. All that's left is a truncated stub of a hallway and a staircase that leads nowhere. Anna showed me the place. She'd hide there to eat the candy and junk food she managed to steal from other girls. Within three years, we graduated from Twinkies and Pop Rocks to cigarettes and weed.

Anna throws down her duffel bag with violence, and it

lands at the foot of the stairs. I make two cigarettes and a lighter appear. Ballerinas always have matches or a lighter because we need them for singeing ribbons on our shoes, so it's not suspicious.

Anna gratefully takes a first puff. Things must be rough—I haven't seen her smoke cigarettes in ages, at least since vape pens became the thing.

"Fuck," she says through her teeth, the cigarette dangling from the corner of her mouth.

"Are you that upset over your Boston guy?" I ask.

She gives me a dirty look. "Huh? What does that have to do with anything?"

"Come on, Anna."

"I told you a million times. There's nothing shady going on. I just can't tell you yet—"

"I get it, I get it. You want to be all secretive, so be it. It's just, if you need another alibi, it'll be easier if I knew what I'm covering for."

Anna sighs and conspicuously changes the subject. "I can't believe they gave me this role. I was sure I bombed at the audition. Did you see how Walter glowered at me? *Sukin syn.*"

Ah, the Russian profanities. Never a good sign.

"Sarah ran out of the ballroom crying, and yet."

"That's because Sarah did just fine, and he knows it. He kept making her do it over to see how far he could push her."

"A soloist part is how far," I mutter.

"I, on the other hand, totally blew it."

"You didn't blow it." Why do the ones who do better than everyone else need the most reassurance? I used to think she did this on purpose, to fish for compliments, but soon realized Anna doesn't fish for compliments. She's internalized her mom's nagging voice so much she confuses it with her own. I don't envy her that. Sure, my mom can't tell a pirouette from a fouetté, so her compliments aren't worth much. But at least she tries.

"I'm telling you, Naomi, he has it out for me."

It's hard not to roll my eyes.

"You did get Nikiya, though."

"And you know why. Because the other teachers vetoed him. I'm not stupid. It's only going to get worse from here because they've challenged his so-called authority, and now guess who he's going to take it out on."

It was Georgina who told her all about the new choreographer as soon as she found out, two weeks before anyone else. And Anna, being the good friend she is, immediately called and told me. Damn, Georgina is a bitch sometimes, but Anna doesn't realize her luck.

"What am I supposed to do, Naomi?" She finishes the cigarette and crushes the filter under her toe. She's looking at me, all supplicating, her china-blue eyes wide in her pixie face like goddamn Princess Elsa. I try not to think that I'm the one who gets to share the stage with her, inevitably looking like Olaf in a tutu by comparison. I got Gamzatti—woo-hoo, lucky me. "What am I supposed to do? Ambush him in his office and blow him? Will that make him like me?"

Oh, for fuck's sake. "You should definitely not do that."

"Well, then what?"

"For one, you could get some perspective. You got the lead role, and a really beautiful lead role too. And it's not just him in there, there's Fabienne and all the others, and they worship the ground you walk on." I'm starting to sound bitter, so I hurriedly change course. "So what you're going to do is rehearse Nikiya, dance in the final performance, and then go to New York or San Francisco or Paris Opera Ballet, because why the fuck not, and Walter will stay behind in this little town, a sad, aging queen taking his frustrations out on teenage girls. Voilà. That's it."

Anna gives me a dubious look.

"Oh, and hey. I'm the one who got the part with the endless Italian fouettés that I have no clue how to do." I put my hand on her shoulder. At least that makes her smile.

"Oh, you'll manage."

"How the hell do you know?"

"Because it's...you."

With that, Anna looks at her phone and decides it's time to go to class, because lead role or not, she's not entirely immune to being chewed out by Fabienne in front of everyone. I follow on her heels back to the Church of Saint Anna, otherwise known as the De Vere Ballet Academy.

You bet I'm going to do all those fouettés and not wobble.

Yeah, because it's me. Thanks for the compliment, prima. After everything—*everything*—I've done. This is what I get. Compliments. You bitch, you fucking bitch.

Because, like I said, it's hard to hate Anna Prescott. But I manage.

5

Now

EVER SINCE ANNA came home with that brace on her foot, time has slowed from a relentless force to something viscous and shapeless. Georgina now finds herself making breakfast and coffee at 10:00 a.m., a time by which she'd normally have been up for hours. But with Anna holed up in her room, Georgina slept off her hangover unnoticed. No poached eggs to make, no bag to check. She wonders how all those tasks that used to structure her days have slipped away, leaving her with nothing. When Anna was little, Georgina would wake her up, blow-dry her hair and style it into a perfect bun, and select her clothes from the meticulously organized closet. There was breakfast to make, lunch to prepare, and the daily drives to school and ballet lessons. Then there were all the other ballet moms to greet, their lives to keep track of so she could ask the right questions: How's your husband's promotion, your other kid's violin competition? Then it was time to take Anna home, make supper, do laundry, and start it all over the next day.

Then Anna left for boarding school, and a terrible emptiness settled in, one that still haunts Georgina. Anna's father refused to move to some small town in the middle of nowhere, sustained only by a musty ballet school and Canadian tourists. A four-hour commute was out of the question. And the truth was, Georgina had never intended for him to join them. She would move there for Anna during the school year, and they'd return to the city in the summer.

In the end, that's what she got, minus the summers in the city. But as Anna grew, there was less and less to do.

Georgina sits at the kitchen counter with her tablet, tapping impatiently at the screen to enter the code. The screen lights up, and she picks up where she left off yesterday.

Naomi Thompson's Instagram page.

How much does she really know about Naomi Thompson? The adage about keeping friends close and enemies closer comes to mind. Of course, she keeps tabs on the competition, which includes Naomi, but Anna doesn't really have competition. Not all second-bests are equal, and Naomi isn't exactly nipping at Anna's heels. Everyone knows that. Fabienne tells her, and Georgina can see from Naomi's Instagram videos: She's technical, stable. She could be better with the right push, but she doesn't have that something that makes the difference between a passable dancer and a great one. She's artistic enough, but her energy is too vibrant, too crude—too American for a school founded on the French ballet tradition, the only such school in the United States. She doesn't know what to do with her hands—they swing around like she's doing karate, not ballet. And her physique, while decent, loses to Anna's in every way that matters. Her legs are shorter, her ankles lack flexibility, and her shoulders are a touch too wide, a downfall for her petite build. What company would cast this tiny linebacker as Giselle or Swanilde?

Or Nikiya, for that matter. But they don't have many options, do they?

If she has the wrong physique for Balanchine, she has the right one for Instagram. She has the face, at least. Pert nose, full lips, a catlike gaze enhanced by fake eyelashes, and she's always wearing gobs of makeup. It's a face made for the selfie camera, and Naomi takes full advantage of this. Georgina scrolls through photo after photo of Naomi's face angled just so, always brilliantly smiling. She looks much prettier than in real life, Georgina thinks. There must be some sort of filter. In the background of many photos, she spies the same ballet poster. In others, she recognizes various places at the academy. But the background is always blurred—the focus remains on Naomi, always Naomi.

Still, Georgina is baffled to see she has over ten thousand followers. Ten thousand people want to watch her stomp through the Raymonda variation, a simplified one at that? How far ballet has fallen.

If this were my time, Georgina thinks, she wouldn't have made it past sixth grade. But the academy isn't Georgina's old ballet school in Siberia. The academy subscribes to new, democratic ideals whereby they don't expel anyone for being, well, bad at ballet. They don't even weigh the students anymore, something unthinkable when Georgina was Anna's age.

But this is America, all about freedom and democracy—words that, even though no one will admit it, don't always apply to real life. Perhaps, Georgina thinks, it's less about democracy and more about capitalism: collecting tuition payments, without which the school would cease to exist. Even with every spot taken, they barely break even and rely on donations for extras like sets, costumes, galas, and heating in winter.

Georgina grudgingly admits Naomi has a future in ballet. Perhaps she'll make soloist at some flyover state's company one day.

At least, that was her perspective until Anna was sidelined.

Naomi had nothing to lose and everything to gain.

Georgina picks up her phone, but before she dials, she takes a few seconds to calm herself. After decades onstage, she's an expert at this. She forces her ragged breathing to slow, a tranquil tide whooshing in and out of her lungs. And even though the person on the other end won't see her, she arranges her face into her stage look: eyebrows arching high, eyes bright, smile wide.

"Hi," she says as soon as the phone is picked up. "Can we meet for coffee at our usual spot? There's something I wanted to discuss."

NAOMI

I didn't sleep a wink last night. Not because I'm excited. I'm not. Really.

I slacked off all weekend. I tried to keep up with my usual schedule, but my mind refused to cooperate. It floated away from my body, and I barely stumbled through the easiest moves.

No official announcements yet, but that's how things are at a ballet school—everyone already knows. The school forum exploded with messages overnight. The thread titled Anna Prescott injured??! has over three hundred comments. Most of them are condolences, emoji of crying faces and broken hearts, and glittering GIFs of flowers.

If you didn't know the context, you'd think she fucking died.

Even my mom crept up behind me yesterday morning as I slogged through my stretching routine. *Are you okay, sweetie?* Yes, I'm fine, thanks, I'd be better if you didn't interrupt. Next thing I know, they'll be setting up counseling booths at school, like we had a shooting or something.

She broke a metatarsal in her right foot, or so the rumors say. Nervous, I roll my ankle, which makes that clicking sound again—or maybe it's all in my head. Phantom pain.

"You're not eating," Dawn says, nodding at my oatmeal.

"I can't," I say, shoving the bowl away.

"You can't just go without eating. They better not call me because you fainted in class—"

"I've never fucking fainted in class in my life, Mom."

She gives me a dirty look: language. Except I'm right, I never fainted. That one time, I slipped and fell on my ass because Gemma put something on the sole of my shoe. And that was two years ago. "I don't want it. I was distracted and put too much Splenda in it, and it's bitter now."

"Then have a PowerBar or something. Don't go to class hungry."

I don't tell her that going to class hungry is the norm, not something exceptional, and that everybody else does it and they're just fine. I don't think I can handle arguing today, so I just grab the PowerBar and throw it into my bag, where it'll get flattened into an inedible, mushy mess by lunch.

As soon as I'm outside, I check my phone. Nothing. The empty screen seems to mock me. Of course, the moment the news was out, everyone swarmed me with questions: What happened? How did it happen? Because I'm her best friend, I'm supposed to know, right? Best friends tell each other everything.

But now I text her and watch my message send with a ping,

only to remain unseen and unread. Just like all my calls that didn't even go to voicemail. She probably took the stupid SIM card out of her phone.

It's probably just paranoia creeping up my spine in a rush of goose bumps, but I feel like people are watching me as I walk into the school. The hairs on my arms stand on end. Of course, that could also be because it's so fucking cold in here. Between late September and late May, the place is an ice palace. I turn my head in time to catch a younger girl's fleeting glance; her group of friends, eighth graders, are less bashful, staring at me overtly.

"What's your problem?" I snarl under my breath as I pass them, and they scatter like little gray mice.

I'm very, very late, and the locker room is already half empty. Gemma sits on the floor, smashing her new pointe shoe in her locker door over and over to break it in: thump, thump, thump, the sound rockets through the windowless space. That reminds me. I'm running low on pointe shoes—it's time to ask my mom. Hell, maybe I can ask Anna for hers. She won't be needing them, at least not for a little while.

I squash the thought and start to get changed. Off with the sweatpants and jumper—this moment is torture because of the cold. The only thing worse is taking off my sneakers and socks. I do my best not to let my bare feet touch the glacial stone floor as I put the tape on my right toes, the ones that always give me trouble. They're misshapen now, covered with bumps I once thought were just bruises, but then I realized it was the bones themselves that had changed shape, bulked up to withstand wear and tear. By the time I'm done dancing, decades from now, my feet will be like the roots of a gnarled tree. I'm never wearing sandals again.

On go the toe caps, followed by the spacers I wedge between my big and second toes, and then the toe pads cover all of them. The pads are filthy and crying for the bin, but I don't have many to spare. Anyway, it doesn't matter because on top of those go my pointe shoes. A new pair today, and unlike Gemma, I took the time to break them in last night, not going to bed until I was sure everything was fitted and comfortable. Nothing like lovely off-white satin to hide all that hideousness. I roll my ankle again, then massage it.

The door behind me bangs open, startling me more than it should have. Sarah storms across the locker room. Her locker is two doors away from mine, so we find ourselves side by side despite being practically alone in here. Except for Gemma. Thump, thump.

She eyes my new shoes briefly.

"So I guess it's you now," she says under her breath. I'm not sure she even meant for me to answer.

"What's me now?"

Her gaze lingers on my face, heavy, as if to say, *Oh, come on.* "Nikiya."

Right. Nikiya. That's why everyone's been staring at me like I grew a hump overnight. They were looking at the new star of the end-of-year performance. "Really? And who's saying that?"

"I don't know. Common sense? Not like there's anyone else who has a shot at it."

"For all we know, that prick is just going to herd us to another bullshit audition."

I should probably get going since class begins in minutes. But for some reason, I linger, watching Sarah change. Her gear is cheaper than Anna's, but it's new. She's a boarding school student—her parents are psychologists with a clinic in New York City. They come to all the recitals. They care. She never has to wear pointe shoes that are falling apart. I watch as she goes through the same routine I just did, familiar to the bone. She puts on her right pointe shoe and ties the ribbons, and only then takes off her other sneaker.

"What?" Sarah barks when she realizes I'm still standing there. "Enjoying the show?"

"How's your ankle?" I ask.

The question, seemingly so innocuous, has the effect of a cattle prod. She jumps to her feet, the one pointe shoe slapping the floor. "It's none of your goddamn business, Thompson," she hisses. "What do you think you're playing at? Yeah, yeah, you're getting Nikiya, big whoop. But you knew that's exactly what was going to happen, so why put on the act?"

I take a tiny step back. "You're psychotic," I say. "Take some more Percocet, it'll calm your nerves."

"Fuck you."

I turn on my heel and head out. Gemma keeps smashing the locker door on her poor pointe shoe that's probably well beyond broken in by now—just broken. What the hell is wrong with everyone?

"Are you going to fucking stop that?" I snarl at her. She stares at me with eyes the size of saucers, with tracks of mascara underneath—she's been crying. "I'm about to lose my mind."

As I leave, I feel their gazes on my back, like the proverbial daggers. No, not really. Daggers you can pull out.

Anna, what's going on?? What happened??
Please please please text me back when you see this!

"Phones away!" Walter's voice rolls through the room. "God help you if I hear another bullshit Flo Rida ringtone in the middle of my rehearsal."

I leave the phone on but turn off the ringer before I shove it into the bottom of my bag. The walk to my place at the center of the barre feels like it takes an hour today, and the feeling that everyone is looking isn't just a feeling anymore. Most of all, Walter is watching me. He makes no secret of it: His head swivels to follow me like he's a creepy bird of prey.

As I take my usual place, the spot next to me is empty, and only now do I realize it's never been empty before. Has Anna ever missed a single day of class? She must have. Even I have, and I've always been the kid who gobbled Advil in secret instead of warming the thermometer on a lamp because I did want to go to school.

But with that spot empty, with Anna gone, the dynamic of the entire classroom is thrown into shambles. It's like we're dancing the final scene in *Swan Lake* but the Swan Queen is nowhere to be seen. Anna, it turns out, was the one who held it all together.

"Well, Naomi…" The sound of my name makes me jump. "What are you waiting for? Please take the central place. Sarah, take Naomi's old spot, please, and Gemma, take Sarah's, and so on." He gives a dismissive wave of his tattooed hand. "Figure it out. Not like you haven't all lain awake all night thinking about it. One thing is for sure—I'm not conducting a rehearsal with that gap in the front row like a missing tooth. And before you ask—since you're all dying to ask—we'll be making some temporary changes to the cast of *La Bayadère*. Honestly, the thought of holding another audition with you lot makes me break out in hives, so let's keep it simple. Naomi will be dancing Nikiya. Let's all put our hands together for our good friend Naomi, please."

Thin applause follows in two uneven waves, like everyone isn't sure if he's kidding. I can't bring myself to look around. Sure, getting the principal role was the plan all along. But this is not how I pictured it.

"As for Gamzatti, we can just figure it out as we go. I won't lie, I have some of you in mind and not others, but I dare you to surprise me."

The rows of girls ripple. That fucking prick. He knows exactly what he's doing, doesn't he?

"Naomi, go see Fabienne in her office—she'll go over the role with you. The three on each side of Naomi, come with me to Room 3A, and let's see what you can show me. The rest of you"—another dismissive nod, which makes his hair flop on top of his forehead—"just do your warm-up, or whatever it is you normally do."

Only when I'm already halfway out the door does it hit me. He's sending me to Fabienne—he's getting rid of me. There's a heavy, leaden feeling on the back of my neck, but when I glance over my shoulder, he's not looking at me at all. He's pacing the rows of dancers, deeply interested—or faking interest?—in how Madison holds her hips in her arabesque.

Only when I'm closing the door do I see him again through the crack. His gaze is on me, still and cold.

But I don't go to Fabienne's. Halfway to her office, I stop in the middle of the deserted hallway and can't make myself take another step. I can only imagine what Fabienne might say to me—me, taking the star role from her favorite. I'd sooner pull out my own toenails with pliers.

The empty hallway is full of strange echoes; the light that filters through the aging, dust-clogged windowpanes has a sepia tone, like I'm trapped in an old photograph. Anna was right, the place is haunted. Perhaps not by literal ghosts, but by the faint echoes of all the dreams of everyone who's walked these halls before me, the boxes of their pointe shoes clacking against the floor. They're so thick in the air that I can practically see them floating in a grayish cloud above my head like smog, obscuring the arched ceiling toward which they rise along with the heat from the radiators. Every little girl enters this place at age ten with all these hopes crowding in her head, big ones and little ones, and then one by one they get ripped away, rooted out, and sent to join the other orphaned dreams under the ceiling. Dancing Odette at the Bolshoi, goodbye. Promoted to principal at nineteen, see ya never. Giselle, Aurora, the Sugar Plum Fairy, Juliet—the real one, not the one that girl barely suffered through last year—never going to happen. Then, for those who didn't quit or get expelled, the smaller dreams take the place of the bigger ones as the third stage of grief sets in, the bargaining: Okay, it doesn't have to be the NYCB or the Paris Opera, I'm fine dancing in Oklahoma as long as I can be onstage. I'm fine with corps de ballet; after all, everyone has to pay their dues, don't they? Everyone tells themselves lies: I'll work my way up, I'll find the right company for me, I'll stop growing at five foot eight. Of course I will. Then the end of senior year looms, and so does the specter of many fruitless auditions. It's harder and harder to tell yourself you've just been overlooked by some cruel quirk of fate and the right person will come along and finally see your spark.

There's a distant rumble behind me that makes me spin around, but I find myself facing an empty hallway. Are those faraway steps? I should do something before I get caught wandering the halls during class. I duck into the washroom and take in the sight in the row of mirrors. I'm a mess. Flyaways are sticking out at right angles above my ears, and the blue around my eyes has deepened. I run the tap, smooth down my hair, take out my makeup tubes and line them up on the edge of the sink. Concealer, mascara, lip gloss, and a smile. I pose in front of the mirror, my hands in second position. Prima material? I've been determined not to let go of my dreams, no matter how hard reality tries to pry them from my hands. I refused to surrender them to the gray cloud, to leave them behind for the future students of the De Vere Academy to pity. But now I realize even I have allowed myself to compromise because it was just easier than accepting the painful reality. Sure, I was second best, but second best to Anna, not just anyone, and that was supposed to be less bad. After all, Anna can't get hired at all companies at once, so I could be some recruiter's second choice.

But now I look in the mirror and put on my ballet face, my stage smile. No. Fuck second choice. I'm going to be the top pick.

For me, the big dream is coming true.

My feet take me to classroom 3A as if of their own free will. When I get there through the labyrinthine hallways, the doors are only open a crack, and I hear music, the thundering of pointe shoes, and Walter's voice barking commands. Finally, all that ballet grace comes in handy: I creep closer and closer to the doors until I can peer in.

I only see a thin sliver of the brightly lit room, but in that sliver, none other than Gemma is dancing the Gamzatti variation. My variation, at least until recently. And, to my dismay, she's nailing it. So maybe the bitch didn't entirely destroy those pointe shoes of hers while eavesdropping on Sarah and me. Sure, she's far from extraordinary, but she's decent. She doesn't wobble, keeps her core tight and her knees straight. It's only her face that's the problem. She looks like she's about to cry again. Finally, she stops, and I can see the crazy, frenzied rise and fall of her chest, her skinny ribs expanding until I think they might poke a hole in her leotard.

"That's fine, Gemma. It was all right. I could work with it."

Now I can only see her face reflected in one of the wall-to-wall mirrors, but it blossoms with relief, and disbelief. Which Walter wastes no time shattering.

"But I don't want to work with it. For heaven's sake. You're supposed to be a princess, and you're seducing your man with your status and beauty. You act like a lovesick nerd throwing herself at the captain of the football team. Desperation isn't sexy, Gemma."

Wow. Who could have seen that coming except everyone?

"But—what would you like me to do differently?"

He groans. "If you can't figure it out by yourself, there's nothing to talk about. Did you see how Naomi did it? That's what I want you to do. Do you think you can?"

I can't make out Gemma's meek, murmured answer. It must not be to his satisfaction because he rages on. "Oh? How so? I'm sure she'd be happy to show you personally. In fact, let's go and get her right now."

My insides turn cold, and no doubt Gemma's do too, because her murmuring takes on a whiny note.

"Well, short of getting Naomi, I'm stuck with you. And you're not performing."

"I can do it," she stammers. "I can do what Naomi does."

"Very well, then. Show me those jumps again."

And then they both disappear from my line of sight. My heart kicks up a frenzy, sending my blood rushing through my eardrums. I'm twisted by the temptation to take just one more tiny step forward, peer closer so I can see.

But before I can do something stupid, I hear the slap of pointe shoes landing gracelessly on the floor, followed by Walter's contemptuous laugh.

She starts mumbling some excuse.

"Get out!" Walter barks.

I barely have time to step away from the doors when one side flies open in my face. Gemma stumbles toward me, then freezes. Tear tracks line her cheeks, and sweat has ruined her makeup. At the same time that I take all this in, shock registers on her face. And then, on its heels, something else—fury. Her nostrils flare, her jaw grinds, and the tendons in her neck pop.

"Were you behind this?" she hisses. "Did you set me up?"

"What the fuck?" I snarl back.

"You bitch," she growls, and pushes past me. She manages a step, then two, three, six. Then she stops, unable to help herself. Her shoulders are pulled up to her ears, her back rounded. She turns around, and the sobs that rise from her chest are already twisting her face.

"You think nobody knows? Everyone fucking knows. And she thought you were her friend."

With that, the tears take over. She cups her hands over her mouth and runs off, presumably to lock herself in a bathroom stall where she can cry herself out and then stuff her face with those chocolate bars she hides in her locker. And then make herself throw them right back up.

I don't have time to ruminate on it all, though. Walter is standing in the doors, his arms crossed. He's surveying me calmly. Too calmly.

"What are you doing here? Why aren't you rehearsing with Fabienne?"

"I—" I search my empty mind for an excuse. But it seems he's not expecting one. He takes me by the upper arm. His fingers are hard.

"Naomi, this is difficult enough. I'm about to find myself without a suitable Gamzatti, and I don't want to find myself without a Nikiya as well. So I don't care how you feel about it, I don't care how Fabienne feels about it, but you two will have to work out your differences. Sad as it is that she must disappoint her crush like this—"

"What happened with Gemma?" I ask. And immediately bite the inside of my lip, hard. What the hell is wrong with me?

"Oh, please. Don't you start." He rubs his eyes with the heels of his hands. "I'm not going to cast her as Gamzatti. I already decided on Sarah. Now you are Nikiya—are you still not happy? What more do you want from me?"

I gulp. "Nothing," I say.

"Good, good. Now off you go to Fabienne before she starts asking me stupid questions."

I barely make it through what is surely the longest day in the history of the De Vere Academy. Rehearsing alone with Fabienne goes about as well as I expected: Nothing is good enough, nothing ever could be good enough, and no one on earth could ever even approach the perfection that was Anna. I exit the morning session drenched in sweat and with bloodied toes and nod off through the day's classes. Luckily, no one calls on me. Right—because I'm the new Anna. No teacher would dare trouble the prima with insignificant questions, like whether she bothered to do her math homework. She has the school's reputation in the palm of her pretty, narrow hand. But despite the relative peace and quiet, I get to the evening dance lessons without a shred of energy.

In the locker room, I have changed into a clean leotard and put my pointe shoes back on when Sarah crashes through the doors and ambushes me at my locker.

"News travels fast," I scowl.

"Shut up, Thompson. I'm serious. I'm not in the mood."

That's when I clue in that she doesn't look excited, like someone about to get cast in a principal part. She looks terrified.

"I need your help."

I know what's coming before she says the words. I grab her arm and squeeze it, hard. Harder than Walter did mine. "Be quiet," I hiss, leaning closer to her ear as if by accident.

"My ankle. It got worse again," she whispers.

Tell me something I didn't know.

"Will you hook me up?" Her ketosis breath brushes against my neck.

"I'll hook you up. Keep your voice down."

"Thank you." She frees herself from my grasp, and suddenly, she doesn't look desperate at all. She's wearing a shit-eating grin. "And why so secretive? Everyone knows anyway."

She takes off, and I'm left behind, hands crushed into fists at my sides until my palms hurt. Another shitty problem I need to deal with.

Luckily, we're all just working on extension while the others rehearse what will be (hopefully, with a prayer and a hell of a lot of practice) the scene of the Kingdom of the Shades. I watch, listless, about 20 percent of my attention on the corps de ballet and the rest on the clock on the wall.

Walter and Fabienne stand on the other end of the room, and for a few minutes I almost forget they're there. Walter is keeping quiet for a change. Fabienne is saying something to him in a low voice. Finally, once the corps finishes yet another lackluster run through the choreography, Walter claps his hands.

"Class, one last thing before you go. Since, from the looks of it, we're going to need all the practice we can afford, I figure I might as well put all misconceptions to rest. Yes, Naomi is dancing Nikiya, no, that's not up for discussion. Gamzatti will be danced by Gemma Cole. The three solos in act two will be, respectively, Sarah, Aimee, and Madison. That's it. The end. Now go home and show up tomorrow in better shape than you were today."

I feel as much as hear Sarah's deep exhalation; she might as well be breathing fire at my back. The class rumbles, too tired to be shocked. Gemma, on the other hand, slings her bag over her shoulder and storms over, her limbs trembling with adrenaline and fatigue. She's sweaty and ghoulish looking.

"I'll destroy you," she hisses at me as she passes by much closer than she needs to. "For Anna."

6

September

THE DAY THE cast list is posted drags on endlessly. Georgina dives into her usual flurry of activity—cleaning, laundry, and wiping down the mirrors in front of Anna's barre. But even after finishing every chore, she realizes Anna won't be home for another hour. With nothing left to do, Georgina collapses on the couch, her gaze fixed on her phone. She opens YouTube and searches for the Boston Youth Ballet Competition 2018. The video pops up immediately, as if the algorithm knows her too well. For the millionth time, she hits play. The music starts, tinny through the phone's speaker. Georgina knows it by heart. Anna looks so small on the giant stage, her pale skin almost ghostly under the lights, her pale blue costume making her look even younger. Georgina had always thought they should do Giselle's act two variation. But no, Fabienne insisted on the grand pas classique, saying it played to Anna's strengths.

Georgina relented, thinking it would showcase Anna's flawless technique. And it does—until the end. Georgina forces herself to watch the final seconds, her thumb hovering over the pause button. She recites the moves in her head: the developpé à la seconde, the precise hops and piqués, Anna's taut muscles, her graceful arms, her angelic smile. Then, at the very end, the easiest part—the finale. Anna trembles, tips forward. It's the smallest of movements, but to the trained eye, it's a fatal error. The illusion is shattered. The video ends with applause, but Georgina hears it as pity. Useless anger gnaws at her.

That girl from San Francisco ended up winning with her Esmeralda variation. Silly, but hey, a tambourine! At least she didn't stumble at the last second. Georgina, feeling masochistic, clicks on the next link and watches the entire variation, fuming. This girl doesn't have a fraction of Anna's talent. How could Anna waste everything like this?

Georgina doesn't hear the front door open. She only realizes Anna is home when she sees her sneakers in the corner of her eye.

"Mom?"

Georgina sits up, her face flushing with guilt. Anna's lips part as if to speak, but Georgina cuts her off. "Why do you have your shoes on indoors? Haven't I told you a million times? Am I your cleaning service?"

Anna kicks off her sneakers. "Sorry, Mama."

"Don't just leave them there! Put them by the door."

Anna sighs and carries the sneakers off. Georgina listens to her daughter's steps fade away, the door to Anna's room softly closing behind her. The apartment is silent again.

Soon, she won't need me at all, Georgina thinks.

But for now, she still does. For now, and for another couple of years at least.

When Georgina enters Anna's room, she finds her daughter on the bed, peeling off her right sock. The sight of the cracked, bruised toenail makes Georgina wince. Anna wiggles her battered toes, rolling her ankles. Georgina, momentarily lost in awe of her daughter, forgets everything.

"I'm sorry, honey," Georgina says, surrendering. "I was just worried all day—and you didn't even text me."

Anna gives her a look from beneath her brow. Georgina feels the urge to confront her about the secret she found, but this is the worst possible time.

"Oh, Anna, don't be mad. Please. I didn't mean to snap at you—"

"You didn't snap, Mom. You yelled."

"I didn't—" Georgina gives up. "Fine. I didn't mean to yell."

"Yes, you did. And now you're only groveling so I'll tell you."

Georgina smiles despite herself. "Whatever. Don't tell me. I'll find out anyway."

Anna shrugs, infuriatingly. "If you can wait until the final performance—"

"I'm not going to wait! You know I'll call Fabienne—"

Anna's face darkens. "Yeah, yeah. Fabienne. Then why do you even ask when you know everyone did what they had to do so I'd get Nikiya?"

Georgina is taken aback by the sudden shift in energy. The force of nature concealed in Anna's small, sinewy body— it never ceases to amaze her. Anna should be dazzling sold-out concert halls all over the world. "So you got Nikiya?"

Anna scoffs. "Yes, I got Nikiya."

"Honey, that's fantastic!"

"Stop it, Mom. What did I just say? You knew all along, so why bother?"

"Of course I knew you'd get Nikiya because you're the best. We practiced day and night—"

"No, you knew because you called this morning. I didn't need your help."

"Of course you didn't," Georgina says, more harshly than she intended. What the hell, Anna? We should be celebrating.

"But maybe, just maybe, I wanted to do it by myself," Anna says. "And maybe, just maybe, I blew that audition."

"You didn't. Fabienne told me—"

"Just a little stumble. Just like in Boston. I saw what you were watching."

Oh. So that's what this is about. Georgina could laugh with relief. "Anna, that was years ago. It's all behind us. You'll do wonderfully as Nikiya. Who cares if you wobbled for half a second? We did every variation ten times—"

"More like a hundred. I thought you might break out the whip any moment."

"Anna, that's not necessary."

"When are you going to forgive me for that bad landing? You've been punishing me ever since."

"That's not true. You know I wish you every success. It's ballet that doesn't forgive."

"For God's sake, Mom. We won silver. The medal is in a display case at school."

Yes, Georgina thinks. To remind you that even when you're the best, one tiny stumble can ruin everything.

"And I'm proud of you," Georgina chokes out. "I've always been proud of you. Just like I'm proud of you for getting Nikiya. You deserve that role more than anyone, and you'll be spectacular in the show." At least she means that last part, wholeheartedly.

Anna gives a tentative smile.

"There you go," Georgina says, encouraged. "Now stop pouting. Your blood sugar is probably low. Why don't you take a shower, dress up, and we can splurge on dinner at Colombina, to celebrate. We've earned it."

"I don't need to shower."

"Come on, Anna. No shower after class? Your hair looks greasy."

That does the trick. Anna heads to the bathroom. Georgina listens to her locking the door and then the rush of water. Only then does she make a beeline for Anna's desk and pull out the drawer.

But the thing that was taped underneath is gone without a trace.

NAOMI

"*La Bayadère*," Walter is saying, pacing the main ballroom. "*The Temple Dancer.* A ballet for the ages. Anyone care to tell me about its origins?"

Everyone here knows *La Bayadère* inside out, and we've all spent the weekend watching YouTube videos of the greatest ballerinas. Finally, Sarah raises her hand, but Walter cuts her off.

"Yes, yes, if you don't know by now, there's a big problem. *La Bayadère*, created by the French in the nineteenth century. But the version you all know was created by Natalia Makarova in 1980, and that's what we'll be basing ourselves on. The story is in the best traditions of the genre. We have our beautiful temple dancer, Nikiya, in love with the brave warrior, Solor. Then the maharaja promises Solor to the princess Gamzatti. Nikiya is forced to dance at their wedding. The jealous princess sends her a basket of flowers that conceals a snake—and Nikiya prefers to die rather than lose Solor. Our valiant lover gets high on opium and hallucinates his dead beloved surrounded by ghosts of other temple dancers, ultimately following her into the afterlife. The end. Now, we already have our Nikiya in the lovely Anna, and

Naomi as Gamzatti, but be assured, there's something in there for all of you. And if you can pull off the Kingdom of the Shades scene with any conviction, you all have a shot at a future in ballet. Am I clear?"

Chins dip in agreement.

"I want to start rehearsing right away. Anna, Naomi, and James, stay here while everyone else goes to join Fabienne."

As the others file out, Anna catches my eye and winks. James stretches in the corner, avoiding us both.

"You two," Walter says, his outfit today a gaudy peacock print that makes my eyes bleed. "Here's something to start you off. You're romantic rivals. You're in love with the same man—"

"Not very feminist, is it?" I chime in. Bad idea, but I can't help it. And what's he going to do—demote me?

But instead of flipping out, he just stares at me, his gaze lingering. "Naomi, your part contains one of the most famous female variations in all of ballet—even though you're no Sylvie Guillem."

Dickhead.

"You have plenty of stage time to show our viewers everything you've got. So what more do you want from me?"

"Naomi is a great dancer," Anna chimes in, and I inwardly wince. What is she thinking? Shut up, shut up, shut up.

Walter glares at her. "I'll be the judge of that, thank you, Anna." He turns back to me. "Since your friend seems so sure—a certainty I don't exactly share—why don't you settle it for us?"

"I'm sorry?"

"Do the variation. And don't give me any excuses. Get up here, get in fourth, and show us."

Thanks a lot, bestie. I step to the center of the room, the necessary smile plastered on my face.

"And go."

He was right about one thing. I do know the variation by heart. It comes naturally, the music playing in my head. Developpé, grand jeté, piqué, piqué, piqué. The jumps are flawless, the first pirouette is great, the second is fine, then the cou-de-pied en dedans runs out of steam. I feel the tension rise in my standing leg, the world slowing tragically, and then, in a flash, it's over. I flop on my working foot.

Walter looks at me with pity, like I'm a shelter dog about to be euthanized. "That's all right, Naomi. Don't feel bad. We have time to practice."

If he'd just flipped out, it would've been better than this subtle assassination. I can't even look at Anna. James scoffs in the corner.

"Mr. Rawley, please mind your own business," Walter snaps. "Now, Anna. Show us what you've got."

"Which part?" Anna's wide-eyed innocence makes me want to slap her.

"Don't be dense. The Nikiya variation, act two."

Anna, at least, gets music. I watch her, unable to blink as she floats through the variation, her movements fluid and effortless.

Walter watches too, as does James. It's impossible not to watch her. She draws you in like gravity. I wouldn't want to follow her onstage.

Oh, wait.

"Stop, stop." Walter waves his hand, breaking the spell. Anna halts gracefully. "Anna, darling, you're dancing at the wedding of the love of your life. You're supposed to be sad. Sad, do you know what that means?"

Anna gulps, her pale skin translucent under the lights, veins visible beneath the surface. If not for her cream-colored leotard, you'd see her heart beating beneath her ribs.

"I can go again," she says. "Sadder."

She returns to the start position, her right hand fluttering just beneath her collarbones, her other arm bent behind her head. The dance unfolds like a flower, her arms and back limber, her feet steady.

Walter claps. I startle, so does James, but Anna stops smoothly.

"Sadder, for real, Anna."

"I am being sad," Anna answers, her jaw clenched.

"That's why they have you dancing Aurora and Coppélia. You kids don't know what true sadness is."

"I know what sadness is," Anna says.

"Pretend your Sephora order got lost in the mail. Internalize it."

"I know what sadness is," Anna repeats, her voice sharp. "Do you?"

"Oh, please. What's your biggest disappointment? Not getting a pony? Silver medal instead of gold? Get back into position and try again."

Anna glares, her eyes icy. Instead of complying, she walks out, the door swinging shut behind her. Anna has never done anything like this before. I'm speechless.

Walter shrugs. "Primas will prima. But if she thinks a ballet company will put up with this—"

"I can do it," I blurt out. "I can dance the scene. I've had plenty of disappointments."

The silence vibrates in the air. Walter stares at me.

"Oh, I don't doubt that."

James chuckles softly. Shut the fuck up, asshole.

"And if my experience as a choreographer is anything to go by, your disappointments aren't over. So thank you, Naomi, but no thank you. Get into positions, you two. Since our diva is off pouting, let's work on the grand pas de deux."

7

Now

THE SECOND DAY after Anna's injury finds Georgina at a coffee shop in the part of town favored by tourists. It's still respectable enough, in case she runs into anyone she knows, but she's unlikely to. The tourist traps make good money here year-round—in summer with the hiking and lake-house crowd, in winter with the skiers. But right now, the old town core is having one of its rare slumps. Only two other tables are occupied, and Georgina's favorite spot in the back is free. The place is charming without the fanny-pack-and-sneakers people. The café kept the original redbrick walls and emphasized the rusticity of the place with antiques-themed decor that she used to find tacky but has gotten used to. Plus, they serve really good skim cappuccinos.

But today, she's not here to sip coffee and gossip. Fabienne is late. Georgina keeps checking her phone and fidgeting until she finally sees her in the door. She's underdressed for the weather, and the giant sunglasses make her look ridiculous. She goes for her habitual two-cheek kiss, but Georgina subtly but effectively distances herself. She's not here for social niceties—she's here to talk about Anna's future.

Fabienne takes off her sunglasses and folds them in front of her on the table's repurposed 1950s tabletop. "I'm so sorry, G," Fabienne says, her voice low and husky. "I'm so sorry about what happened to Anna."

"Anna will be fine," Georgina says through clenched teeth. The waitress, some girl who can't be older than a high schooler, comes at the worst possible moment, asking if they want anything to drink.

"Do you have cognac?" Fabienne asks.

"Uh. If you want to drink alcohol, you have to order food. Those are the rules."

Georgina groans. "Fine. Bring us whatever menu item is the big, greasy, salty crowd favorite and two cognacs."

"We have brandy."

"Brandy is fine."

"So that'll be a crab cakes platter and two brandies. Do you want two sets of utensils?"

"No."

The waitress leaves, finally. Georgina follows her with a mildly horrified look; having spent most of her life marinating in the world of ballet, first ballet school, then years of dancing, and now ballet school again, she manages to forget what the outside world looks like. In this case, it looks like hunched shoulders and a short neck, and high-waisted baggy jeans that nobody should ever wear. She must be Anna's age and already has flabby arms. What'll they look like by the time she's thirty?

"Thank you," Fabienne mouths. She looks like she could use a cognac—pardon, brandy. Fabienne works hard on the whole French-girl shtick, even though she's from Quebec and has only set foot in France on vacation. When she lets her hair down, she likes to regale Georgina with tales of her childhood in the Centre-Sud of Montreal, running past massage parlors to her after-school ballet classes.

"So Anna will be coming back? In time for the show?" Fabienne half whispers. "What exactly is her injury? A break, or just a hairline fracture, or—"

"She won't tell me," Georgina says. "And she won't tell me what happened. She says she fell, except that makes no sense. How do you break your metatarsal by falling down the stairs?"

"It's possible," Fabienne chimes in. "Unlikely, but—"

"Unlikely," Georgina snaps. "Don't you think it's too much of a coincidence?"

Fabienne sinks into silence. The crab cakes arrive, piled on a greasy plate next to a mountain of fries. The smell of cooking oil makes Georgina nauseous.

"That's because it's not a coincidence," she says, lowering her voice. "Think about it. Too many people benefit from Anna being out of the picture."

Fabienne shakes her head. Is she in denial or just this dense? "What are you talking about, G? Everyone at school loves Anna. Always have. She's—" Fabienne cuts herself off.

She's the star, Georgina thinks. Exactly. If Fabienne had more cunning, her own dance career might have been that much more illustrious.

"You think this has to do with the Christmas gala?" Fabienne whispers.

"I don't know. Maybe. That boy James, does anyone know what he was doing that day?"

Fabienne gives her a look.

"Or Walter. You know Walter would do anything to get rid of Anna."

"If either of them had anything to do with it," Fabienne says, "Anna would have told us."

Georgina exhales. "Precisely. But she's protecting someone. Who would she be protecting, and why?"

"Georgina, I'm sorry to say this, but could you be over-thinking this? If someone else had been involved...if you really think someone...pushed Anna...she'd have had every reason to tell us."

Oh, but you don't know Anna like I do, Georgina thinks.

"I need your help more than ever, Fabienne," she says. "I need you to find out everything you can about Naomi Thompson."

"Naomi?" Fabienne blinks her tired eyes. "What about her?"

"What about her? Are you joking?"

At that moment, the short-necked girl returns with the brandies. The amber liquor sloshing around the bottom of the glass, clinking with ice cubes, smells cheap. Georgina takes a sip that confirms her suspicions. Fabienne looks at the drinks doubtfully.

"You think Naomi had something to do with Anna's fall?"

Is she thick in the head? Georgina can hardly contain her fury. "Yes, I think Naomi had something to do with it. She had everything to gain. Like I said, it's just too much of a coincidence…"

"But I thought," Fabienne cuts in artlessly, "I thought you said that because…your own career, that ended when you broke your metatarsal, didn't it?"

In that moment, Georgina's old dance training rears its head. For years and years, since she was a little girl, her language hasn't been Russian or English or the French of the ballet vernacular so much as it has been dance. Her feelings manifest first in motion and only then in thoughts and words. And now it's a peculiar mix of shame, indignation, and surprise that moves her. She leaps to her feet.

"Fabienne," she says, "you must help me. I helped you and Alexandra and your school, didn't I? Don't you think you owe me?"

What she reads in the other woman's gaze isn't quite what she hoped for. "I'll help you," Fabienne reassures her. "Of course

I will. I didn't mean to offend, Georgina. Not at all. I'm sorry I brought it up."

Georgina gets her purse, pays the short-necked girl, and heads out.

NAOMI

Another day as Nikiya, and I could be doing better.

"Piqué, piqué, piqué, pirouette." Walter's voice drowns out the music, at least in my ears. Minkus's frantically simple little melody fills the room to the ceiling. The volume is earsplitting, yet it seems like I'm the only one who can't hear it properly. At least according to Walter. "Can you actually dance, and not just go through the moves to get it over with? You're dancing the lead in *La Bayadère*, not doing Zumba for seniors at the Y, Naomi."

It's weird enough to be doing these same moves that only a week ago belonged to Anna. Anna's role, Anna's costume (which feels like it's about to burst at the seams, thanks for asking), Anna's perfect little steps that I just can't replicate. How the hell did she make this look so easy?

I glance at the mirror for reassurance, but all I see is my own sweat-drenched self, wobbling slightly on pointe. The worst part is, I did everything right! I nailed every move, didn't stumble, yet it's still not enough. I've always tried to convince myself that maybe, just maybe, the differences between me and Anna were trivial, purely subjective, affectations of our ballet teachers who were biased to begin with, not to mention brainwashed by some unattainable Balanchine ideal. Now I truly realize there's a chasm between me and Anna, one I might never, for all my training and determination, be able to cross.

Ballet, it turns out, is built on all these uncomfortable truths. All creative fields are, to a degree, but especially ballet. It'll never be egalitarian and fair. It flies in the face of the cliched American dream, but what can you do? You can't really be anything you want, no matter how hard you work. If you're born with a certain sort of feet, body, turnout, you will always look better than someone who works just as hard as you but was less lucky in the genetic lottery. Anna was born to dance. And it would be silly to expect otherwise, with a heritage like hers. She's royalty, and the rest of us are peasants in tutus. The end.

"Naomi, do you care to tell me what the matter is today? Yesterday you weren't great, but you were nowhere near this bad."

"I'm doing the exact same thing I did yesterday," I snap, unable to help myself. I'm only too aware of Gemma on the periphery, smirking. She hasn't yet had my epiphany, and for now, she's sublimating all her deep-seated envy and rage into hating me.

"And yet it's not working. This is a key scene, Naomi. The death of Nikiya. The sorrow of seeing the love of your life betrothed to your rival, then the last, desperate élan of hope. And then you choose death over seeing your beloved with someone else. It's supposed to be brimming with emotion. Why can't you get it right?"

I can't answer that question truthfully without disgracing myself and admitting defeat. I might as well just hang up my pointe shoes, walk out of the school, and never come back. So I choose the only other option that seems sensible: I double down.

"Because I don't believe it," I say, and the moment it comes out of my mouth, it becomes the truth. "It's dumb and makes no sense. Why should I kill myself over some guy? So he wants to marry the other chick, good riddance."

Walter groans. He rubs his eyes with the heels of his hands. "Ah, yes. That. Why, how stupid of me. Let me just rewrite the whole ballet to fit your modern sensibilities. We've still got a couple of weeks before the performance, right?" He crosses the distance between us in slow, heavy steps. "You know, that's the problem with you. Not your poor stability or your balance. The problem is much bigger, and your dancing is positively infected with it."

He's standing right in front of me now, not enough distance between us to breathe. "The problem is between your ears. You treat dancing like some sort of gymnastics competition. And it is, for sure, but it's an art first, and that's where you fail. Art isn't one-note. It's not just a scoreboard with grades of one through ten. *La Bayadère* is art. It's nuanced, it's ambiguous, it doesn't try to spoon-feed the audience what they're supposed to think and feel. To dance Nikiya, you must be able to reconcile within you both love and hate, anger and forgiveness, all at the same time, in a perfect balance within your soul. That's why *La Bayadère* is one of the great ballets. That's why it's memorable. And you are not. You are one-note, just like your dancing."

Blood rushes to my face. Walter steps back, then strides to the other end of the room like nothing happened. Everett watches me intently. Gemma, on the other hand, is looking everywhere except at me.

Walter claps his hands. "Well, don't just stand there like wax figures. Everett, you're up. Let's leave the death scene for another time and practice the Kingdom of Shades pas de deux."

But to my dismay, Everett shrugs. "Sorry. I can't do another PDD today—I'm supposed to rest my shoulder."

I don't believe my ears. He's doing this to me now? He got to dance Solor instead of some bit part, and he's repaying me like this? Traitor.

Walter heaves a sigh and then waves his hand dismissively. "Yeah, whatever. I know you've got to lift Naomi, and that's no easy task. You can go, but that shoulder better be in good shape when we need it."

Blood rushes to my face, and I'm grateful for being already red and sweaty.

"I'll do it," Walter says.

What?

"I'll stand in for Solor. This is about you, Nikiya, so go ahead and impress me."

He circles me like a predatory cat, longer than necessary before taking his starting position. The music starts. Feelings, huh? That dickhead wants feelings. I'll show him feelings.

I bourrée around Walter before he puts his hands on my waist so I can do my pirouette turn, and that's when he breathes in my ear:

"Love and hate, right? That can't be too hard."

"Shut up," I mutter through my teeth, even as I keep up the necessary sorrowful expression the scene requires.

I transition smoothly to the arabesque, balancing on pointe on one leg. It's one of the harder moves of the pas, and I always wobble, but right now, my standing leg is solid, taut as a string, and the balancing comes almost naturally. A beat, two beats, three beats, and I feel like I could go on for another full minute when it's time to transition out, into a graceful jump followed by a developpé, my leg raised high. Walter's hands glide along my waist, just firm enough to support me in this complicated move, cold, light, respectful.

Appearances truly can be deceiving, can't they?

Anna isn't the only one who knows how to pretend.

8

October

Rehearsals have only just started, and already Georgina has a bad feeling.

"This is not okay, Anna. I'm going to speak to Fabienne."

Anna stops halfway through the pas chassés sequence she's practicing, her feet moving with the usual efficiency and precision, practically a blur.

"What's wrong with it?"

"What's wrong with it?" Georgina repeats with an incredulous chuckle. "Are you kidding me? Why don't they send you out in a bikini while they're at it?"

"But it's the Nikiya costume for the death scene. It's the same in every production I've seen, Mom."

"Yes, well—every production you've seen isn't danced by children. He's sending you out onstage in a bra. You're fifteen."

"Almost sixteen," Anna mutters.

"As if that makes a difference! This is a show for ballet recruiters, not a sex-slave auction."

"Mama!" Anna exclaims indignantly.

Georgina dismisses her with a wave of her hand. "Don't. If you want to act all offended, be offended at Walter for dressing you up like eye candy. At least that'll be productive. They might listen if it comes from you."

Anna takes off the headpiece. It's a lovely costume, in a way, Georgina has to admit—adorned with an intricate pattern of high-quality rhinestones, and the headpiece has a veil attached, made of a soft, flowing fabric that follows Anna's every move like a living thing. All very well, except for the bra. But why does this girl have to argue about everything?

"I'm not going to say anything to anyone, Mom," she says, and Georgina knows she means it because she gets that obstinate look she's had since she was a child. It's not an attractive look. Her nostrils flare, and her mouth all but disappears, and she looks—no matter how much Georgina hates to admit it—just like her father. Not Georgina's favorite side of her. "Everyone will make fun of me forever."

"So what? And if they tell you to dance naked, you'll just go along so that no one laughs at you? You have to have principles."

"I do have principles." There it is again, that square-jawed, narrow-eyed expression. Oh, how she wants to slap it off Anna's face sometimes, even though she'd never act on that urge. "And yes, it makes a difference. Sixteen is the age of consent, so I decide—"

"Age of consent!" Georgina laughs. "Just listen to yourself. Age of consent. Consent to what, exactly?"

Anna folds her arms across her chest—across that ridiculous sparkly bra. But whatever nonsense she's about to say to Georgina, Georgina interrupts before it can leave her mouth.

"You're still my daughter. And I still have some say about whether it's a good idea to dance half-naked. And if you want to talk about the age of consent, maybe you also feel like telling me about those birth control pills I found taped under your desk drawer."

Georgina regrets it the second she says the words. For the last month, she's managed to put the birth control pills out of her mind. There were more important things to think about, like that arabesque balance in the third act that Anna got right about one time out of three. And, whether or not she admitted it to herself, she hoped to keep the knowledge secret for the time being—as leverage to be used at the right moment. And now she's gone and wasted it on this silly argument over a costume. Is it so bad after all? Anna has a point; every Nikiya she's ever seen wore a variation of that same outfit.

But now the bird is out of the cage, and Anna's expression becomes livid.

"You went through my things again?"

"I was cleaning your room, which you always leave like a pigsty. Your desk drawer was jammed."

"That is none of your business!"

"Like you yourself just pointed out, sixteen is the age. And you're not sixteen just yet. And I'm pretty sure you need a prescription for those things—"

"I only got them for my acne, Mom," Anna snaps. "Because no one will care about my dancing with all the crater zits glaring through the pancake foundation under stage lights. And I didn't tell you because I knew you'd freak out!"

Georgina's face warms. She's not entirely sure she should believe Anna, but she has a point—stress has been making her break out, especially around her hairline, where all that hair spray clogs pores and makes it even worse. But it's embarrassing to have made such a scene for something so banal.

"You should have asked me first! I would have gotten you some Retin-A cream or something. Not the pill, for God's sake. Don't you know what that garbage will do to your body? Everything you eat will go straight to your tits. And with that—stripper bra they insist on having you wear..."

"Mom, please." Anna looks so over it. She sits down and starts to take off her pointe shoes.

"You're not done!"

She momentarily looks up. "Yes, I am."

"And you still didn't answer my question."

"Question? Were there more questions?"

"Yes. Where did you get the pills?"

Anna heaves a deep sigh, gets up even though she's only had time to take off one shoe, and plods to her room. The door slams, and Georgina is left alone in the middle of the living room.

Who does she think she is, she catches herself thinking, and immediately cringes with guilt. This isn't one of her old ballet rivals—this is her own Anna, and what matters most is that she get every opportunity, secure every success. Even if she acts like she hates me, Georgina thinks, deep down she appreciates everything I do for her. Or at least she will, one day.

And if that day hasn't yet come, Georgina refuses to be discouraged. So Anna doesn't want to tell her—so what? Georgina has her ways. And she's never let anyone stand in her way before.

So, without wasting time, she grabs her purse, puts on her shoes and her fall coat, and heads out.

Dawn's head throbs from too little sleep and too much coffee. She excuses her lack of energy by saying she had insomnia, which makes every other night nurse nod sympathetically: That upside-down schedule is almost as hard to get into as it is to get out of, and it'll mess you up. But the truth is, she stayed up way too late—early?—watching YouTube videos of ballet dancers. She'd never heard of *La Bayadère* before, which she reluctantly admitted to Naomi—who, in turn, reacted with abject horror. She explained to her mother all about the ballet, the story, the characters. "And I'm dancing Gamzatti," she said. "The princess who steals the warrior from Nikiya."

"The second role," Dawn clarified. She hadn't meant anything by it, she swears. She hadn't even thought of what she was saying. But Naomi, as always, took it to heart. She started pouting and said it was a principal role. Of course it is, but it's not the main role—that would be Nikiya. But by then, Dawn knew to keep her thoughts to herself.

She watched endless clips on YouTube of the so-called Gamzatti variation. Variation, apparently, just means a solo dance. At first, she found the combination of bland classical music and bizarre, anachronistic Indian costumes jarring and a little ridiculous, but then she had to admit it grew on her. The ballerina dancing Gamzatti wore a classic tutu that stuck out at a right angle while everyone else wore those wide pants and headpieces. All the jumps and turns and the seemingly impossible footwork—could Naomi really do all that? She felt awful for doubting her daughter, but it just looked so...difficult.

She scrolled through all the search results. All the names of the great ballerinas meant absolutely nothing to her, and she tried to imagine her daughter among them: the great Naomi Thompson, principal dancer at This or That Ballet. Naomi had all the determination in the world and talent to match, but Dawn still had a hard time picturing it. The competition had to be more than fierce. Did Naomi realize how many hurdles she had yet to face? To get into a ballet company at all, she'd have to beat all the best dancers from all the other ballet schools. It wouldn't be like at the academy, where a handful of girls had real promise and the rest were just having their ballet phase.

Oh, how Dawn once hoped it would turn out to be a phase. She'd never tell her daughter, not if Naomi had her at knifepoint, but more than a few times, she's regretted ever taking her to that production of *Swan Lake* when they visited her family in Boston. After that, it had to be ballet class or nothing. And what a coincidence, their town was home to one of the most prestigious schools in America!

But now, she simply has to think in terms of sunk costs. After all these sacrifices, the least she can do is be encouraging and do her best to help Naomi get a fair shot at her dream.

She's so lost in her thoughts, she doesn't hear her own name being called. Then the voice says it again, and it's familiar but in that wrong way, out of place. She turns around, and sure enough, it's not one of her colleagues. The woman stands out against the stark bareness of the hospital hallway. She's little, but she's wearing vertiginous high-heeled boots, and her carefully dyed hair is pulled back to show off a pair of heavy diamond earrings.

"Dawn," she says for the third time, "we should talk."

"Georgina," Dawn says. "Hi. What are you doing here?"

She finds Ms. Prescott terrifying. She always has. When Naomi first became friends with Anna, in fifth grade, Dawn took pity on the slight, pale little girl who looked so much younger than her age, left to her own devices at boarding school. She welcomed Anna into her modest home for dinner on many nights and for sleepovers on the weekends. It was nice that Naomi had such a close friend, and the girls adored each other.

But then, two years later, Georgina moved to town and promptly took Anna out of the dorms. As far as Dawn understood, there had been a divorce from Anna's father, and so Georgina had moved from Boston into a spacious condo that she'd bought with her settlement. When she first introduced herself, Dawn committed the mortal sin of not knowing who she was. Apparently, she was some great dancer once upon a time, born and educated at a ballet school in what was then the USSR, with a career spanning two continents. It wasn't personal—Dawn hadn't heard of her any more than she had of any other ballerina, famous or not. But since then, even though Georgina Prescott née Mironoff is nothing but cloying sweetness to her in public, Dawn has known she doesn't like her.

Georgina looks her up and down. It would be enough to irritate Dawn, but in the years of ballet recitals and school events, she's gotten used to that once-over that seems to be industry standard, useful for sizing up competition and evaluating the wealth of potential patrons. Right now, though, Georgina is her usual self in impeccable, expensive-looking clothes, and Dawn is wearing scrubs, her hair up in a messy bun. The glance confirms what Dawn already feels: Georgina sees her as a natural inferior.

"Hi, Dawn. So sorry to interrupt you, you must be busy. But—"

"I kind of am, actually." Two can play this game. Dawn mirrors Georgina's fake grin.

"Oh, I hate to bother you. It won't take long, I promise. I just wanted to know, who the fuck do you think you are to go behind my back, prescribing medication to my daughter?"

The smile slides right off Dawn's face. Instinctively, she checks around her to see if anyone can overhear. Thank God they seem to be out of earshot. "Georgina, is this about the birth control?"

She hates it, hates it with every fiber of her being, but she will have to grovel. What she did was technically wrong. "I didn't mean anything sinister, I swear—Anna said it was for her acne. She does have some stubborn breakouts on her forehead—"

"Did you think I wouldn't find out? I went to the drugstore. They didn't want to show me the prescription, but I explained that Anna is underage, that I'm her mother, and that the prescription may have been made without my knowledge. And imagine my shock when I recognized the name on the scrip. Thompson."

Dawn scrambles for something to say. Why did she do it? She was just trying to help. She always wants to think of herself as the good grown-up, the kind of parent—and adult in general—that her daughter and other children can come to with their problems, someone they can trust. She supposes she got carried away this time, but you know what they say about hindsight.

"Anna came to me for help," she stammers, mortified at her voice's betrayal. "I—I didn't know how to say no. She said there was no one else she could ask—"

"Except there was, wasn't there? Me. Now listen here, Dawn. I hope you realize these are decisions a girl has to make with the advice and guidance of her mother. Not some holier-than-thou stranger so desperate to be the cool mom she's willing to break the law. I wonder what would happen if I went and told your superiors."

Dawn's insides clench.

"But I won't. Purely for Anna's sake. I know she loves Naomi and would be terribly upset if her best friend's family had to leave town."

All the breath goes out of her lungs, but Georgina, having gotten her pound of flesh, seems satisfied. The look of rage is replaced by one of cold smugness.

"Have a good night, Dawn. Don't wear yourself out."

She turns around and leaves, all perfect posture and grace, floating like a vision down the hospital hall. Dawn notices a couple of her coworkers unabashedly staring from around a corner.

Dawn clenches her fists at her sides. You smug, self-satisfied crow. Whose fault is it that your daughter didn't feel it was safe to come to you? And who can blame poor Anna? A great white shark would make a better mother.

And she wonders what Georgina would have said had Dawn

told her the real reason Anna wanted those pills. She'd shit her perfect pantyhose right in the middle of the hallway.

NAOMI

It's official: I'm having the day from hell.

The moment I cross the threshold of the front door, I know my mom is in a bad mood. When I left this morning, she hadn't come back yet, and now she's clearly had time to sleep on whatever had pissed her off. The house is sparkling, and there are sounds of furious vacuuming coming from another room.

My room.

Forgetting to kick off my sneakers, I race across the house and stop in the doorway of my bedroom. Sure enough, she's vacuuming under the bed.

"Mom?"

The vacuum doesn't stop, but she turns around. Some of the tension goes out of my shoulders when I see the look on her face. She clearly hasn't had time to find anything incriminating. Yet.

"Naomi. You're home early."

"I'm home on time," I say—more like yell. I gesture at her to turn off the vacuum, which she does. Silence at last.

"Oh, I never know anymore. You're always staying after classes since you got that role."

And that's your excuse for ransacking my room? "I'm not staying after classes—I'm rehearsing. Along with Anna."

At the mention of the name, a shadow goes over my mom's face.

"What's the matter? Why are you in my room?"

"Because someone has to clean in here. Obviously."

Okay. What's gotten under her scrubs? "I clean my room myself. As you know."

"Then try doing it more often than once a year, Naomi. I swear, at this rate we're going to get mice."

But she unplugs the vacuum cleaner and gets up. "Are you going to eat dinner?"

"Already ate."

"Ha. Nice try. We're having spaghetti and meatballs, and *we* includes you."

Once I'm reasonably sure she's not going back to my room to snoop around, I quickly hop in the shower. I need it; I stink. In all senses of the word.

I'm not going to tell Dawn in a million years, and even if I did, she wouldn't understand. She'd either brush it off as insignificant or, even worse, try to sound like she actually cares, which achieves the opposite effect because she so blatantly has no idea what she's talking about. In all these years, you'd think she'd have taken at least some interest in what I do. I'm not asking her to learn the choreography of an entire ballet by heart, but she could have googled some of the moves so she's not looking at me with glassy eyes when I tell her about my day.

I mean, what am I supposed to tell her? That her daughter, wannabe principal dancer, can't manage the end of the grand pas de deux between Gamzatti and Solor? Yes, I got it right once, but then I just couldn't seem to replicate it. I wanted a principal part, and now I have one. But the sequence, Italian fouettés followed by twenty fouettés en tournant, proved too much.

In the finished version, it's supposed to be this grand scene with the corps de ballet in the background and two soloists on either side of me. One of the most spectacular scenes in a ballet that's chock-full of spectacular scenes. But there was nothing spectacular about me floundering through the routine time after time. All of Walter's yelling made no difference, except that I think my ears are still ringing. *Fine*, he said at last. *If she still can't manage by showtime, we'll just have to modify.* Yes, the recruiters from all over the country will have come all this way for a modified Gamzatti.

Fuck my life.

I get out of the shower to be greeted by the nauseating smell of burned meatballs, and I know my day is only going to get worse from here. Dawn is, sadly, one of those people who are inherently bad at cooking but love doing it.

"Mom, I really ate," I say as I emerge from the bathroom, my hair in a towel. I realize I sound like I'm whining, which is okay, because after all, I am whining. "I swear."

"Nope." Dawn doesn't turn away from the stove as she pours oil into the frying pan in a vain effort to save the meatballs.

"Then just…give me some plain pasta and let's call it a day."

She brings the oil bottle down on the counter harder than she has to. A little bit spills out over the edge.

"I'm making you dinner," she snaps. "You could at least say thank you."

"Thank you, Mom. It's just—"

"And don't take your bad day out on me. I had a crappy day too, by the way. Night. Whatever. You know why? Because your friend Anna's psychotic mom showed up at my work and made a huge scene."

Blood freezes in my veins. "What?"

"Oh, yes. You know what they say, no good deed goes unpunished? Well, I feel like I've gotten my money's worth. When your Anna asked me for those birth control pills, I agreed, because I believe in responsibility and safe sex and a woman's right over her own body. And if she doesn't feel secure talking to her mother about things—better she comes to me than goes unprotected, am I right?"

Jesus. It's about that. I collapse like a deflated balloon. "Mom…"

"No, don't *Mom* me. This is the last time I meddle in your teenage problems. I wonder what a fit Georgina would have had if her precious Anna had gotten pregnant instead."

"Mom, please stop. I'm sorry Ms. Prescott yelled at you—"

"I have been nothing but a fairy freaking godmother to that girl. From the start. Back when she hid in corners at the school dormitory while her mother lived the good life in the city, I took her in. Let her into my home, treated her like my own child. And that woman never said a word of thanks. She treats me like dirt. Like it's such a step down to work at a hospital instead of doing something worthy, you know, something creative, like hopping around on my toes all day with my ass hanging out of my skirt. Is she right? If you think so, Naomi, just say it to my face."

"No, Mom. She's not right. She's crazy, you know it, everybody knows it. Even Anna knows it, that's why she came to you." It all comes out on autopilot because I've said some variation of this spiel a number of times before.

"You know what? I've been patient and tolerant and accepting of all this ballet stuff. I pay that crazy tuition and pretend I don't notice that you're a couple of pounds away from starvation. But to have that psycho show up at my place of work and threaten to get me fired? That's a bit too much. Sometimes, I swear, I want to just pull you from that school and put a stop to all this dance nonsense."

I glare at her across the tiny, cramped kitchen. The burning reek from the frying pan intensifies.

"Naomi, I didn't mean it like that. I—"

"Smoke," I say, and it's true. Thick gray smoke rises from the frying pan and floats under the ceiling, where it awakens the ancient, grease-crusted alarm. Its hoarse screeching fills the small room. My mom curses and rushes to open the window, which does nothing to diminish the smoke.

Fuck it. I've had enough. And she knows where she can shove her spaghetti. I go to my room, close the door, and prop up the handle with the back of a chair. Only then do I check my secret hiding place. The little booklet is still exactly where I left it, undisturbed, and so is the roll of bills as thick as my wrist.

9

Now

GEORGINA CHECKS HER phone, even though she knows there's no new message. She dials her ex-husband's number, anticipating voicemail. When it picks up, her anger resurfaces.

"Colter," she begins, straining to keep calm, "it's me again. It's about Anna. She broke her foot, and I don't know how severe it is—whether she'll dance again or even walk." The lie sticks in her throat. "I also haven't received any payment from you since July. We could really use some help. I don't want to go through the court, but you know I will if I have to." She grimaces, knowing he's a top lawyer in Boston and could stop paying anytime he wants. "Anna would like her dad to call and check on her." She ends the call, knowing he won't respond, and dials another number, one she found online, this one for a law firm.

"Are you out of your fucking mind?" Alexandra hisses.

It's nice to see Alexandra be candid for once. They're in her office, alone, with the door closed, and this must be the first time Georgina has heard Alexandra use a curse word. Right now, she looks like an angry cat; the lines around her mouth that she diligently pumps full of filler every few months are nice and deep, and while her forehead is immobilized, the veins on it pop out like gnarly roots of a tree.

"Anna fell on school property, and her entire ballet future is at risk. Think, Alexandra. If this were your daughter, what would you do?"

Alexandra doesn't have a daughter. She diligently danced through the entirety of her childbearing years with a big and prestigious company—in the back of the corps de ballet, but still. She could have headed down the well-worn path to oblivion, alcoholism, and pill popping, but luckily, she's a better socialite than she was a ballerina. After a short stint as a teacher, she charmed her way up the ladder to the job of principal.

It occurs to Georgina that perhaps Alexandra just doesn't like children, and her hopeless career was merely an excuse. In that case, she's found her dream job here at the academy, torturing young ballet hopefuls, deciding fates with the stroke of a pen.

"You're suing the school."

"Not suing just yet. But yes, it's in the works. For now, I'm also open to settling, if the terms are agreeable."

"You're shitting me. Terms? You can't sue us. This stuff isn't within our control. Can you imagine if every ballet school and company got sued whenever a dancer is injured?"

Georgina swears she sees an evil glimmer in the woman's blue eyes. Yes, indeed, Georgina herself would be rich enough not to have to beg her ex-husband to pay for Anna's physical therapy.

"This isn't just any injury," Georgina says.

"What are you implying?"

"You know Anna didn't just trip and fall. And I have information suggesting another student was involved."

Alexandra pales. "What information? Georgina, don't do this. We're friends. We both care about Anna. If you know something—"

Georgina cuts her off. "You will find out what when we go to court." She can't deny that she feels a certain satisfaction at seeing the other woman's distress. Friends, yeah, right. *What were you thinking when you brought in that tattooed vulture as choreographer? That's when it all came apart. This is all your fault too.*

"Georgina, please. Don't do this."

"My lawyer will get in touch to see if you want to negotiate a settlement," Georgina says. She's already spoken to the police so far, an impertinent, impatient woman whose name is already slipping away from her—Tyler or something. The conversation was brief and inconclusive, so Georgina is bluffing like there's no tomorrow, but she knows how to keep a poker face. Unlike Alexandra, who's coming apart at the seams right in front of her. "And you really should consider it. Because I know you don't want it to go to court. Imagine, a trial, a formal investigation. When they get to your office, to your filing cabinets, what will they find?"

Alexandra grows livid. "You cunt," she spits through clenched teeth. "After everything we've done for you—"

Georgina gets up and picks up her coat. "If anything, I'm the one who's done everything for you. Without me, all your galas would look a lot more...spare, don't you think?"

"I wish I'd never accepted your help," Alexandra hisses. "I wish I'd never, ever let you cross this threshold—"

"But you did," Georgina says with a satisfying feeling of finality. "And here we are."

NAOMI

I just finished rehearsing Nikiya's scarf dance from act two. Finished, as Walter bluntly put it, for today. The scene, for now, is far from ready.

At least this scene doesn't require many lifts, so we manage with Everett's unreliable shoulder. Now I get to slump against the wall, water bottle in hand, while he continues dancing, this time with Gemma.

Maybe he's doing this to piss me off—he probably is—but suddenly his shoulder seems fine. He's not dropping Gemma nearly as much as he did me. Yesterday, after rehearsal, Gemma just happened to enter the bathroom as I was leaving, and as she brushed past me, she hissed, "Maybe lay off the tacos. You'll be easier to lift."

She doesn't have that problem. I guess all the puking is finally paying off.

Truth is, I've lost weight over the last month—enough that my jeans need a belt, and my mom is starting to get on my case again. But I eat all the burnt slop she makes, and still, every time I step on the scale in the locker room, I weigh less. Maybe by the final performance, Anna's costume will actually fit me.

Gemma's been doing a decent job, much as I hate to admit it. She's improved, not just in this role but in other rehearsals too. Teachers praise her, and no one calls on her in class—a bad sign. She's like the potted plant from that experiment where people say nice things to it all day and yell at the other plant. The praised plant looks better and better while the other one slowly dies.

Walter watches her, and I watch him whenever I think he's not looking. He's got his chin propped on his hand—a sign he's pleased. Or as pleased as Walter gets. Lately, he hasn't propped his chin when looking at me. Not at all.

Today, though, there's a thin smile on his lips that I can't quite read. The music reaches a crescendo, the grand pas concludes—still without the fouettés—and Gemma returns to a still position. Sweat soaks the front of her leotard like a bib.

"Do you have any notes?" she asks, breathless.

Walter lets the silence hang. "Gemma, Gemma," he says finally. "Everett, good job. Keep at it. No more wobbling or dropping. If you can lift Gemma without a problem, Naomi should be a cakewalk since she's at least ten pounds lighter."

Gemma's ballet smile fades.

"Gemma, dear, what can I say? Not bad, not bad at all. Unfortunately, you're done here."

Her arms drop by her sides. "I'm—I'm sorry?"

"I said you're done. You're good, but not good enough for Gamzatti. You'll be doing the pas de quatre instead of Monica. Now, can someone run quickly to classroom 4G and tell Fabienne I need to borrow Sarah?"

Before I can think better of it, I'm on my feet.

"Go, Naomi. Hurry. We still have thirty minutes, and I want to make the most of it, especially since we're having a last-minute change in casting."

I hurry down the hall to classroom 4G. What did Gemma do wrong? He wouldn't change the cast with just a month to go before the show just to mess with us. Would he? Even for Walter, that's too much.

When I reach classroom 4G and deliver the news, Fabienne hardly seems surprised. Sarah takes everything in stride—too much in stride.

"What did you do?" I whisper as she falls into step next to me. "Blow him during lunch break?"

"Fuck off," she replies, but with a smirk. It doesn't sound like something Sarah would do, anyway. She's smart enough to know not to play those games with Walter. At least not yet.

Poor Gemma. I can't help but shudder.

Sarah takes her place to rehearse the variation, and Walter tells me I can cool down since he won't need me for this rehearsal. So I change, wash my face, and let my hair out of its bun, rubbing my aching scalp. But instead of relaxing, I'm drawn back to the rehearsal room.

As I get closer, I tiptoe, heart racing. The music pours through the wide-open doors, and I forget to be quiet.

The music swells. It's not the variation anymore; it's the end of the pas de deux. I reach the doors and peer in just in time to see Sarah, on pointe, her leg extended behind her as she flips effortlessly through the developpés. As the fouetté sequence begins, she notices me. She beams, spinning flawlessly through all twenty fouettés without a tremor.

Before anyone can see me, I retreat like a coward. I back away, terrified that any moment now, they'll spill out of the doors, pointing and laughing at me.

The music crashes to a crescendo, and that's when I finally turn and run.

That whole thing with the bad ankle, the buddy act—it was all fake. The entire time, she was planning her takeover. She will pay for this.

She will pay.

10

November

"GEORGINA! HI. I'VE been meaning to talk to you."

Then you could have called, Georgina thinks coldly. She isn't here to talk to Alexandra—she's here to watch the rehearsal for the Christmas gala show. Along with the usual numbers from the other age groups, they plan to showcase select scenes from the upcoming end-of-year performance by the graduating class. Anna and her partner, a nice boy from a wealthy New York family, are dancing the act one pas de deux. Georgina interrogated Fabienne, of course, and Fabienne assured her that he was reliable and had never dropped anyone. She mentioned they'd had a little trouble with chemistry at first, but both Anna and her partner had really leveled up. So Georgina isn't here for quality control as much as to admire the magnificent sight that is Anna onstage. In those moments, she almost forgets that she's Anna's mother, and even that she is a ballerina in her own right. She retreats into the comfortable zone of admirer rather than stern evaluator, allowing herself the luxury of just sitting back and enjoying.

Or she could, until Alexandra spied her waiting at the doors to the auditorium and pounced.

"You look tired, Alexandra," Georgina says. "Are you getting enough sleep?"

"Look, I'm so sorry about Walter," Alexandra says, her voice all honey. "He'll mellow out once he gets to know you. He's just protective of his creative vision."

Yes, the creative vision of my daughter in a tiny rhinestone-studded bra, Georgina thinks. "I don't see how he's going to get to know me since I'm not even sure I'm still allowed within these walls."

"Then I have the perfect opportunity for you to prove just how irreplaceable you are," Alexandra says. Here it comes, Georgina thinks. "I'm having some issues with this year's Christmas gala."

"What sort of issues?"

"Well...I had some last-minute cancellations. And this year, we've had budget cuts that mean we can't afford to provide accommodation for some of our guests, and the champagne isn't quite...what it was last time. And under those conditions, it's kind of hard to get people to donate."

Georgina sighs and pretends to think it over, feeling triumphant. Just like that, she's back in favor. They know they depend on her for so much. It doesn't matter how Walter feels about it. The school needs her.

She agrees. She'll do it. Of course she'll do it, just like every year. She'll work her magic, reach out to all her old fans with deep pockets, and everything will appear—the champagne, the funding, everything.

"Wonderful. Stop by my office after the rehearsal."

Georgina gracefully acquiesces. What else is there to do? It's for Anna. There's nothing she wouldn't do for Anna.

NAOMI

I watch them on the stage doing the final rehearsal. The view is so different from my angle, from behind one of the heavy velvet curtains. I see what nobody in the audience can see.

Anna is wearing an all-white outfit, from leotard to pointe shoes, reminiscent of Nikiya's act one costume, all flowy and angelic and innocent. James is dressed, as always, in all black. He picks her up with no effort at all, and she looks ravishing, as if she really did just run into her lover's arms, full of spontaneity and joy, not fake, rehearsed perfection. She looks great. Hell, *great* is too small a word. She looks ready to tread a world-class stage. In this moment, she *is* Nikiya.

"Careful," says a voice above my ear. "I think they can see those green glowing eyes out there in the audience."

I turn, but it's just Everett. He got cast as the Golden Idol, a short but extremely challenging role that will showcase him in a good light since his great strength is in his jumps.

"I'm so not in the mood," I say.

"You can't even tell that he dumped her last year," Everett points out. "Unless, of course, they're back together."

"They're not getting back together."

He shrugs. "How much did you pay him to pull that stunt?"

My heart gives an uncomfortable little jump. But, as the trained ballerina that I am, outwardly I don't move a muscle. I turn my head so I can see his face and speak carefully. "What the hell are you talking about? What stunt?"

He gives a soft guffaw, concealed in the shadows of the curtain. "Everybody knows, Naomi. If Anna doesn't know, she will soon."

"There's nothing to know. They dated. He dumped her. He's James, he's fucked the whole school twice over since eighth grade. What did she expect? Wedding bells?"

Everett shakes his head. "They look like they're getting along fine out there, if you ask me."

I look up just in time to catch Anna coming out of a pirouette, James's hands on her waist, and glimpse the beaming look of happiness on her face as she turns to him. That's not real, I remind myself.

"In that case, she sure fakes it well," Everett says, and I realize I've spoken out loud. "What can I say, she's the best. Right, Naomi?"

I ignore that.

"I guess even your powers have their limits."

"Oh, shut up," I snap. "Don't you need more Vicodin?"

He raises his chin, his look mocking. "My shoulder is just fine."

"Yeah. Whatever. That's why they gave you the role where you don't have to lift anyone."

"Bitch, please. You can barely hobble through your own role. It would make sense to be jealous—if you actually had a shot."

He turns to leave.

"Then don't come to me with your problems anymore," I hiss. "You're on your own."

Out there, on the stage, the music comes to a pompous grand finale. Anna and James take their bow. I can't make out all the rows of empty seats from where I'm standing; the light overhead is too bright, and the audience, or lack of it, is shrouded in darkness. But I imagine it. Rows and rows and rows of eyes, of people holding their collective breath, their gazes trained with an irresistible compulsion—on Anna, Anna, Anna. Anna who doesn't even want this! Not as much as I do, anyway. Anna doesn't know what it means to want. She's always had everything handed to her on a platter—roles, dreams, boys.

It has to be me, I think. It will be me. I will do whatever it takes. Time for the big guns. I really hoped it wouldn't come to this, Anna, I really did.

But this time, I want it to be me.

Georgina feels as though her blood is vibrating. It's fantastic. She hasn't felt this way since it was she who trod the stage in front of an adoring audience—so many years ago, it makes her head spin. Where did the time go?

"You were incredible," she says to Anna. Her daughter is in the passenger seat, gazing out the car window, but since darkness descends so early now, all that she—and Georgina—can see is her own reflection. Her expression is gloomy, her lips slightly pursed, her brow furrowed. She's had that look often lately, and it worries Georgina: It's becoming a habit. A bad habit. She's too young to start developing mimic wrinkles.

And on any other day, she wouldn't hesitate to tell Anna exactly that. But tonight, it's time for praise. Well-deserved praise. They're almost there. If Anna dances like this in the final performance, they'll have their pick of companies all over the world.

"Now there's something I don't hear every day," Anna murmurs.

"Oh, that's not true, honey. I may not say it every five minutes like some moms at your school, but you know I'm thinking it. And if anything, saying it too much dilutes the meaning. When *I* say it, you know it's deserved."

"Yeah," Anna says with a shrug. "Except it doesn't matter what you think. It matters what Walter thinks."

"Oh, Walter can go to hell. You were incredible, and if he doesn't think so, he's a complete idiot."

"He's not an idiot," Anna says softly. "He's a genius."

Now it's Georgina's turn to frown. Where is this coming from? "Did he say something to you after the show? Now, whatever he said, you put that nonsense right out of your mind, because—"

"He didn't say anything. He didn't have to."

"Well, then. You need to stop worrying, Anna. You did great. I tell you that with all my ballet experience, and I wasn't educated at some backwater American school—"

"Gee, thanks."

"You know perfectly well what I meant! My point is, your technique was flawless. I knew some primas who would have struggled with that choreography, and you didn't so much as tremble. And the emotion, it was spot on. You're not just a great ballerina but a great actress. I believed it. Every move, every step. You were running out to meet your beloved in secret after dark. I swear, I was *there*."

Anna says nothing. Georgina takes a turn in the direction of their home, and only then Anna stirs. She stretches and sits up straight. "Do you think we can grab a bite to eat? I'm starving."

"Oh, I have dinner ready to go. I just need to press the button on the steamer."

"I was wondering if we could go out. It doesn't have to be Colombina or anything. I'm up for Chinese, or . . ."

"Is that a good idea? All the salt will make you puffy. And you shouldn't eat at those fast-food places. It's so bad for you. Why don't we just have our nice home-cooked meal? Besides, I already cut everything up and put it in the steamer basket."

"Fine."

They pull up to the condo building. It's part of a development project from a few years back, and while the excessively angular architecture isn't much to Georgina's liking—it definitely doesn't have the cachet of the centennial they used to live in back in Boston—it looks cozy right now, shrouded in the Christmas lights that the condo board puts up every year right after Thanksgiving. There are only four units per building, and they have the nicest one, with the most natural light. Georgina supposes she could have bought a house, but she decided to put the extra money toward Anna's tuition and expenses. Pointe shoes don't pay for themselves, and she can easily go through six pairs a week. In the time they've lived here, she has almost grown attached to the place, but she won't be sorry to leave it behind next year. She's just about done with this town; she's ready to live in the heart of it all once again.

"You said Walter didn't have to say anything," she tries again as they enter the apartment. "What did you mean by this? Did he do something? Has he been inappropriate with you?"

Anna rolls her eyes. "No, Mom. Everything is fine."

"You bet. He's just resentful, because next year you'll be dancing in New York and he'll still be here, a has-been, stuck at the school forever because there's nothing else for him to do with his life."

"Mom, I think you made your point. You can leave Walter alone. He didn't do anything wrong."

Georgina only shakes her head. As soon as she takes off her shoes, she heads to the kitchen, where she starts the steamer and sets the plates and cutlery on the table. "You're young, Anna. You haven't seen much of the world yet, apart from this town and the school—"

"And Boston," Anna corrects as she hovers near the counter.

"That doesn't count. You were a child when you left . . . But don't worry. There's a whole world out there, and I can't wait for it to meet you. You'll see, next year, when we're living in Manhattan . . ."

Anna seems to perk up. "We?"

"Of course. I can't let my sixteen-year-old daughter move to the city by herself! What kind of mom do you think I am? I'll get us an apartment, and we can go to all the galleries and theaters and museums . . ."

"Yes. It'll be great."

"Why are you so glum? You'd never know you just danced a textbook-perfect pas de deux."

"I'm not glum."

"Then stop sulking and come help me serve dinner."

Anna huffs.

"Oh, what's the matter now?"

"Nothing."

"Doesn't look like nothing."

"Nothing," she repeats, and that frown is back, tracing a line between her fair eyebrows. "It's my birthday. I'm sixteen today."

And, as Georgina watches helplessly, she heads to her room and shuts the door.

ACT
TWO

11

December

"Hi, thank you for taking my call. This is Georgina Mironoff. How are you?"

She speaks in her best voice, a trick she learned early on. It's all as much a part of a successful ballet career as good turnout and musicality, to be able to socialize, to charm, to convince. Something that Anna has yet to learn, Georgina thinks in the back of her mind as she makes small talk with one of the school's donors. And perhaps it's about time she did. That sullen demeanor won't get her far at a ballet company. No one's going to tolerate a diva attitude; it's not the 1960s anymore.

"I'm calling on behalf of the De Vere Academy," she says in her honeyed voice, going in for the pitch.

"As I don't doubt you do." Ysobel Harrington sounds like a benevolent grandmother, but Georgina senses something amiss at once. A chill passes between them even through the rustling static in the speaker. But she promised Alexandra donations, and she will have to get her donations, come hell or high water. Now, of all times, when she had to prove herself more than ever, they all decide to play hard to get. Is it her fault that the economy is on the downswing? This is just as bad as being a fledgling dancer all over again. Injury or no injury, bad day or good day, you get up and dance because you'll be judged the same regardless of the circumstances. Georgina momentarily feels relief that it's all behind her, and, to her surprise, she finds herself feeling sorry for Anna, who may think she's going through hell but who hasn't even started.

"I wanted to thank you," Georgina says, not giving up, not yet. "For the generous donation you made last spring. Fifty thousand dollars, all of which went towards top-of-the-line equipment and accommodations for our students—"

The woman on the other end makes a sound that could mean anything.

"A hundred, you mean?"

"Ysobel?"

"A hundred thousand."

"I'm—I'm sorry?" For a moment, Georgina fears that her English has failed her, which would be a first in many, many years. But it's not that she doesn't understand what she just heard, she just can't seem to grasp the significance.

"It was a hundred thousand dollars that I donated. Surely you remember." The woman still sounds impeccably polite even though Georgina feels like the floor beneath her has dropped out. She winces, glad the woman can't see.

"Of course, of course. My mistake. I must have you mixed up with someone else." She is burying herself deeper with every word, she can tell.

"And if a hundred thousand isn't enough, I don't know if I can help you. Perhaps there are some cuts your school could make. So many superfluous things. Those extravagant galas while the students room like ants in poorly heated dorms. And now the choreographer in residence. And what a choreographer!"

"Ysobel, I'm not sure I—"

"People are talking. My great-niece goes to your school, as you well know, and she's told us all about that. It's bad enough that the school itself is so poorly run, Georgina, and apparently, so are your donor records. But that man? Did anyone even look at him before they hired him?"

"Ysobel, I have no influence over these things. You know that!" She's defensive, which means she has already failed. She grinds her teeth.

"Of course, Georgina. But if I were you, I'd distance myself from that school. Do some research on that choreographer and see for yourself. Until then, I'm afraid I must suspend my patronage of the De Vere Academy."

The woman hangs up, leaving Georgina to stare at the phone in her hand with a bewildered expression. What was that all about? And how could she have made such a mistake? The frustration gives way to rage of a different sort. How dare this woman speak to her this way? That great-niece—Georgina has seen her, an eighth grader with the grace of a manatee. The only reason she's still there is Great-Auntie Ysobel's generosity.

She pushes away the fury. She must focus, find a way out of this situation.

The spreadsheet in front of her came straight from Alexandra's computer, so there can be no mistake. If it says $50,000, then it had to be $50,000. But the other thing—

Georgina closes the spreadsheet and pulls up the browser. Her hands hover over the keys as she hesitates, frowns, and finally opens the search engine.

Within a few minutes, she has a list of contact numbers, and with a decisive sigh, she dials the first one.

"Hello? I'm calling about a former employee of yours who listed you as a reference. This is about Walter Graf."

NAOMI

This is the first Christmas gala where we're allowed to celebrate with the parents and the patrons. The younger grades go up on the stage to perform age-appropriate numbers from *The Nutcracker* but then have to decamp home, leaving the grown-ups to sip their champagne in peace. But us, the graduating class, we're expected to be there, dressed up and on our best behavior, except we get Snapple instead of the bubbly.

I bought myself a dress and lied to Dawn about how much it cost. No way am I going to show up in a discount prom dress when other girls wear designers. In the end, I had to find a middle ground because the thought of parting with all that money made me a little nauseous. But the dress looks good. It's a deep wine red with a plunging neckline and a full tulle skirt.

"You look fantastic," Anna says, and I can't return the compliment because Anna isn't wearing hers yet. I'm the only one wearing my gala dress because I'm not dancing in the show. Anna is wearing her costume for act one, a flowing white skirt and a cropped, rhinestone-studded top. She already has her perfectly-broken-in pointe shoes on and is warming up with pliés and tendus.

"Thanks," I say. "Are you wearing the silver one?"

"No," she says, and rolls her eyes. "Georgina bought me a new one. It's expensive as hell, but I think she feels guilty that she forgot my birthday." She does a truly prodigious backbend. Anna's true strength is her fluidity: She can do all the hard moves yet never look like she's worked on them. For all anyone can tell, she just has an innate ability to bend her spine backward into a U shape, and she maintains a serene smile throughout, right until she stands up straight again, her elegantly curved arm over her head.

She throws a glance around. We're alone in our corner.

James hasn't gotten here yet, and the rest of the space is taken up by the eighth graders in snowflake costumes, doing sissonnes with dead serious faces. It feels like we were them just days ago, yet now, they look like little kids to me. And yet I know from experience that they already have the same hierarchy in their ranks that we did: Everyone already knows who's going to be the star and who will get booted from every audition.

Anna's eyes sparkle. "I have a secret," she says. "James and I got back together."

I really should have seen this coming, but still, I feel like I've been punched. "Really?"

She nods. The huge fake gemstones in her headpiece catch the light.

"And you're just going to take him back?" I ask carefully. "After what happened?"

"That wasn't his fault," she says. "And anyway, it's all in the past. He told me he loves me! Imagine, Naomi. He actually said it. Love."

My vision splinters, swimming with circles of light. Whose idea was it to glue two pounds of rhinestones to her head? She looks like a human disco ball. "And you believed him," I say.

"Oh, don't start. I know you're the big cynic, but yes, I think he really meant it." And she gives me a significant look that cuts me to the bone. For a fraction of a moment, I'm a million percent sure that she knows something she's not supposed to. What did that idiot say to her? I swear, I'll cut off his balls with my pointe shoe razor. But then the look disappears, and she's just Anna again, a lovestruck teenage girl.

"I'm not a cynic, I'm a realist," I huff. "And you're being just like those ballet heroines we always laugh at. He breezes in, causes this huge disaster, and then makes puppy-dog eyes, and you just forgive him!"

"There was no disaster," Anna says. "It was a disaster to Georgina, maybe. For the rest of the world, it was a silver medal at a world-class ballet competition."

"He dumped you the day before. Over text."

Anna scoffs. I've never seen her like this—obstinate, stubborn. Disdainful, almost. "Well, no wonder," she mutters under her breath.

"No wonder what?"

"No wonder Walter thinks you're a robot. Can't you believe in something magical just once?"

My breath catches. "Walter doesn't know what the fuck he's talking about," I snap. God, if she only knew the half of what I know about her precious Walter. "And no, I'm not going to believe in anything magical because magic isn't real."

"Well, maybe if you did, you'd be the one dancing onstage and not sitting in the audience."

Okay. She went there. "Fine." I realize I've raised my voice when the eighth-grade snowflakes throw glances in our direction. "Believe in magic. Believe in whatever you want. I'm going to take my seat."

"You do that," she yells after me.

"I hope he drops you," I snap over my shoulder. "Maybe then you'll understand."

I'm probably going to regret this. Fuck no—I'm certain I'm going to regret this.

But I guess it's time for the last resort.

"I don't understand. At the rehearsal, she was perfection."

Fabienne puts her hand on Georgina's forearm, discreet but firm. "Anna did great," she says with that subtle accent of hers.

"You don't have to say that. I know my daughter. She was off her game."

"G, you're seeing things. We all have better days and worse days. Maybe she was just having a spectacular day then."

"Yeah, yeah. Never when it actually matters. That's my Anna."

"You're overreacting," Fabienne says gently.

"Did you see when he was this close to dropping her, towards the end?"

"Well, that's hardly on Anna. Now let's focus on the positive, okay? There's still half a year until the final performance. And she's a vision in this dress! She's coming this way, so please be supportive."

Indeed, Georgina turns to see Anna floating toward them. Floating—there isn't a better word. In the floor-length gown of silvery blue silk, she glides as much as walks. In the muted light of the chandeliers, she looks like a vision from the third act of a nineteenth-century ballet. Naomi is by her side, as always, decked out in a trashy red dress that looks like it came from a sex shop.

"Anna, you did a great job," Fabienne says, and goes to kiss her student on both cheeks. "Everyone was so impressed."

Anna nods and thanks her. Only Georgina can see the strained look on her face. She knows she could have done better. And she knows that Georgina noticed.

"Wonderful, wonderful," Fabienne is saying. "We're all looking forward to the final performance. You're going to blow everyone away."

"We'll try to make sure she's a tad more stable by then," says a familiar voice, and Walter sidles up to them, making himself instantly the center of the conversation. How does he do that? He's dressed ridiculously, as Georgina expected, in a leather jacket over a shirt embroidered with gold flowers. "And hopefully, she won't embarrass the school."

Anna looks at her hands. She's turning the sapphire ring Georgina lent her over and over on her finger, and Georgina sees for the first time that her daughter's nails are bitten to the quick.

"Not bad, Anna, but it could have been a lot better. You understand what I mean by stability, right?"

"I wobbled on the pirouette," Anna says, eyes still on the ring. She looks like she's about to pry the big central stone right out of the tongs. "I'm sorry."

"It was barely noticeable," Fabienne rushes to reassure her.

"It was noticeable," Walter corrects, offhandedly. "But that's not what I'm talking about. A real prima always dances impeccably. Even when she's had a bad day. Even when someone said something mean to her that morning or her dog died before she went onstage. If you can't show up and give a stellar performance no matter what, there's no place for you in ballet." He pats Anna on the shoulder. She still won't look up. "Now go, girls, go. Have fun. Socialize. I need to speak to my colleagues."

They leave, and he turns his gaze to Georgina. "How very gracious of you," he says. "The champagne is excellent. You outdid yourself. However, as I must remind you again, you're not an employee of the school, and so I kindly ask you to go enjoy yourself elsewhere while I speak with Fabienne. We must discuss some casting choices. Thank you!"

With that, he puts his hand on Fabienne's waist and leads her away, leaving Georgina standing there, glaringly alone, utterly humiliated, brimming with useless anger and shame. Her attention refocuses on the glass in her hand. How she'd like to snap its fragile stem in half. She rarely drinks these days. But here she is, and it's Cristal—Cristal she managed to hustle up, just like she hustled up half the guest list. And so she raises the glass to her lips and drains it.

NAOMI

I'm working my way steadily through my glass of sugarless cranberry cocktail concealing a heavy splash of vodka. Sure, the students aren't allowed at the open bar, but everything is allowed if you know who to ask—and how. But I don't have time to get anywhere near drunk enough when I see Anna gliding toward me in that new dress I haven't seen. Goddammit. Next to her, my red dress instantly makes me feel like I should be perched on a stool in a hotel bar somewhere, not at a ballet academy gala. What made me decide cleavage was a good idea?

But I guess I shouldn't worry, because all eyes are on her anyway.

"I'm sorry," I murmur when she comes close. "I never should have said that."

"That's okay," she says, "I know you didn't mean it. James and I are back together, and it's all behind us."

I take a generous gulp of the spiked cranberry juice and spot Georgina standing near the champagne table next to Fabienne. She looks horrible. All the former ballerinas look so young from far away, but up close they look older than their age. All those years of starving oneself into a Balanchine ideal have consequences. But right now, she doesn't just look gaunt; there's something in her eyes, something utterly savage. They're riveted to us—to Anna—like two all-devouring black holes.

"Come on," I whisper to Anna, "your mom is here. Let's go say hi."

Anna winces. But if anyone can take her down a notch right now, who better than her own mom? So I drag her over.

It goes about as well as can be expected. When she storms off, I follow, ready—as always—to pick up the pieces.

"I'm so fucking sick of her," she whispers once we're in a corner alone, hopefully out of Georgina's earshot. She's also holding a glass of what looks like juice but I suspect isn't juice.

"It could be worse," I say with a shrug. "At least she bothers to come. When was the last time Dawn showed up to anything?"

"I wish she didn't. That's why I fucked up the second lift. I could feel that glare of hers trying to bore a hole in my head. It's like suddenly I weighed three hundred pounds. James almost fucking dropped me."

"Nobody saw that."

She throws a hateful glance in Georgina's direction. Well— at the spot where Georgina stood a few minutes ago. She's nowhere to be seen now. "She clearly did," Anna hisses.

"She's a has-been. Who even cares what she thinks?"

Anna sulks. "Walter saw too."

"Walter just has it out for you. You could have danced like Fonteyn and Sylvie Guillem and Zakharova rolled into one, and he'd still find something to shit on. Because that's what these types of people do."

"What types of people?"

Of course it's him. Speak of the fucking Devil. I turn to face him with a shit-eating grin. "The genius types," I say.

"Well, you wouldn't know anything about that, Naomi. I'm here to borrow Anna, actually. Anna, it's time we do the tour. All these patrons and donors came here to our humble gala and our performance—don't make them leave without having met the star. Come on, I'll introduce you around."

"Naomi should come with us," Anna says, chin high. "She dances in the final show too."

So I trudge along as we do the tour, or Anna does, since I didn't dance onstage and no one apart from the teachers knows who I am. Anna shakes hands with the school's patrons, all sparkling jewelry and Rolexes peeking out from under shirt cuffs. After she introduces herself, or Walter introduces her, she always manages to squeeze me in. *And this is Naomi Thompson, she dances Gamzatti in the end-of-year performance.* People acknowledge me with a nod, or not at all. One elderly lady mutters something about how she's looking forward to it before turning her attention back to Walter so pointedly that I take my cue. It's time I leave them alone. This humiliation is both unwanted and unnecessary. Sometimes I wonder if Anna is actually aware of what she does and is doing it on purpose. To put me in my place.

But just as I make the decision to put a stop to it, the crowd parts, and then, out of nowhere, Georgina appears in the center of the room.

From the looks of it, she's had a few. Her eye makeup is

bleeding into her fine lines, making them look like gulfs. She's holding a champagne flute, and her knuckles are white, like she's barely holding herself back from crushing it.

"Hey, Walter," she says. Georgina always has a loud voice, but now it's different. Usually, with her poised speech and her sharp accent and her sharper, sky-high heels, she asserts dominance. Right now, it doesn't seem . . . controlled at all. "Yes, you, Walter Graf. We should talk."

"Hello, Georgina," says Walter. His smile falters. "Do you need a glass of water? Or a cigarette?"

"No," she says, "but you might need one, after I've said what I have to say. You think everyone doesn't realize how pathetic you are? Anna is the only good dancer in this whole school. You only treat her like garbage because of your weird little grudge with me. Well, let me tell you—it's not going to work."

Walter throws a quick sideways glance. People are watching while pretending not to be watching, an art perfected by this social class. I can tell they sense they're about to get a show much more interesting than Anna's stupid pas de deux of love-struck teenagers.

He steps toward Georgina, lowering his voice.

"Grudge? That's interesting. You've wheedled your way in, you've ingratiated yourself to Alexandra and to Fabienne and everyone else, all to get Anna ahead."

Georgina sneers. "I didn't have to do anything to get Anna ahead. Anna is the best. And you know it."

He makes a motion to gently take her by the elbow, but she pulls back, yanking her arm away. And I swear to God I can't tell if it's accidental or she does it on purpose—she was a great ballerina once, after all, with perfect command of her every muscle, presumably even when drunk off her ass. But the contents of the champagne flute end up in Walter's face.

Right on the money. The crowd around them holds its breath.

"Are you out of your mind?" Walter snaps. He blinks his wet eyelashes, his nostrils flaring.

"I as good as paid for this damn party," she says, sneering. "And the champagne. So I do what I want. I made a couple of phone calls. To the company you worked for in Boston, and then the one in the UK. Everyone, would you like to know why Walter was politely asked to go back to America?"

Fabienne arrives in the nick of time. She comes up behind Georgina in a rustle of black silk and clings to her arm. "G, please," she murmurs.

"Let me fill you in. And then you decide if that is the kind of person you want teaching the ballet stars of the future."

"Georgina!" Fabienne urges. "Stop."

"Such great values to teach at a ballet academy," Georgina goes on, but she's faltering. She's way too drunk. Fabienne clasps her forearm and pulls her away, into the crowd.

Only now do I notice that Anna is gripping my hand. Hard. Her strength is surprising for someone so ethereal looking. In this moment, I almost feel bad for her.

"Ladies and gentlemen!" booms a voice overhead. Not a moment too soon. The DJ has decided it's time to take over. "Dear patrons. On behalf of the De Vere Ballet Academy, I'd like to thank you—"

It goes on and on, and gradually, reluctantly, everyone turns away from the scene and toward the podium. Alexandra is there, smiling a smile so strained her face might burst at the seams of her last facelift.

"…please help yourselves to our canapés and the open bar. In the meantime, on the screen behind me, we're happy to show some of the highlights of our student performances."

The screen lights up, gentle classical music begins to pour from hidden speakers, and the crowd returns to a semblance of calm. I glance sideways at Anna: Her face is hard, pretty but hard and shiny like a porcelain doll's. Once again, I almost feel bad for what I did.

But, as Walter would be quick to point out, almost just isn't enough.

I look at the screen, where last year's *Romeo and Juliet*'s death-of-Tybalt scene comes to a stop and winks out.

In its place, another image appears.

At first, the screen is completely dark, but that only lasts seconds. Then the shadows move, slowly taking shape. The light is weak but it's enough so that the shapes of two bodies are distinctive. A pale, slender leg, a stomach, a chest, and the girl's arms wrapped around the man's back as he thrusts. Then the camera shakes, the girl sits up, blond hair tumbling around her face, and it becomes clear that the girl is Anna, giggling at first but then frowning, confused. She pulls a sheet over her chest, too late. A moment later, James pops up next to her, his hair disheveled. He reaches forward, and then something dark falls over the camera, the image vanishing from the screen as quickly as it appeared before starting again, in a loop.

Anna lets go of my hand. She ignores me calling her name, turns on her heel, and storms out of the ballroom.

As she reaches the door, I see her rip Georgina's sapphire ring from her finger and throw it into the trash.

12

January

"HER? YOU WANT to suspend *her*? Are you out of your mind?"

Alexandra wrings her hands like a heroine from a tragic ballet. And she has every reason to be a wreck, Georgina thinks, except she seems worried about the wrong thing. But she'll set Alexandra straight. Oh, she will.

"I want to suspend them both," Alexandra says, fidgeting. They're in her office, alone, with the door firmly closed, but still Georgina winces because the other woman talks way too loudly. The school is supposed to be empty at this hour, but you never know, do you? "Anna only for a few days. James for three weeks."

"That makes it look like she's guilty!" Georgina explodes. "When she hasn't done anything wrong. He has. And I don't want him to be suspended—I want him to be expelled."

Alexandra grimaces. "Look, it could have been much worse. We stopped the projection quickly—"

"I can't believe what I'm hearing!" Georgina snaps. "Could have been worse? I can't imagine it being any worse."

"I'm handling this situation the best I can," Alexandra says, her tone strangely flat. Georgina suspects this isn't the first time she's uttered this phrase in the last few days. Probably not even the tenth time.

"The only way to handle this situation," Georgina says icily, "is to expel him. Make an example out of him. Make a statement. This sort of thing cannot, and will not, be tolerated."

"I can't expel anyone without a thorough investigation into what happened," Alexandra says plaintively.

"What are you talking about? Of course you can."

"And the investigation," Alexandra persists, "has gone nowhere. Everyone is denying knowing anything. No one knows where this recording came from or how it ended up on the projector."

"Of course James is denying," Georgina says. "I'll bet."

"But here's the thing. So is Anna. Won't tell me a thing. Can't you talk to her? If you could make her cooperate…"

Georgina grits her teeth. Anna? Cooperate? Now there's a tall order. Why that girl does anything she does is a mystery. But how can she admit it? How can she admit to Alexandra that she has so little control over her own daughter?

"It's not up to Anna to cooperate!" Georgina retorts. "This is a school. You're the principal. And your students, may I remind you, are underage. The responsibility is on you to protect Anna!"

"Well, Georgina, I hate to say it, but James was in the recording too. And he's the same age as Anna. So unless we figure out how all this came to be...I can't expel him any more than I can expel her."

This is it. Georgina will not hear another word of this nonsense.

"Alexandra," she says, "you and I have been friends for a long time, haven't we?"

"That has nothing to do with—"

"Oh, it has everything to do with it. I'd hate to ruin the friendship, but if I have to, I'll get the authorities involved."

Now, this gets the job done. Alexandra pales. "Georgina—"

"Expel him. Expel him, send a clear message about who's in the wrong and that such things will not be tolerated."

"But..." The other woman stammers, licks her already dry lips. "His parents—"

"Ah yes, the well-to-do New York parents. The parents don't want the authorities involved any more than you do. They'll pack him up and take him home, and that'll be the end of it. Everett can dance Solor, if that's what you're worried about."

"I—I can't do that." Alexandra's mouth twitches, and then understanding dawns at last. Georgina feels that victorious rush, like she just danced a fiendishly difficult part to perfection on opening night.

"Oh, I think I know the reason. It's not the end-of-year show. It's not about fairness. His parents, the Rawleys. They donate to the school. How much? Let's see if I can remember." She narrows her eyes, knowing she's already won even before the other woman's face crumbles.

"I had an interesting conversation with one of the donors," Georgina says.

"Wait," Alexandra chimes in. "You don't understand..."

"And then I called up some of the other donors," Georgina continues mercilessly. "I think you already know where I'm going with this."

Alexandra glares at her as Georgina holds a long pause. The tension in the room practically sparks in the air.

"You were counting on their yearly donation," Georgina says, "to cover what you already took? Isn't that right?"

"Without their contribution," Alexandra says, "I'm fucked."

Silence descends onto the office once more.

"Well, if I get the police involved, you're even more fucked," Georgina says happily. "So I think you're going to do what I say and expel James Rawley for what he did, effective immediately."

Once outside, the crisp winter air cools down Georgina's overheated face. She tilts her head upward, letting the small snowflakes that spiral from the dark clouds melt on her skin.

Everything has been saved, yet again. She did it so many times before, and she's done it now. And that means she's still got it, and that means there's still hope for the future.

Because the show must go on, isn't that how it goes?

13

February

NAOMI

"It's your favorite part," Walter says as he stands facing our small group. "Time to rehearse the pantomime. Can anyone here tell me what a pantomime is?"

He doesn't wait for an answer—and most of us have learned this habit by now, so no one raised her hand in the first place. "The expression of meaning through gestures set to music. Gamzatti, there isn't even pointe work in it for you. Nikiya, you do need to dance, sorry. But worry not, you'll love it, because this is where you try to stab her for stealing your man."

I've watched every YouTube clip of this scene in existence. The gist is simple: Gamzatti summons Nikiya and tries to bribe her with jewelry, but she refuses to abandon her love and tries to stab Gamzatti, who orders her death. And Walter isn't quite right: In many iterations, my character does dance on pointe.

But I suppose he decided to go with the easier version because he already thinks I can't hack it.

"Places," he calls out, clapping his hands. "This is your chance to show you've also got acting chops. That way, if no one can lift you, at least you can be a character dancer. And go!"

Not surprisingly, everyone is still talking about the show-down at the Christmas gala, although not nearly as much as one might think. When we all came back from Christmas break, people stared, some whispered. But Anna is Anna—she ignored it. In fact, she's been pretending like nothing happened. Except ever since then, she's been absolutely insufferable with her perfectionism. Every step has to be just right. And whenever anyone else makes a mistake or a misstep, whenever I sneak a glance at her, I'll catch her glaring, her eyes gleaming darkly, almost gleeful.

It's not like her.

Despite what you might think, Walter has actually been less of an asshole to Anna since classes started again. And since Walter obviously needs to let off steam, I've been unwillingly cast as scapegoat.

He saw me in the hallways before class and cornered me before I could make a quick getaway. "It's your favorite scene," he said with that smirk of his. "The roles are reversed, for once."

"I have no idea what you're talking about."

"You're the princess, and Anna is the one who wants to stab you."

"I don't want to stab anyone," I said coldly.

"No, you just want her role."

"Everyone at this school wants her role. What's your point?"

"Oh, cut the crap, Naomi. With me, you don't have to pretend. I know exactly what kind of person you are. And by the way, I know it was you."

"You're not going to get a rise out of me, if that's what you're trying to do."

"What I still haven't put together is why no one has come forward, and how you convinced James to do it. I do have some theories—want to hear them?"

I glared at him.

"Oh, no comeback this time."

"You said you would help me get that role," I snarled. "And you've done exactly nothing."

"If you keep this up, there's not much I can do. Be nice, and I won't tell Anna my theories. Unless—I already did?"

"You wouldn't," I snapped, knowing well that indeed he would. "And she won't believe you anyway."

He gave a shrug. "Run along. And don't be late for class."

I take my place at one end of the room while Anna waits at the other. My prop in the scene is supposed to be a wedding veil, but right now, an old towel is taking its place. I circle the room with an appropriately agonizing look on my face, pining for the warrior I'm supposedly in love with.

"Stop," Walter calls out. "More emotion, Naomi. You love him but he has someone else. A beautiful temple dancer. But you're a princess—you can have anything you want, including him. You're conflicted…"

"I don't understand."

My head snaps sideways, as does everyone else's. It's Anna who has spoken from her spot at the other end of the room.

"Yes, Anna, what is it?"

"I never could quite pinpoint it. *Is* she in love with Solor? Really in love?"

"What else would you kill somebody over?"

Anna gives a small shrug. "Pride. Vanity. *I* think she just doesn't like to be told no because she's spoiled."

Walter sighs and rubs his eyes with the heels of his hands. "Of course, leave it to Anna to decide to psychoanalyze the daylights out of it instead of dancing. How typical. Anyway, Anna, thank you for that reflection, but for the purposes of this show, let's say Gamzatti really is in love with Solor, truly, madly, deeply and all that."

"In that case," Anna says pensively, her head tilted, "this ballet treats her kind of terribly, doesn't it?"

Walter groans. But Anna goes on as if unaware. "She truly loves this guy who's in love with someone else, which is bad enough. Her love drives her to a reprehensible and amoral act, and then she's either killed by falling rocks for all her troubles or just ignored, her plot thread left hanging."

"Yes, yes. There goes the character development. Now will you two please—"

"She's really a tragic character," Anna says. "I think the dancing in this scene should reflect that."

"Excuse me, did I miss some big news? Are you the new artistic director? Since you think you know so much better than everyone, why don't you show us what you think it should look like." He gives me a nod. "Can you dance Nikiya for this scene? Do you have even an approximate idea of the sequence?"

I know the sequence in my sleep. But all I manage is a tight little nod. I'm dancing Nikiya. Even if it's just this once, in this one rehearsal for this one scene, I'm dancing Nikiya.

Whispers race through the crowd of girls behind me, but I barely notice.

Anna takes her place, and Walter starts the music. She's wearing her pointe shoes, so she just brazenly goes for the version with pointe work.

Under all our gazes, she glides across the room to where Solor's portrait is supposed to loom over her. And I believe it. I believe every movement. The towel she clutches to her chest and then holds out, supplicating, becomes the gauzy wedding veil, and the blank wall becomes the image of the man she's desperately in love with.

And as she clutches the prop to her chest, I see on her face such a hungry, naked longing that it's impossible not to recognize it. It's the look I glimpse every time I look in the mirror, the fleeting face that I sometimes spy when I unexpectedly encounter my own reflection. One millisecond and it's gone, replaced by the face I always wear, the ballet face with its three prefabricated expressions that cycle one after another based on the musical cue.

"Nikiya," Walter murmurs, somewhere on the periphery of my personal hell. "Ni-ki-ya! Naomi, what are you waiting for?"

And so I stumble on pointe toward where Anna sits, graceful, her feet pointed. She pantomimes taking off a bracelet that she pretends to offer me, and I push it away.

"Not so aggressive," Walter barks. "She's your superior, remember?"

Anna tilts my chin up. I've seen this in one of the YouTube clips, Bolshoi or Mariinsky, who the hell knows anymore. Her expression is one of dismay and resentment as she takes in her rival's supposed beauty. Then she gets up, and I imitate her, her hands gentle on my shoulders.

"This is how it's done," Anna whispers, her breath hot on my ear.

"Oh, shut up, prima." I meant for it to be playful, teasing, but maybe it's the whispering that makes it sound like a threat instead.

The music reaches a crescendo, and suddenly, Anna's hands turn from gentle butterflies to a bird's claws that sink into my shoulders so hard I choke on an exclamation. She spins me around, and this is where I'm supposed to finally see Solor's portrait and figure out what it's all about. But all I see is a blur of faces and mirrors.

"Keep up." Anna's voice is a growl in my ear. "Walter told me everything."

With that, she gives me a shove in the back, pushing me toward the portrait. I stumble, and there's nothing calculated about it. I do my best to recover and resume the dance. The princess is done pleading—now she's giving orders. What the hell do you think you're doing, bitch?

I back away but she comes after me, a fearsome creature, a delicate monster. "He's replacing you as Gamzatti," she whispers. "He told me as much."

What? I expected anything but this.

"What did you say to him?" I say under my breath. We're breaking from the choreography—hell, we've left the choreography behind some time ago. I'm faintly aware of every pair of eyes in the room trained on us. Drinking it all in. "What did you do, you crazy, vindictive cu—"

She gives me another shove, sending me off pointe and stumbling back. This is where I'm supposed to grab the dagger, except there isn't one, of course, because Walter didn't really bother with props.

"What do you think you're doing?" I pant. "What was that fucked-up theory? Tragic character? What the fuck?"

"I'm trying to help you!" she snarls.

"Why are you dancing my part? Nikiya isn't good enough for you? You want mine too?"

"I'm saving your role, dumbass!"

"I don't need your help. I don't need anything from you. Fuck you, Anna. Fuck you!"

"Oh, you wish."

I lunge at her, forgetting the pointe shoes, forgetting the music, forgetting everything. My hand, as if of its own free will, reaches toward her perfect blond bun, the braid curled up like a snake. I watch with detached fascination as my fingers sink into it—

"Girls! Jesus Christ, break it up! Somebody! Everett!"

The next thing I know, Walter is grabbing me from behind while Everett pulls Anna away. Her hair is tumbling down, free from its bobby pins. Her eyes glitter, wild.

"Well. Who would have thought." Walter claps slowly. "To be honest, this is the best performance I've gotten so far. Out of either of you."

"That was one hell of a show out there today."

Alexandra glances over her shoulder to make sure the door to the choreographer's office is shut. He's looking up at her defiantly from his seat, his arms crossed, but the smirk on his face doesn't fool her. He's nervous. His gaze darts back and forth, unable to settle on any one thing.

"I'm serious, Walter. What was that?"

He shrugs. Finally he lets his arms drop by his sides.

"Ballet wunderkind, huh," Alexandra mutters. "Maybe you're just coasting on your reputation."

"You have to agree," he says, cornered. "Both their dancing has greatly improved."

"That was no dancing. That was a catfight in the middle of rehearsal."

"Well, the school did hire me to shake things up."

Alexandra clenches her fists, her hands hidden behind her back so he can't see.

"I'm going to have parents complaining. I can't have that."

"Georgina doesn't count."

"This isn't about Georgina."

He chuckles.

"I'm serious, Walter."

"So am I. You wanted me to put the school back on the radar, and I'm doing that. The sad truth is that your students are unprepared for the ballet world. Yes, even Anna. Especially Anna."

"Is that why you're doing your damnedest to give her role to Naomi?"

She watches him keenly as she speaks, and for all his decades of dance training, he can't help giving a start.

"Naomi can't hack it," Alexandra says with finality. "I don't know what you're playing at, but she can't dance Nikiya, and she won't."

"Of course she won't. You think I didn't know the Anna fan club would veto my casting?"

"We vetoed your casting because we all thought you'd fallen on your head."

She steps forward and plants her hands on his desk, leaning in closer. "Anna has the body," she says. "She has the legs, the feet, the arms, the stability."

"And Naomi has the nerve," Walter says blithely, a bit too quick—he probably anticipated what she'd say and came up with a retort in advance. "She has the adaptability and the mental fortitude. It'll take her farther in ballet than Anna and her perfect feet. I wanted to show you all. I wanted to show all these recruiters that there's something beyond superficial perfection. That there's beauty in grit and persistence. They'll walk away dazzled. Isn't that what you wanted?"

A thread of electricity passes between them. Alexandra's spine pulls taut, her muscles tighten, like in her faraway ballet days. She doesn't fully realize what she does next, or why, she just decides to go with it. He's so close, she barely needs to lean in. Her lips touch his, searching, hungry.

For a moment, it seems like he's answering the kiss. Then he breaks away, and she stumbles back from his desk, nearly losing her footing, her face hot and her heart hammering.

"What the hell are you doing?" he demands. He's glowering at her with a look that cuts her deep, deeper than she expected. Not even because there's disgust in it—if there is, he works hard to hide it. It's the incredulity. Like it's the last thing he expected. All her signals have gone over his head, it seems.

Shame and anger mingle within her. Now that he's on his feet, they're face-to-face. In her heels, she still stands taller than he, but it fails to restore her dignity.

"What?" she snarls. Her face twists into an ugly sneer she doesn't realize is a mirror reflection of his. "Too old for you?"

"I don't know what you're on about," he says coldly.

"Oh, really? I brought you in. I gave you a job. When no one else would have you."

"So now you expect those kinds of favors in return."

His smirk adds insult to injury. "There isn't another ballet school that'd let you sweep their floor, Walter."

"If you regret your decision, go ahead and fire me. Figure out how to make them dance all by yourself."

"I'm wondering if I should do exactly that."

"I'd advise you to wait until the final performance," he says. "The result will be worth it. The recruiters will talk about it for months afterward—"

"As long as they're talking about it for the right reasons," she says.

The smugness slides right off his face, at last.

"That's what I thought," Alexandra says, and storms out. As the door bangs open, she spots a lone figure at the end of the hall, and it takes her only a beat to recognize her. Naomi.

Great. Just great.

NAOMI

The school is empty. The day is over, everyone has gone home. Except me, because guess what, I got detention for physically fighting with another student. I wonder if they would have bothered if it had been anyone other than their Saint Anna on the receiving end. Who cares. It'd do her good to have her hair pulled from time to time.

I head to detention like a good girl, except my feet carry me in an altogether different direction. Past the empty classrooms, past the locker rooms, to the other end of the school. Just as I turn into the final hallway that leads to my destination, I hear a door slam, and then Alexandra storms right past me like I'm not even there. I wait for her steps to fade in the distance before making my way to the office door where the plaque still reads EDITH SPENCER because they never got around to changing it.

Edith—I haven't thought about her lately. It's crazy, she was one of our teachers for years, and now she's been gone for a few months and it's like she was never there. Good riddance. *Madame* Spencer and that Yorkie she lugged with her everywhere. To add insult to injury, of all the Yorkies in the world, hers turned out to be the one that didn't get the hypoallergenic gene, so she left a trail of dog fluff everywhere she went. The sound of her name is enough to make my eyes itch.

Edith, too, was a longstanding member of the Anna Prescott fan club—hell, more like its president. She had nothing but disdain for anything that didn't conform to the Balanchine ideal in every last little detail. When a girl dared get a haircut in ninth grade, Edith had such an epic freak-out that everyone thought she'd have her expelled. And anytime I'd land a touch too noisily after a jump, she'd joke about how I should be dancing male roles.

So goodbye, Madame Spencer, and don't let the door hit your ass on the way out.

For a moment, I think that Walter's not there and I just wasted my time, not to mention risked getting into even more trouble. The door is shut, but through the insert of colored glass, I see a glimmer of light. And so, with a deep intake of breath, I raise my hand and knock.

"Come in."

I turn the door handle and the door opens. I slip inside and, after half a moment's thought, shut it behind me.

Walter is behind his desk, and he has glasses on, looking at something on a laptop screen. The sleek Mac is the only thing in this little office that doesn't reek of Edith Spencer: It's still the same desk, the same ugly velvet chair, the same musty posters from 1960s ballets on the wall.

That's okay, Walter. Don't bother redecorating. You'll be out on your ass soon enough.

"Naomi," he says, closing the laptop. He does it in a single smooth, ballet-honed movement that still seems a bit too deliberate to me. "How can I help you?"

"For starters," I say, and find, to my surprise and dismay,

that my mouth has gone dry, "you could cut the crap. I'm not just another one of your students."

His skinny eyebrows inch up his forehead. "Of course you're one of my students. What else would you be? Unless you went and dropped out and I haven't been told yet, in which case, thanks for the heads-up."

"You tried to play us against each other," I say. "Anna and me. We talked earlier. She didn't believe you, by the way. That I was responsible for the video."

Infuriatingly, he nods. "She told me as much. She refuses to think badly of you, her best friend. However, she did believe that I was going to replace you as Gamzatti. What do you think that means?"

"You're not going to replace me," I snap. "And we both know why."

He chuckles. "I was never going to replace you. If only because we have no one else for the role, short of cloning Anna. But you really should take some cues from her. I thought the interpretation was spot on."

"Not only are you not going to replace me—you're going to make me Nikiya."

I don't know where the boldness comes from. Just five minutes ago, I never would have imagined these words coming out of my mouth. "You're going to make me Nikiya and make Anna whatever you want. Shade number three on the left in the second row, if you like. But I want to be Nikiya."

"So this is why you're here? To ask me to change my casting choice?"

"I'm asking you to get rid of Anna," I say. "Like you promised."

"I never promised any such thing."

"You said you would get me a principal role."

"You have one. And God knows you're struggling enough with that."

"Walter," I say, "don't fuck with me. Or you know what I'm going to do. Especially after the Christmas gala, how do you think it's going to go over? It's not ten years ago anymore. It's a whole new culture. I don't know if you're aware, but these things are viewed kind of negatively right now. They'll believe me. And even if they don't, I have proof…"

I take my phone out of my pocket, unlock it, tap on an icon, and swipe. Then I put the phone on Edith's old desk and slide it over so he can see.

August

It's Anna who calls me. From her other SIM card, which is how I know things are serious. Georgina scrutinizes her phone bill every month, and a lengthy call after bedtime is bound to get her attention.

"There's a new choreographer," Anna whispers into the phone. "She said it was some kind of dandy with a weird haircut and hand tattoos. Can you imagine, Naomi? Hand tattoos! He'll be replacing Edith. Isn't that wild?"

"Not so wild," I say with a shrug. "Anyone who gets rid of the old bag is an improvement, if you ask me."

"I know she was mean sometimes, but she's brilliant," Anna says. Such an Anna thing to say. "She launched so many great careers."

"Yeah, and they're all in care homes by now. Time for a change?"

"It's just, it's kind of like if Ozzy Osbourne just waltzed in casually and said, *Hi, I'm here to take over for Mozart.*"

I puff with laughter. "Can you even name one Ozzy Osbourne song?"

Anna giggles in turn. "You know what I mean! And how many careers did this Walter Graf person launch? How many iconic ballets did he stage? Other than, you know, some weird modern-dance, writhing-naked-in-mud thing."

"Walter?" I ask, my gaiety suddenly gone. "Walter Graf?"

"You've heard of him?"

"Here and there," I say, even though the answer is yes. "I've seen some of his stuff on YouTube." And it's not writhing naked in mud. Although to someone like Anna, with her pink satin pointe shoes and tutus, it's all the same.

Walter Graf is a ballet wunderkind. He's breathed new life,

new energy, into stodgy old classical ballet pieces. I've read that in a few decades, he'll be today's equivalent of Balanchine.

"And? What's it like?"

It's not for people like you, I almost say. Or Georgina or Edith or any of the old hags propping up the dusty classical dance institution on their bony shoulders.

"It's a different style," I say. "More like ABT's."

"You didn't hear this from me," Anna says, "but the end-of-year performance won't be *Sleeping Beauty*."

I lick my lips, glad she can't see me through the phone. "He said that?"

"Yeah! My mom was shitting a brick. She really saw me as Aurora, I guess, but hey, I'm glad I won't have to dance the damn Rose Adagio!"

I tune her out, letting her go on and on about all the difficult moves and all the awkward lifts she'd have had to do as the star of the end-of-year performance, poor thing.

"It's going to be *La Bayadère*," Anna whispers feverishly, instantly getting my attention back. "Our school has never done *La Bayadère*. Isn't that exciting?"

Yes, so exciting. To Anna, maybe. Does it matter to everyone else what corps de ballet number they'll be bourrée-ing through for two-plus hours? The vision pas d' action from *Sleeping Beauty*, the wilis from *Giselle*, or the Kingdom of the Shades. We'll all be part of a pretty backdrop in gauzy costumes—a backdrop for her.

"Georgina must be flipping out. Wasn't *La Bayadère* her last ballet?"

I can't see Anna, but I can picture her rolling her eyes on the other end of the line. "Oh yeah. Now I'll never hear the end of it. She had a hairline fracture in a metatarsal that apparently split apart in the act two pas de deux. They got the B-cast girl to dance the last scene."

Just hearing it makes me flinch. I hope she can't hear me gulp. She speaks so glibly about it, but it's pretty much the worst thing any dancer can imagine.

I actually feel bad for Georgina. Hell must have frozen over.

"And wait, get this," Anna whispers. "Walter made quite the impression on everyone. He cussed left and right, and then he asked if anyone knew of a decent watering hole to take the edge off this dull little town. If it's so dull, I wonder what he's doing here. They must not have wanted him anywhere else."

I get off the phone with her. It's getting late. Dawn left for work hours ago and won't be back for many more hours. I go to my room and throw open my closet. My tightest jeans, the lowest-cut top I own, and then forty minutes of careful shading and blending, false lashes like little hairy caterpillars over my eyes.

Then I slip out, fake ID in my back pocket and some cash stashed in my push-up bra.

It's not hard to guess the watering hole someone like Walter would prefer. We are tourist central for everyone not ballet initiated, so we too have a hipster cocktail bar. We've had it for only a couple of years, since the ski-in-ski-out condos started to pop up. I needn't have bothered with the ID because no one asks for it; it's the end of summer, they won't be busy again until ski season and could use all the hot girls they can get.

Inside, I take a spot at the bar and get a vodka soda, hold the vodka. I'm not here to get hammered at fourteen dollars a drink, thank you very much. It would be a crime to waste my hard-earned cash like this, especially since summer is low season for me as well with so many people at school back home for the break.

Obnoxious, generic techno music is playing too loudly, which has the unintended opposite effect of what they probably hoped for: It makes the emptiness of the place even more starkly obvious. After a few minutes of sipping my empty soda water, I start to wonder if I was wrong. I feel foolish. Why am I so sure he even decided to go out? He probably just said it to shock and scandalize these old bags.

Just as I'm debating going home and kicking myself for the waste of perfectly good makeup, here he is.

I thought he'd bring me home. Instead, he brought me to his office. Naughty, naughty. For a quadragenarian. I giggle, pretend-drunkenly, as he leads me through the very halls I walk through every day, not letting on that I know the way much better than he does. He's only just had his first day, he says apologetically.

Up close, Walter Graf is not how I pictured a ballet wunderkind. He's disappointingly human. When he's had a few, he has bad breath, which is hard not to cringe at when we make out. He has crooked teeth too. Too proud to get braces? That faux British accent is irritating, but, thankfully, it slips after the third drink, and he sounds like the Jersey Shore kid that he is.

"This way," he motions. I tactfully duck past the glass display, where my image lurks in the class photo from last year. What do you know? For once, not being the star has served me well.

"Come here," he slurs. I put a little something in his fourth drink, and I worry it's kicking in too fast. Don't want him to pass out too soon. I tug him unobtrusively in the direction of his office, but he comes to a halt in front of the display, and all my gentle pulling on his arm is in vain. On the contrary, he grabs me and pulls me close.

"Look," he says, stabbing his fingertip into the impeccable glass. I look. Behind his greasy fingerprint is Anna's face. She's in the blue tutu she wore for the grand pas classique at that competition.

"A bunhead," I say with a shrug. "They all look kind of alike to me." *Please don't look at the class photo.*

"But this one is supposedly special. Everyone here is obsessed with her. Apparently, she's the next big thing."

This seriously can't be happening. "Is she?" I ask.

He shrugs before breaking into a grin and eventually collapses into laughter. "I have no idea. I saw her YouTube video. She dances like a pretty puppet. Good technique, zero emotion. But who knows, she might be different in person."

Eventually, somehow, we do make it into Edith's former office. As tempting as it is to have sex on that antique desk of hers with all its coasters and doilies, I'm not here for that. Walter is on the edge of passing out anyway. I have time for a few compromising photos, and that's all I need. All he'll remember tomorrow will be picking me up at a bar, and for all he'll know, we fucked each other blind.

I position him at his desk, his shirt unbuttoned and his belt undone. He snores softly, and a small puddle of drool has already formed on the desk's flawless lacquer as I tiptoe out.

14

February

NAOMI

"Put your phone away," Walter says. His voice is dripping with disgust. "Are you a ballerina or are you—"

"You're not in the position to call me names," I say, even though, treacherously, blood rushes to my face. It's dark, but not so dark he can't see me flush red.

"You know, from day one, I thought there was something wrong with you. Not because you turned out to be the girl I picked up at the bar the night before. But something off, in an undefinable way. And I was prejudiced against Anna because of her repulsive mother. But then I watched the two of you. Anna dances. You just swing your arms and legs well."

"Walter," I say, "you're digging your own grave, don't you think?"

"Anna nailed it today," he says, ignoring me completely.

"Right before you started your meltdown. You should have paid more attention."

"We talked about this," I hiss. "On the second day of classes, remember? You said—"

"That I'd get you a principal role. But I'm not an idiot. You want to dance Nikiya? Then level up. Because as long as Anna is around, no sane person would cast you as the lead."

"Then make Anna not be around anymore," I whisper. "Make it happen."

"This is your last resort, then?" He nods at the phone still sitting on the table between us. "You've tried everything else. Blackmailing me?"

"I wouldn't call it blackmail," I say. "More like justice."

"Naomi, we both know justice has nothing to do with it." He sounds bored.

"Is that how the police are going to see it?"

He sighs and rubs his eyes with the heels of his hands. Like he does when we're not dancing well enough for his liking. And judging by how long it lasts, I'm really doing the shittiest job of my life right now.

"Fine. Call the police. Call Alexandra, call everyone. Have me thrown in prison if it makes you feel better. But be aware that it's not in your best interest. You'll still be the loser in that situation because then you'll never dance Nikiya. You probably won't even dance Gamzatti—because, let's be frank, Sarah would do as good a job, if not better, minus all the drama because somebody can't stomach playing second fiddle to their best friend. If I'm gone, you'll lose your only advantage because the only way you'll ever, ever outdance Anna is by scheming and plotting."

I take a tiny step back. He slides my phone toward me squeamishly with the tips of his fingers. "Go on, call. I'm sitting right here."

I reach out and snatch the phone from the desk and then slide it into my back pocket.

"See you tomorrow," Walter says as the door swings shut behind me.

When I get home after detention, my hopes for some alone time are shattered because Dawn hasn't left for work yet. On the contrary, she just got up, she's had her coffee, and she is insufferably chipper and energetic. And determined to make me "eat a real dinner," which, by her definition, turns out to be some sort of stir-fry made with frozen vegetables and swimming in a lake of soy sauce.

"How were rehearsals?" she asks. I hold up a piece of broccoli on a fork, watching the dark soy sauce drip from it onto the pristine white rice.

"Great," I say with a rictus grin. "I did forty-eight fouettés en tournant and then jumped twelve feet."

"That's great, honey. Can't wait for that show of yours."

I groan. "That's not even possible, Mom."

But she doesn't get it, of course. "What, I can't look forward to my own daughter's ballet recital?"

"Never mind."

"Oh, I know I missed my share of rehearsals. But it's only because I had to work to pay for all those rehearsals. I know you don't hold it against me." She serves herself a heaping mountain of stir-fry and sits down, fork in hand. "They say if you're a prodigy, they let you study for free. But sadly, no one at that academy of yours has heard of it."

She didn't mean it to, but it still stings. I push the rice around on my plate. "I think I'm done. I'm not very hungry. I'm just too exhausted to eat."

She gives me a shrewd look. "No, you're not."

"There's too much salt in this," I plead. "Tomorrow's the first general run-through. I can't be bloated."

"You can't faint onstage either."

"I didn't faint!" I jump up from my chair, only now noticing my hands are in fists. "Will you let it go? It was forever ago, and only one time!"

"I haven't said a word about the tuition or all the crazy hours," Dawn says, "but I won't let my daughter be malnourished. That's not something on which I'm willing to compromise."

"You literally just complained about the tuition two seconds ago," I mutter. "You've complained about it every day for as long as I can remember. *It's so expensive, Naomi. Can't you make those shoes last another day, Naomi? You're too thin, you're too sinewy, you'll wear out your joints before you're thirty. Why don't you put more effort into physics and math—in case the dance thing doesn't pan out?* How do you think it makes me feel?"

Dawn looks me up and down. "Stay calm," she says. "I won't have this conversation in such a tone."

"It's not a five-year-old's tap dance recital you're going to, it's the freaking *Bayadère* with the real Bolshoi choreography. And I'm dancing the second-biggest role. Would it kill you to be supportive for once?"

"I've always been supportive."

"Bullshit!"

She forgets to snap at me about the language. "Would you rather I was one of those psycho dance moms? Would you like that better? If I started weighing you twice a day and forcing you to sleep in pointe shoes like your friend Anna's mom? That would be so great. That would turn you into a real well-adjusted individual, wouldn't it?"

I cover my face with my hands. That way, I can imagine none of it is real; all I can see is the red pulsing under the skin of my fingers. This cramped kitchen isn't real, Dawn isn't real. The reality where I'm stuck forever in Anna's shadow, hobbled by things utterly out of my control, shitty genes and shittier luck, doesn't exist.

"Don't ignore me, Naomi. Answer me when I talk to you."

"I fucking wish Georgina was my mother," I snap.

I hear Dawn put her plate down with a clink, and then steps fade in the hallway. When I lower my hands, she's gone.

The day of the first run-through, there are no other classes. Just as well, because no one is in the mood to try to focus on trigonometry. We start with warm-up, followed by a pep talk from Fabienne. Funny—just yesterday we were lazy snails asleep at the barre, and today we are the academy's bright future stars, every single one of us. I guess perspective *is* everything.

There's a chill between me and Anna, even though she goes out of her way to be nice and normal to me in front of everyone. I get the feeling that she does this not so much for my benefit but to show off how wonderful and forgiving Anna Prescott is. It's easy to be magnanimous when you're about to dance Nikiya in the full version of *La Bayadère* for the first time.

"Okay, everyone. Girls." Fabienne claps her hands for the final time. "Go out there and dazzle us all like every recruiter in the world was sitting in the audience. And, finally, I say to you all, merde."

"Merde," everyone echoes.

When they let us out of warm-up, Everett smirks at me as he passes by on his way to the exit. "Break a leg," he whispers.

"Drop me, and I'll kill you," I snap back.

In the big auditorium, all the seats are empty except for the first row, where I spy Fabienne, Walter, Alexandra, and most of the other teachers. Walter is sipping from a giant Starbucks thermal cup. I can see the bags under his eyes even from here, and his pallor is more blue tinted than usual. If I didn't know better, I'd think he got hammered last night. Alone, I'll bet.

In spite of myself, I smirk. For the first time, I feel a tiny bit better. If he got shit-faced, he must have taken my threat more seriously than he lets on.

He's talking to Alexandra, who's wearing a new pair of earrings. I can tell because they're like disco balls attached to her ears—the light reflects off them violently. She dressed up like she's going to the actual end-of-year show. Walter gets up, about to head backstage and start yelling at us as usual, but in that moment, the doors in the back of the auditorium open with a crash that echoes through the room thanks to its great acoustics.

I almost do a double take when I see none other than Georgina Prescott sashay down the aisle to take her seat next to Alexandra. A hush falls over the row. The look on Walter's face suggests a violent headache.

Sure, Georgina always shows up for the first run-through. Anna told me so. But this year, clearly no one expected her to, not after the showdown at the Christmas gala. Georgina, though, looks like her usual self, dressed to the nines and smug as a snake. I get as close to the curtain as I can without being seen from the audience.

"Hello, Walter." Georgina unwittingly helps me, speaking as she always does in her poised, too-loud voice. "I can't wait to see this genius in action. Hello, Fabienne. Alexandra, such beautiful earrings. Real diamonds. You can always tell."

The principal's hand shoots to her earlobe self-consciously.

I half expect Walter to have a meltdown, maybe even have her thrown out. But instead, he clutches the Starbucks cup. "I have to go. The show is starting in fifteen minutes."

Alexandra gets up to let him pass, but Georgina remains planted in the way, and he has to awkwardly squeeze past her. She follows him with a condescending look.

"You're looking good, Georgina," Alexandra says in a strained voice.

"Never better."

Fabienne studies her fingernails.

"You know I wouldn't miss this for the world," Georgina says. "Anna would want this. I've never missed a single run-through in all her years at school, have I?"

I look around, searching for Anna backstage, but I can't seem to spot her anywhere. Just a moment ago, she was by the barre, dressed in the white Nikiya costume for act one and busily warming up with that look of blank concentration she always has before a show, staring straight ahead but not seeing much.

When I turn my gaze back to the auditorium, I nearly do a double take. A slight, white-clad silhouette appears to the left of the stage and glides, not walks, toward the first row, where everyone has seen her and frozen midmotion, not sure what to make of this. Her hair is up in its perfect bun, and the rhinestones on her costume sparkle every bit as brightly as Alexandra's diamonds.

"Anna," I hear Georgina say. Her voice has lost some of its cocky assurance, but she clings to the illusion of confidence for dear life. "You're a vision."

Anna stops cold a few feet away from her mother. Not one muscle twitches. "What are you doing here?"

Her voice carries well. I, and I'm sure everyone else too, can hear every word.

"I've come to watch the run-through. Like always."

"I want you to leave."

"Don't be ridiculous." An awkward laugh bubbles out of Georgina. "You knew I was going to be here. I'd never—"

"Well, this year, you're not going to be here. And anyway, aren't run-throughs for school personnel only?"

Even at a distance, I think I can see Georgina's throat move as she gulps.

"Anna, I have to be here. I need to watch you so I can give you my notes."

"I think I have teachers here for exactly that purpose. Right, Fabienne?"

Fabienne starts to stammer.

Georgina speaks up. "Well, they don't know you, or your dancing, like I do. My feedback—"

"Yes, yes. You do a better job than them. Why don't you turn around and tell them that to their faces?" Anna lets a beat pass and then smirks. "Nobody wants you here, Georgina. Leave."

"Georgina." Fabienne speaks up softly. Georgina's gaze darts to her sidekick, her face slack at such a betrayal.

"I think Anna can manage by herself today," Fabienne finally says, her gaze once again on her fingernails.

"Naomi!"

I jump. The voice behind me takes me completely by surprise.

"What are you waiting for?" Walter barks over my ear. "Costume! Where's your costume, Naomi?"

Right. I tear myself away from the scene and go over to the rack where my Gamzatti tutu is hanging under a plastic sheath with my name written on it in Sharpie. NAOMIE T. Fabienne was in charge of the costumes. Spelled my name wrong on purpose. Bitch.

I hurry to put it on, and, to my consternation, it's tight. Like, really tight. Which is impossible, because I weigh myself every day in the locker room. But the zipper in the back of the stupid rhinestone-studded bodice didn't get the memo, it seems, because it gets hopelessly stuck halfway up my back.

"Need help?"

I spin around so fast I almost trip and fall. Everett holds out his hands to steady me by the waist. "Wait, wait. Save your falling for the stage."

"Shut your mouth," I say. "And help me get zipped."

He circles me, and his hands brush against my bare skin as he pulls the two sides of the bodice together and then tugs at the zipper so hard I fear I hear stitches popping.

"Mission impossible," he says over my ear. "This thing is two sizes too small."

"That can't be," I snarl. "I actually lost weight since the start of the semester. All my clothes are baggy."

"Right, wasting away from envy," Everett says cheerfully. "You need to write a diet book. It'll be a bestseller."

"Just keep pulling," I mutter under my breath.

Inch by painful inch, the zipper moves up until I'm encased in the bodice like it's a suit of armor. I can barely breathe. This is no accident. This is sabotage. I scan the surroundings: Anna is still gone; in the other corner, the girls who dance the Shades are warming up by jumping in place.

"Places in five," I hear Walter yell on the periphery. The corps de ballet girls slink to their positions. Anna strides out of nowhere, her face unreadable, her chin high.

"You're welcome," Everett reminds me.

"Why don't you go to your beloved Nikiya?" I nod in Anna's direction.

The music starts. I kind of zone out through the opening act of the corps. Everett bounds past me onto the stage for his first variation. Then Anna joins him without so much as a look or a word to me.

And today, she's magnificent. Once again, she embodies

Nikiya. Watching her dance, it's easy to forget that there is no audience and no set and that half the cast isn't even in costume. You might as well be sitting in a velvet seat at one of the world's greatest theaters, watching a prima.

Before I know it, the pas de deux is over, scene one has drawn to a close, and a slightly breathless Anna is backstage again. There's barely a sheen of sweat underneath her makeup. She stretches her swan neck, takes out the pins that hold her sparkly headpiece in place, and, without looking, plunks it down into my hands.

I'm speechless. As if on cue, the entire corps de ballet bursts out in applause. Anna bows her head, all grace and humility.

"Naomi," she says, finally taking notice of me. "Is everything okay? Your lips are blue."

"I'm fine."

Fabienne appears, takes Anna's hand, and pulls her aside. "Magnifique, magnifique," I overhear before she starts to give her pointers for scene two in a low voice.

I lose track of her after that because the music is playing and it's time for scene two. Which means the pantomime. The moment I set foot on the stage, I glance at the front row. Georgina is nowhere to be seen.

I float through the scene in a sort of numb haze. Anna is in character and doesn't break it for so much as a breath. Here she is, subservient, then tragic, despairing, and finally furious. And exit. Done. Thank God.

"More energy, Naomi, more energy," Walter mutters as he rushes off to help someone with a pointe shoe.

I've never felt more like a piece of the backdrop. Although that's what I am, I guess. It's what I've always been. "Everett," I say hoarsely.

"What is it? Not too late to change and just go on in your leotard."

"The costume is fine," I snap. "Come here. I have to talk to you."

It's time for our pas de deux. And I nail it. The whole thing. The Gamzatti variation goes off flawlessly. The coryphées flank me on all sides, but I can feel everyone's eyes on me; I've overshadowed them.

"Do you still wanna do it?" Everett whispers anxiously as he lowers me after a lift.

"Yes."

And instead of the modified version, I go for the original, Italian fouettés and all. Developpé, developpé. I think my heart might explode and all my tendons and muscles rupture, but then I land on my standing foot after the last one, and it's done. I do one fouetté, then two, three, four. I have time to glimpse Walter's astonished face in the audience.

I can do it, Walter. I can outdance Anna. I'm becoming short of breath, and dizziness sets in. Eight, nine, ten, eleven—

I manage thirteen before I lose my balance and have to come to a somewhat graceless stop in fourth position. I'm panting, and sweat is pouring down my chest, soaking through the satin bodice. The music still plays. And plays and plays. That's seven fouettés short. Which apparently takes an hour in real time. Finally the music comes to a crashing crescendo, and I can bow and get the hell offstage.

The rest is a sort of painful blur. Nikiya dances, gets bitten by a snake, and dies. The curtain falls. And that's it for my turn to shine. There's a lump in my throat, and tears are burning in my eyes.

Everett gives me a hug. "You did great," he says, and that's when I know it truly is a disaster. If only he'd poke fun at me or mock me, then there could still be hope. But this is a mercy kill. Even Walter isn't the storm of wrath that I expected. "Very nice, Naomi, but at the actual show, let's stick to the choreography we settled on, okay?"

Act two begins. From backstage, I watch the Shades in their white tutus do their hypnotic dance to soft, sad music. Souls of dead temple dancers. I used to think it was just a rip-off of *Giselle*'s wilis. What dead temple dancers? It made no sense to me. Did so many girls get bitten by a snake after being thrown over for a princess? Is that a normal temple dancer thing? But now I watch them in their robotic melancholy, stuck forever in their pattern of arabesques and adagios like they think they're still spinning in the spotlight under the adoring gazes of the audience. Like they don't even realize they're dead, dead and gone, just shadows in someone else's opiate delirium, and it's all over.

And then I see it, one of those rare and despairing glimpses of a bleak future stretched out in front of me. My moment in the light, the one I've worked my entire life for, here and gone, just a flash, and after that, it's the backstage and the darkness. A whole life of never getting to hold the thing I want the most in the palm of my hand. The bite of a snake concealed in a basket of flowers seems like a gift in comparison.

Then the run-through is over, and we're summoned to a classroom for notes, but I can't focus on anything. No one mentions me anyway, so it doesn't matter.

At last, Fabienne tells everyone to go home and recuperate, that we start the final phase of rehearsals tomorrow and we must all be well rested and ready to do our best. I jump to my feet before everyone else, pick up my bag, and head for the exit.

I think Anna is calling my name, but I don't turn around. You all wanted me gone, well, I'm going to grant your wish. Instead of turning down the hall toward the main exit, I turn left and head to Alexandra's office.

I'm officially dropping out.

15

Now

"Mom?"

Georgina gives a start. It's late; she's perched at the kitchen counter, the screen of her tablet the only source of light in the room. That and the clock on the microwave, which blinks 12:00 because there was a power outage a few weeks ago and no one bothered to reset it.

She didn't think Anna was still up, but here she is, standing in the doorway. Somehow, she managed to sneak up on Georgina, to creep up quiet as a shadow despite the clunky brace on her foot.

Georgina smoothly closes the tablet, plunging the room into near-total darkness. "What is it? Shouldn't you be in bed, recovering?"

Anna fumbles, a mere silhouette in the dark doorway, and then the overhead light flickers on, making Georgina squint.

"I'm hungry."

Georgina mulls it over. Normally there's no nighttime snacking in their house. But she supposes that rule, like so many of the other rules, has gone out the window. Either way, there used to be nothing to snack *on*, but now there's leftover takeout and the remains of a frozen pizza—Georgina had more pressing concerns than steaming vegetables and cooking brown rice. Anna doesn't wait for an invitation. She plods to the fridge, and Georgina can't help but notice that *now* her every footfall makes the entire house shake as that brace hits the floor.

To Georgina's surprise, she comes back with only a hard-boiled egg. She sits down at the counter and methodically peels the egg as Georgina watches her with the same fascination she always had for her daughter's dancing. Anna's thin fingers move quickly and seamlessly, like spider legs, as she chips away at the egg's white shell. Her bitten fingernails have grown back, although she hasn't bothered to file them, let alone cut her cuticles. They're staring to look savage, a bird's claws. The ceiling lamp is directly above her head, casting strange, sharp, contrasting shadows on Anna's face and her hunched figure. There's something wild and feral about all of her, her rounded back, the lunar landscape of vertebrae, her hair, loose and tangled, framing her face, her look of intense concentration, mouth pressed into a hard line and brow furrowed. In a split second, a scene flashes through Georgina's mind: a cutting-edge contemporary ballet, Anna thrashing around in wild stripes of light, each movement equally fascinating with a touch of grotesque, an embrace of the ugliness in beauty and the beauty in ugliness.

Georgina shakes her head, and the vision vanishes. What kind of stupidity is that? Georgina hates modern dance with a passion. There is no beauty in ugliness—that's why it's called ugliness. It has no redeeming value.

And Anna is the opposite of it. Anna is beauty, made for, trained for, and perfectly suited for the classical, the sheer wonder of grand jetés, elegance of cambrés, lightness of pas de bourrée.

If she ever gets that brace off.

As if responding to Georgina's thoughts, Anna looks up. She's holding the egg in her hand, the shell pieces a messy pile right on the quartz counter. She takes a bite from the egg, grayish yolk crumbling around the corners of her mouth.

Georgina fights the urge to reach out and wipe the crumbs away. But Anna is no longer a small child. Anna, as Anna never fails to remind her, is sixteen.

"What were you doing?" she asks.

"Nothing," Georgina says in exasperation. "I was looking things up online."

"Not more physical therapy, I hope. Because I won't be getting any."

"That's nonsense, Anna. Of course you'll be going to PT. Otherwise—"

"Otherwise I might never dance," Anna mimics, rolling her eyes.

"You may think you don't care now," Georgina says, "but a few years from now, you will beat yourself up over it. Trust me, you will never stop beating yourself up."

Anna stuffs the rest of the egg into her mouth. As if she's doing it on purpose to rile me up, Georgina thinks. She reaches out and wipes the damn crumbs off Anna's lips. Anna winces but doesn't pull back.

"Maybe," she says. "But anyway, I don't see how I'm going to get PT when we can't pay for it."

Georgina gives a start, like her daughter slapped her. "What did you say?"

"I know we have no insurance anymore," Anna says. "Don't ask. Is there anything you want to tell me, Mom?"

"Anna, it's nothing," Georgina rushes to explain. "I'll sort it out. It's your dad. He must have forgotten to renew, and I can't seem to get a hold of him lately, but—"

Anna groans. "You know," she says, and gets up, not without some difficulty, "I think you're right. I'm never going to dance."

NAOMI

When I come to school on Monday, I don't notice anything odd right away. I've gotten used to the stares, to the locker room suddenly falling quiet as I walk in. Is this how Anna always feels?

But I have to concede that today, it's worse than usual. I walk into the morning rehearsal to find everyone huddled in the corner of the room, hunched over their phones.

At first no one notices me. One girl looks up, and then, like dominoes, others follow her gaze and look up one after another. There's something choreographed about it. Almost beautiful.

"What's up *your* ass?" I mutter, more to myself than to any one of them. I take my place at the barre and start to warm up. But nobody comes to join me.

Finally Fabienne walks in and shuts the doors behind her. You'd think that would get these bitches to simmer down, but it's like nobody notices she's there.

"Girls," she says. "Girls! Take your places, please. I will not have disruptions in my class."

They finally snap out of it and go take their places, but the tension is thick enough to cut. The absence of the usual chitter-chatter and giggles borders on eerie. I wait until it's my turn to do the run-through of the act one dance with Everett, and as he lowers me from one of the many complicated lifts, I murmur, "What's going on?"

"You don't know?"

"Less talk, more dancing! Everett, I don't want to see straining. You're in love, not sitting on the crapper." Her accent makes the word funny, not quite right. She's trying to copy Walter's devil-may-care attitude, but she can't quite make it work. "Naomi, you're stiff and wobbly at the same time. How is that possible? From the top. Do better."

The music starts again. I run at Everett, he catches me, we embrace. I can't help but flash back to the Christmas gala show, to the image of Anna, clad in white and sparkles, ethereal, light as air. Compared to that, I feel like a stampeding elephant. Why did I have to meddle? Why couldn't I just let her have what was hers?

"Stop!" Fabienne bellows. "Stop. Naomi. The pirouette. How hard can it be? He's holding you, for crying out loud. Again."

"What don't I know?" I whisper loudly at Everett as we do the damned pirouette, his hands gliding along my waist.

"Read it yourself. The school forum. But don't say I didn't warn you."

The school forum is not a place where I spend a lot of time. It's just a cesspool of hypocrisy and bullshit. And it's gotten worse since Anna left, so now I don't even look at it. Oh God, what is it now?

"Naomi!" Fabienne yells so hard she's spitting. "Heavy. Too heavy. You are heavy, your feet are heavy, your arms look like you're barely holding them up. You are an innocent, young girl in love. Again, from the beginning. Show me Nikiya."

Oh, I'll show you Nikiya, you skeletal lesbian dinosaur. We take our places, and I start again, light this time, *light light light*. My pas de bourrée is a work of exquisitely crafted perfection as I glide around Everett. I do the pirouette, the other pirouette, the developpé. And then it's time for the big lift. I run at him once again, and he catches me by the hips and lifts me over his head. At least that's what's supposed to happen. In reality, I don't stop in time. Or maybe my foot slips. In any event, I plow into him like a bulldozer and nearly knock him over. His hands slip from my hips.

"What the hell?" he hisses under his breath.

"Enough!" Fabienne snaps. "Enough. Listen, class, if you think I don't know what's going on, you have another think coming. I know what this is about. At this school we don't let ourselves be affected by gossip and unsubstantiated rumors. And while we're here to ensure you all have a safe and welcoming environment—"

There are some chuckles in the ranks of students, which Fabienne ignores with steely resolve.

"—there will be no tolerance at all for anonymous accusations of any kind. There is no reason not to come forward if you have anything to say. But any anonymous statements will be treated as pure fiction."

And that's when I start to feel seriously alarmed.

I'm sorry I have to hide behind a pseudonym, but I'm afraid of speaking out. We're all still reeling from what happened to Anna, but I can't stay silent any

longer. The truth is, I saw everything. It was on the
old stairs near the demolished wing, the ones that
don't lead anywhere. I was at the very top, and
when I heard voices, I crouched so no one could see
me. But I saw Anna there, with Naomi. They were
fighting, and Naomi was saying something about
how Anna didn't deserve her role. I couldn't see
everything from where I was hiding, but I know what
I did see: Anna turned around to leave and Naomi
pushed her down the stairs.

I turn off my phone.

For some reason, I remember my seventh-grade exit exam
four years ago. That was the year we were all supposed to start
pointe work in earnest, but I sprained my big toe at the start
of the year and had to stay back from pointe class for weeks. I
was terrified I'd fall behind, and when I finally got the okay, I
threw myself into it like my life depended on it. Because it did.
The exit exam included pointe work, and if I flunked out, that
would be the end. Of everything. Even if I did manage to get
into another school—and I'd have to spend the entire summer
desperately practicing to get up to level—Dawn couldn't afford
board and would never agree to move. No other place in town
offered advanced ballet classes; the little studio where I started
was for ages five through ten only. It would be public school for
me, and that would be it.

Luckily, I bounced back. Within weeks, I was progressing alongside everyone else. But I guess that fear left an imprint on my soul, like a hair tie you forget around your wrist overnight: a deep groove that refused to fade. As the exam approached, I was a wreck. Somehow, I just knew I would fail it: I would stumble, fall on my face, flop disgracefully. Dawn didn't get it—what else is new? When I showed her my less-than-impeccable pas de bourrée, she'd just shrug and say some version of *But what do they expect—you girls are twelve years old!* I wanted to shake her. All over YouTube, twelve-year-olds at competitions did the White Swan variation. And Anna—Anna was ahead of everyone, as usual. It was also the first year we had Fabienne as a teacher, and she kept saying you could let Anna out onto the stage any moment and no one would know she'd been doing pointe for less than a year. We were still close then, even closer than we are now because she still lived in the dorms, which meant she was at my house four days a week.

But when I finally dared share my fears, she just didn't seem to give a shit. *Naomi, you'll do fine. You're overthinking it. The less you think about it, the more stable you'll be.* It's like she just didn't get it. And I suspected she'd never get it—how could she, when every step she made was perfect?

And so the exam day came. Anna acted weird. We warmed up, and everyone was all nervous giggles—back then, we still had some sense of camaraderie left and didn't have the full understanding we were each other's competition and thus mortal enemies—but Anna was silent. I'd never seen her like this. We had numbers at random pinned to our leotards, and mine got called before hers. I remember the blank look on her face as I went ahead. She didn't even bother to wish me luck.

Thing is, I nailed that exam. I didn't stumble once. It was Anna who fucked up. She, who hadn't so much as trembled all year, lost her balance not once but three times. If I'd done that, I might not have made it to the next year. But it was Anna, of course, so it made no difference.

It wasn't until weeks later, when Georgina made her grand entrance in town and moved Anna out of the dorms, that I learned that was the day her parents divorced. I guess it was understandable that the teachers went easy on her because of it. But for me, it was too late—the resentment already imprinted itself on me, indelible.

And reading this missive on the school forum, I feel the tug of that familiar dread. This is a lie. A vile, vicious lie. None of this happened. Whoever posted this couldn't have seen anything.

I slide my phone under my textbooks and go back to pretending to pay attention to the history class lecture. When it's time to go change for the afternoon rehearsals, I linger outside the locker room.

"...I mean, everybody knew it. It's so obvious."

"I don't know about that..."

"Oh, please. She wanted to get her out of the way since day one. If you're surprised, I have a bridge to sell you." I recognize Gemma as the one speaking.

"It's just—wouldn't Anna have said something?" asks a third voice.

"It's Anna. She's too good for that. She knows that Naomi will get booted from the school faster than she can blink."

"But wouldn't Anna *want* her booted from school? Instead of, you know...dancing her principal role? I would!"

"That's why you're doomed to be in the corps, Madison. And always will be."

I clench my fists as tears well in my eyes. A part of me wants to burst into the locker room and kick Gemma's ass, but I doubt it'll make me look any better. It's just that, God, how I've had it with this whole cult of Saint Anna. It's so easy to be a fucking saint when everyone already loves you! When you never have to really work for things in your whole life. When the stakes are never all that high, so you can afford to sit back and float, ruled by your little feelings and emotions. *I* could never afford to fumble through an exit exam. *I* could never get away with almost getting dropped by my partner. And if a sex tape of me ever surfaced, my life would be ruined, not inconvenienced for a couple of days. No matter how I feel, what my day was like, how many toenails I left inside my pointe shoe after last week's fifteen run-throughs of the second-act variation—I have to show up and do a stellar job or lose it all.

Anna broke her fucking foot and all anyone can talk about is whether she might still make it to the final show. If that had been me, everyone here would have forgotten my name by now.

And the worst part is, she doesn't even realize how lucky she is! She takes it all for granted.

She doesn't deserve it.

"Shut up, you gossipy twats." Sarah's voice cuts through the murmurs. "You know that post was made by some troll to fuck with you. And you're all too happy to take it and run. None of that happened, and you know it."

"Whether or not it happened, you can't deny that Naomi benefits from it," says Gemma.

"Yeah, yeah. And if *I* break my leg tomorrow, then I guess everyone will say you kneecapped me like Tonya Harding."

That shuts Gemma up. At least for a few seconds.

"Still. Something about all this is just...so...fishy." Madison speaks up again. "Does anyone know what really happened? How did she fall? Was she alone? What was she doing there alone anyway?"

"Maybe it's not any of our business."

"And if the post isn't true, then who posted it, and why?"

"To stir up drama. Why else?"

I step away from the door before anyone can catch me eavesdropping. No one ever said anything publicly about Anna falling on the old staircase. It happened late in the evening. No one else was at school. And who even knew about the old staircase in the first place?

The person who fell, for one. Anna.

And I think it's high time I paid Anna a visit.

The noise wakes her. Georgina nodded off without realizing it, and she's pulled back to reality with a sense of disorientation. She fell asleep on the couch. In front of her is her tablet, the familiar video frozen on the screen: Anna's grand pas classique, paused, as usual, right before the stumble.

And the doorbell is buzzing. She sits up and rubs her eyes, forgetting about her eye makeup. According to the clock, it's way too late to have visitors. She walks to the door, barefoot, and peers out the peephole.

Her heart gives a jolt, waking her up instantly. What is *she* doing here?

"Anna, open the door!" Naomi's voice is muffled and indistinct, but Georgina can still make out everything she's saying. "Open the door. I know you're home. We need to talk."

"Anna is sleeping," Georgina says through the door. She reaches up and makes sure the chain is in place. "And you should go home, Naomi."

"I only need to talk to her, real quick," Naomi answers. "Please, Ms. Prescott. It'll only take a minute."

"I said she was sleeping."

"But it's really important." Georgina watches as she raises her hand and pounds on the door with her fist. "Anna, wake up!"

Cursing under her breath, Georgina opens the door a crack, just enough for the chain to pull taut. She glimpses the side of Naomi's face, practically pressed to the door. She looks unkempt, her hair a mess.

"Naomi, you're not welcome here," Georgina says. "Is that so hard to understand?"

"At least tell her," the girl stammers, breathless. "Tell her to stop spreading lies. She knows I didn't do anything wrong. Tell her to remove her post."

"I have no idea what you're talking about," Georgina says smoothly.

"Oh, but Anna does." She presses herself to the door; Georgina can feel the heat of her breath. "Anna!"

"Stop it," Georgina hisses.

"She's lying. I know she resents me, and hell, I get it, but this is just evil. I didn't do anything wrong! I didn't push her."

"Really, now?" Georgina lowers her voice to a loud whisper. "Then maybe you can help me out. What did happen? How did Anna fall?"

"I have no idea!" Naomi's voice trembles, inching closer to a wail. "I wasn't there. All I know is that I didn't push her! Just let me talk to her, please!"

"Absolutely not. I won't have you upsetting her. Does your mother know where you are?"

"Please!" Naomi shrieks. "She won't answer my calls or texts. I just want to talk to her!"

"If she doesn't answer," Georgina says, "it's probably because she doesn't want to talk to you. And I'd say that's a good decision."

With that, she throws her weight against the door and manages to shut it in spite of Naomi's desperate attempts to wedge herself into the crack. Georgina turns the lock and takes a step back, struggling to calm herself. She expects Naomi to start pummeling the door with her fists and yelling, but nothing happens. She can't hear any steps, but when she tiptoes to the door and peers through the peephole, no one's there. As if the girl vanished into thin air, like a ghost.

The next thing she knows, she hears a loud crash somewhere behind her, deep in the dark apartment. She gives a start, spins around too fast, and for a moment, she thinks she might be having a heart attack. Her vision goes dark before blooming with fiery flowers. Not feeling her legs, she rushes down the hall and throws open Anna's door. Anna stumbles out of bed, like a specter in her white nightgown, her hair a pale blond halo around her head. Only the brace on her foot keeps her tethered to the earth.

"Mom?" Her voice is not sleepy at all. Has she been awake the whole time, hearing everything? "Mom, what's happening?"

Georgina pushes her aside and runs to the window. Or what's left of the window. It shattered inward, and the rock that did it sits in the middle of the floor. Glass is everywhere, and before she knows it, searing pain lances her bare foot, triggering a flood of memories. Georgina exhales sharply. Anna looks down at the blood that spurts from the cut on her foot and screams.

Georgina looks up. The pain woke and sobered her; she feels more clearheaded than she has in weeks.

"Calm down," she says to her daughter. Anna stands there, her hands clasped over her mouth, her eyes bottomless pools that look black in the near dark. "And call the police."

When Dawn's alarm goes off, she drags herself out of bed to realize that Naomi isn't home. Her shoes aren't by the front door, so Dawn figures she hasn't come home from school yet.

As Dawn plods wearily to the kitchen and starts the drip coffee machine, she wonders if she should take some time off. Naomi has gotten out of hand. Then again, when has Naomi ever been *in* hand? For as long as Naomi has been sentient, it has always seemed to be Naomi pulling her mother along through life, not the other way around. Dawn's life has changed laughably little in the last decade and a half. Hell, the coffee machine that sputters with steam on the counter is older than Naomi.

There was the divorce, and then life became a string of hospital shifts and bill payments, punctuated by driving Naomi to various dance classes.

Dawn remembers watching her five-year-old daughter prance in that studio for little ones, the one on the other side of town. From the outside, it was just another sporadically occupied rented space in a strip mall, but when you walked in, there were mirrored walls and classical music. She thought it was nice. Naomi jumped and tiptoed through the performance, the first in a line of girls dressed like fairies: Dawn had had to make the costume herself. She remembers the look on her daughter's face, a look she hadn't seen before but would often see afterward. A look of complete and utter concentration. It was a five-year-olds' dance recital, but clearly, for Naomi it was the most important thing in the world.

The teacher—who Dawn wasn't even sure had ever danced professionally herself—said Naomi had promise, and Dawn wondered if she was just needlessly stoking Naomi's enthusiasm so Dawn would keep enrolling her in classes. Promise of what? Of astronomical dance school bills, apparently.

And then there was the audition at the De Vere Academy. Dawn drove Naomi over, and they waited and waited amid a swarm of lanky preteens and their mothers—always moms, not a dad in sight. She looked around in fascination while Naomi stretched and warmed up, jumping in place and scissoring her legs, bending this way and that until Dawn worried her spine might snap. All the other moms were Botoxed and dressed smartly, and all of them had the same look of deep focus. All of them seemed to know exactly why they were here and how it was supposed to go. *Remember, Maddie, focus on the upper body. That way they won't be able to tell your turnout isn't perfect.* Dawn felt a wave of shame and a terrible fear that one of these birdlike women might look at her and magically guess her awful secret: that she didn't even know what number her daughter had prepared for the audition.

She was also keenly aware of how poorly she and her daughter fit in. All around her, she saw nice, expensive dancewear—on ten-year-olds who would grow out of it by the time their first year started! Naomi, on the other hand, wore a leotard from Walmart, $12.99 and the second one half price. Dawn had always thought it made no difference. Now she saw plain as day that yes, in fact, there was a difference. A glaring, huge difference that instantly set her daughter apart, marked her as an outsider.

And she found herself hoping that everything she'd been secretly thinking would turn out to be true. All the hype in Naomi's head was the work of the dance studio lady; she'd realize she was nothing special compared to all these girls who clearly had even more training under their belts. She'd fail the audition, they'd go home, and life would resume as normal.

"Naomi," she called. Naomi was using a windowsill as a makeshift barre and practicing that little move where she tapped the floor with her toes, the move that drove Dawn nuts with its noise to the point where she was beginning to hear it in her sleep. Naomi didn't turn around, so she called her again.

"What is it?"

Dawn looked in those wide green-gray eyes and braced herself. "You do realize that there are hundreds of girls here, and only a handful of places."

Naomi rolled her eyes like someone five years older. "Mom…"

"I know you think I'm boring and a nag, but I just want you to know one thing. Your self-worth isn't tied to the outcome of this audition. Even if you don't get in, you're still just as good and worthy and special."

"Thanks for the vote of confidence," her daughter scoffed, and went back to tapping the floor.

"I'm not saying you'll fail," Dawn tried, but it was too late. Naomi counted out whatever number of reps was necessary and turned around with a swish of her leather-soled slippers. She now faced away from her mother, and *tap tap tap* went the other foot.

But then their number was called. Dawn made a motion to follow Naomi as she rushed toward those double doors, but a look from her daughter made her stop in her tracks. It was true, she realized, feeling herself flush with embarrassment. The other moms stayed outside.

So time passed, and then Naomi came running out, and

the next thing Dawn knew, her daughter had been accepted. An official letter arrived in the mail a few days later, on fancy cream-colored paper stamped with the school's insignia, sealing the deal. She never knew what exactly Naomi had done to wow the admissions committee.

But to this day, Dawn thinks, to this day, she hasn't forgiven me for that little spiel.

And now she feels doubly guilty. Triply. For the spiel, for all her secret thoughts. *This is what Naomi wants, and I should be supportive.*

In the face of everything that's happening, she simply has no choice.

She opens Instagram on her phone. She only installed it to keep track of what her teenage daughter posts. And in the last couple of days, the comments on Naomi's beloved, carefully cultivated Instagram have been flooded with hatred and abuse.

Underneath a photo of Naomi in a truly death-defying balance on pointe, complete strangers let loose.

How do you like your friend's role? Hope it was worth it.

You don't deserve to be in ballet.

I've never seen anything so bad in my life. She has no musicality whatsoever. See how she misses all

the beats? The only way she'd ever get to dance
Nikiya is by shoving someone down the stairs.

You are a disgrace.

I hope you fall and break every bone in your body.

A chill runs down Dawn's spine. This is over the line; these are threats. The other day, she suggested meekly that they call somebody. This could be dangerous. But Naomi brushed her off and vanished into her room as usual. She's trying to pretend nothing is happening but she's failing, although she'll never admit it. At least not to her mother.

But Dawn can't let it go. Not if it continues. They can't just keep harassing Naomi over some unfounded rumor.

She didn't tell Naomi, but she read the post on the forum. It fascinated and repulsed her in equal measure, and she had to reread it several times before trying to make anything of it. She concluded that it was all made up from beginning to end. It had that quality to the writing, melodramatic and overwrought. And the situation described—it was from a cheap soap opera, so very on the nose. Sadly, this same quality made it perfectly calibrated to play on stupid people's heartstrings. The people who wanted to believe it clearly did.

Besides, how much more ridiculous could it be—Naomi pushing Anna down the stairs? They've been best friends since fifth grade. Anna was the one who helped Naomi get caught up on pointe work when she injured her toe when she was twelve. Naomi told Dawn herself. And Naomi, too, always looked out for Anna. It's a role, for heaven's sake. A role in a ballet, not even a real ballet but a high school production. There will be so many more ballets in Naomi's future.

The people who talk are just jealous of Naomi's success. Dawn remembers this. She saw it in their eyes all those years ago at the entrance audition. Naomi, with her cheap leotard and worn slippers, drew their ire-filled stares like a magnet. Like they knew even then that she'd be the threat. Dawn was worried her daughter would be the target of bullying, but then things seemed to mellow out once Anna became the class's big star.

Could Naomi really have done this? No. Was she capable of such a thing?

Dawn fears the answer, even only whispered to herself.

That's when the doorbell rings, making her jump. It rings loudly, insistently, as an unseen somebody mashes their thumb into the button. Dawn jumps to her feet, her legs still sore from the long shift, and races to open the door.

Naomi is standing outside on the porch, looking ragged, flanked on either side by police officers.

16

Now

DAWN CALLED THE hospital and told them she wasn't feeling well and needed someone to cover her shift. She's rapidly losing all sense of time, but according to the clock, it's nearing 1:00 a.m.

Naomi sits at the kitchen table, one foot tucked under her, like she always used to do as a child. She's staring into space, like she'd rather be anywhere but here.

"What were you thinking?" Dawn asks for what feels like the millionth time. "Throwing a rock through Anna's window? You're lucky they didn't press charges. They still could!"

"They won't," Naomi says. It all strikes Dawn as utterly surreal. She couldn't have imagined it only five years ago, when Anna was a skinny eleven-year-old, the best friend of her own skinny eleven-year-old, who used to come over for dinner to eat spaghetti with canned sauce and pretend-practice fouettés with

Naomi until late into the night. The two of them would bounce around the small house in tutus and whatever makeshift ballet costumes they could put together with the scarves in Dawn's wardrobe.

And now all these sordid stories, ballerinas shoved down stairs, rivalry to the death—over what? It's all so absurd she could laugh. But right now, she doesn't find it funny.

"I know you didn't mean to break the window," she says, softening her tone. "You only wanted to talk to your friend—"

"She's not my friend," Naomi mutters. "Not anymore. She's a lying, scheming—"

"Language, please. I don't believe this. How did it come to this? You used to be thick as thieves…"

"And now we aren't."

"Anna didn't write that post," Dawn says. "I'm certain."

"No one else could have written it," Naomi spits. "No one else knew. She's just mad because she can't dance Nikiya anymore, so she decided that if she can't have it, no one else will."

"Well, somebody will," Dawn points out. "Someone else at school. Might as well be you. If you don't do stupid shit like this!"

She realizes she broke her own rule and swore, but she no longer cares. Naomi looks up and meets Dawn's gaze for the first time since the police dropped her off. To Dawn's surprise, she's smirking.

"What's so funny?" Dawn snaps.

"You know, Mom, this is probably the first vaguely supportive thing you've said to me since I started the kid ballet classes at five."

Dawn draws a breath, but there doesn't seem to be enough air in the kitchen. She lets it out of her lungs, calmly comes over to where Naomi is slouching in her chair, and, with vehemence that shocks the breath out of both of them, slaps her daughter across the face.

After nearly twenty minutes, the bleeding from the laceration on Georgina's foot starts to slow. The folded paper towels she holds to the ragged cut are no longer soaked through in seconds. It's a shame about the mess she made, the bloody tracks on Anna's floor and down the hall and all over the bathroom. But that can be easily cleaned up.

Anna peers through the half-opened bathroom door, her eyes like saucers in her pale face. "Are you okay, Mama?" She sounds almost like her little-girl self, the Anna Georgina knows and loves, the child who looked up to her like she was some kind of god. When she was five and started her first ballet lessons, whenever anyone asked her what she wanted to do when she grew up, she'd say pertly, *I want to be a prima like Mommy.*

"I'm fine," Georgina says. For the first time in weeks—ever since she got the fateful phone call that ruined everything—she feels her mood lift. This is the first good thing that's happened. Good *how* she's not quite sure, but there are many ways she can make it work for her. For them. "You think this is the first time I get a cut? This is nothing. A paper cut at worst. When I was about to dance Myrtha in *Giselle* after being promoted to soloist—"

"Someone put glass in your pointe shoes," Anna finishes. She's wincing, putting her hands over her ears. "No need for the details. I remember."

"And I still danced it like everybody's business," she finishes cheerfully. "Because a real ballerina dances no matter what!"

"*Nobody's,*" Anna murmurs. A smile lurks on her pale lips.

"Hmm?"

"*Nobody's business.* That's how that expression goes."

Georgina chuckles. "I don't care how it goes. I always danced like *everyone* was watching."

"That's a different expression." Suddenly the shy smile flutters away, replaced by a new look of horror. Anna's mouth forms a mute O as she points at Georgina's foot. Georgina looks down—oh, damn, it started bleeding again, coming out in little spurts.

"Maybe you need stitches," Anna says.

"I don't need stitches."

"We should have called an ambulance instead of the police."

"I called who I meant to call."

"There was no need to call the police on her, Mama. She was upset—"

"She threw a brick in our window, Anna. Was I supposed to invite her up and offer her a cup of tea?"

"It wasn't a brick. It was a little stone. I think she just wanted me to open the window. She didn't mean for all that to happen."

Georgina rolls her eyes. "How nice of you to always see the best in people. I could never afford that. When I was young and starting out—"

"Yes, Mama, enemies were everywhere, everyone was scheming against you."

"Yes. Because they were jealous. They wanted what I had. And you should be aware of it too, Anna. You're way too trusting."

Anna crosses her arms on her chest, and that new stubborn expression is back on her face. The little girl is gone, and the teenager is back with a vengeance. Well, Georgina isn't going to give up.

"And look what you got for all your trust. You got shoved down the stairs."

"No one shoved me down the stairs," Anna snaps. "I told you a million times. Naomi didn't do it, Walter didn't do it, nobody did it. Will you let it go? You're only making us look bad. Someone posted on the—"

"School forum," Georgina says, nodding. "I know. It was me."

She doesn't realize the full severity of her mistake until five, ten seconds go by without a reply. She looks up from her foot to see Anna's face, so livid that her skin looks translucent.

"What the hell?" Her voice is deafening, echoing off the tiled walls. "Why would you do that?"

"I figured if you don't tell the truth, somebody has to."

Anna's arms drop by her sides artlessly. Like whips, Georgina's erstwhile ballet teachers used to say. "You're crazy," her daughter says, shaking her head as she backs out of the bathroom.

"Anna—" Georgina gets up, ignoring the blood that starts pouring from her foot once again. But Anna slams the door shut.

Georgina sighs. I never should have told her, she thinks. That was a mistake. Should have just let her think it was...whoever. Then again, Anna would have figured it out eventually. To sound as realistic as possible, Georgina included too many details. She knew the school like the back of her hand. She knew all about the secret place by the old stairs because Anna used to sneak away there to call home back when she lived at boarding school. Anna told Georgina herself, although she probably doesn't remember.

Everything I do for this girl, she thinks. And she's never happy. Never so much as a smidgen of gratitude.

She eyes the door, thinking that Anna will probably come back any moment to apologize and make peace; her little girl was never able to stay angry for long. But after a few minutes go by and nothing happens, Georgina shrugs. Fine, let her stew. Georgina was once a teenager too, after all. Not that she understands all this childish sulking and ingratitude. What she would have given, at fifteen, to have one-tenth of what her daughter has! To have a mother who cared—about ballet, about her dreams. Her own mother couldn't even be bothered to give her a nice name. No one who expects great things for her child names her Zoya. She changed it as soon as she could. And Anna has everything: pointe shoes, tutors, a mother who takes her to every class, a name that looks great at the top of a ballet program. Everyone assumed she'd named her daughter after Pavlova, when it couldn't be further from the truth. It's just that Colter and his insufferable family (who names their child Colter, for that matter?) had a whole list of despicable names at the ready. So Georgina played the ballerina card: so many great dancers named Anna, and she will be one too.

Georgina runs a bath—not the best thing for her foot, but necessary for her nerves. She adds some sea salt and a dash of lavender, and at once, the astringent scent that wafts into her nostrils calms her down. She'll smooth things over with Anna. They're stuck together in this apartment for at least six more weeks, after all. So she might not dance in the final show—big deal. They'll work around it. Georgina will make some calls, and they'll have a leg up in auditions when they go to New York in the fall. Anna is a perfectionist, she can't help it. Another thing Georgina gave her: She raised her right. The moment the brace comes off her foot, she'll be back at the barre. The pull of ballet is irresistible. She has six more weeks to sit around and brood and stare into her phone only to understand, finally, what every dancer has understood. What Georgina herself understood at a crucial juncture in her life, when she was this close to throwing everything away: Without ballet, she's nothing. Less than nothing.

This time next year, she'll be making her debut on a world stage. Then everything will be all right.

Georgina steps out of the water, mindful of her foot. She towels off and puts on a bathrobe, then bandages the cut carefully—she's had lots of practice—and eases her foot into a slipper.

She exits the bathroom, half expecting to find Anna pouting on the living room couch. But the kitchen and living room are empty and dark. Georgina finds a light switch. The light of the ceiling lamp pushes the shadows back into their corners, but Anna is nowhere to be seen.

She can't have gone back to her room. There's glass everywhere. Georgina walks over to the door, which is open a crack. She peers in: The room is cold, filled with the humid scent of approaching rain. The wind howls through the broken window, shards of glass like teeth. The gauzy curtains flap wetly against the windowpane. No Anna.

Georgina calls out her daughter's name, but there's no answer. A rotten, heavy feeling rises in her chest. She steps into the hall, peers into her own bedroom—this is where Anna would go, of course, to sleep in Georgina's nice, warm bed. Georgina's hand creeps along the wall until she finds the light switch and flips it. The room is as she left it. Her bed is unmade and empty. Her pictures and framed posters adorn the walls from floor to ceiling. Her makeup and perfume bottles are lined up like little soldiers on the vanity. There's no Anna anywhere.

"Anna, this isn't funny," Georgina calls out. She rushes to the entrance. Anna's coat is still there, and she breathes a sigh of relief, scooping the coat up and holding it to her face, breathing in the weak scent of Anna's shampoo. Only to notice a moment later that the crutches that stood by the door are gone, and so is Anna's light spring jacket.

In a rush of panic, Georgina turns the locks with shaking hands and peers out into the lobby. But it's empty. How much time did she spend in the bath? How far could Anna have gone?

"Anna!" she calls out once more, and her voice cracks. She clutches Anna's coat to her chest until something falls out of the pocket to land at her feet. She picks it up: a sheet of paper folded in four.

She opens it. Typed words, in all caps.

Her knees buckle, the second time ever that her legs have betrayed her, and she slides down the wall to sit on the floor.

17

Now

*DON'T TELL LIES ANNA. YOU
KNOW I CAN MAKE THINGS VERY
DIFFICULT FOR YOU. SO STOP
SPREADING RUMORS AND KEEP
YOUR MOUTH SHUT.*

"She must have gotten it earlier," Georgina says. Her mind is a jumble of incoherent thoughts she can't force into a pattern. All the lights in the condo are on, and she feels like she's stuck in some kind of human-size aquarium. She and the police officer stand in the middle of the brightly lit living room, adding to the feeling.

"How much earlier, ma'am? Earlier today? Yesterday?"

"How should I know?" Flipping out at the police officer isn't going to help, but Georgina needs to flip out at someone.

"I found it in her coat pocket. Do you have someone out there looking for her?"

"She can't have gone very far on crutches, ma'am," the woman tells her.

"If she left of her own free will."

The woman gives her a look.

"Did she say anything, did she act strange?"

"She's fifteen!" Georgina snaps. "Sorry. Sixteen." She ignores the judgmental look she's convinced she sees flashing through the officer's eyes. "Of course she acted strange. She's been acting strange for the past year, if not more."

"This injury, when did you say it happened?"

Georgina wrings her hands. She doesn't see how that has any bearing on what's happening. She names the exact date. Like she could ever forget. "It was a big deal. She was supposed to dance the star role in the graduation performance..."

"So I suppose there was some jealousy?" the woman— Officer Tayler, according to her ID—asks. "Anyone specific?"

"Are you kidding me?" Georgina explodes. "This very evening the specific someone threw a rock through her window."

"I see that."

Do you really, Georgina thinks. The sky is lightening; it's nearing 5:00 a.m. She hasn't gotten a moment's sleep tonight. Her bones hum with adrenaline and exhaustion.

"Was there a boyfriend or something like that?" Officer Tayler asks.

"What?" Georgina's blank stare meets the officer's gaze.

"I'm just making a list of places we should check first."

"No, she didn't have a boyfriend," Georgina says, annoyed. "Ballet was her whole life."

"Have you called her friends? If not, you should. She might be at one of their houses."

Georgina opens her mouth to tell her that no, Anna isn't at a friend's house. Anna has no friends at that school. She has competitors—rivals who dream of making her go away.

"What about family? Relatives?"

"No."

"Anna's father lives in Boston, correct?"

"Anna's father," Georgina says, "abandoned us and wants no further contact with his daughter. Anna is heartbroken about it."

The woman makes a noise that could mean anything. "We'll be looking for her, ma'am, don't you worry. I recommend you try not to leave the house for too long in case she comes home."

That's it? Georgina wants to scream. *In case she comes home*, indeed.

The woman leaves, and Georgina finds herself alone once again. She shuffles to the living room couch and collapses onto it, covering her face with her hands. The apartment practically vibrates with emptiness.

How did it come to this? This was not what she wanted, not what she pictured. Not that she ever had a clear image in mind, a precise end goal she hoped to achieve after all the hard work at the ballet school lost in a frigid Siberian town and then the corps de ballet. All the hours of practice, all the injuries she overcame or ignored. If someone asked her back then what she wanted, she would have been stumped. To dance Giselle, Odette, Aurora, sure, that was easy. Beyond that, it mattered little. All the other stuff, the bows and ruffles, came after: She didn't just want to dance, be in the spotlight, be seen and applauded and adored. She also wanted the nice things she saw all around her, the big apartment, the diamonds. And it was all achieved easily enough. You only had to know what you were doing. She simply followed the steps.

But now it is all gone, and so is Anna. Georgina finds herself here, in this backwater little tourist trap of a town, all alone, abandoned and forgotten. The last Shade in the back row of the school performance now has more than she does. Without Anna, there is nothing to look forward to.

No, she would never accept that.

She picks up her phone, but she doesn't follow Officer Tayler's advice to call Anna's friends, or, heaven forbid, Colter. She dials Fabienne.

18

Now

NAOMI

It's the day of the costume rehearsal. Today it'll be me wearing Nikiya's white dress and then the flowing red tulle and then the act two Kingdom of the Shades tutu. It'll be me doing the pas de deux and being bitten by the snake and dying. It'll be me, last woman standing at the end.

And it doesn't matter what any of these bitches have to say about it.

As I change into my costume, I spot Sarah in the corner, rehearsing what I recognize as the Gamzatti variation, my old part. She looks sweaty and haggard.

Oh well. Not everyone is made for principal roles.

I put on the headdress, the same rhinestone-studded headpiece that Anna thrust so thoughtlessly into my hands after the first run-through, and secure it with extra bobby pins. They dig into my scalp, but I don't care. I won't let anything go wrong. I checked every inch of the costume and of my pointe shoes: no needles, no glass. The costume slips on like it was made for me, not too tight or too loose, even though I don't think they've had time to adjust it since Anna. I check myself in the mirror and freeze, transfixed by the sight. I'm a vision. The white satin flutters around my slight form, making me look ethereal, and the rhinestones suddenly look like they could be real diamonds. My heavily made-up eyes are huge, devouring my face.

This is what I was made for. This is the role I was meant to dance all along.

"Don't fuck this up." Walter, who's been watching the warm-ups from the corner, comes out into the center of the backstage area and claps his hands. "God knows there's been enough fuckery already, so please don't add to it by tripping over your own feet. That's all. Now merde, girls and boys, merde, get out there and prove me wrong."

"Merde," the class echoes. Except Sarah, who's staring ahead, glassy-eyed.

As he passes me by, Everett tips his water bottle in my direction. "To living your dreams," he says.

The act one music begins, and I take my place. In the audience sits the same small group as at the run-through, minus Georgina, of course. Good. Let her and her daughter fall off the face of the earth. This part is mine. It belongs to me.

I do the entrance variation without any major fails—do it

quite well, actually. But anytime I glimpse the teachers' faces, they're grim. Alexandra looks a decade older, glassy-eyed like she's having a hard time remembering there's a ballet being danced right in front of her. Fabienne's lips are pursed. Walter taps his fingertips.

I leave the stage, my heart thundering. Blood pounds in my eardrums, drowning out the music. I notice the Shades standing there, immobile, all of them watching me.

"What?" I snarl at them under my breath.

Before any of them can answer, it's my cue to go back. I race breathlessly through the pas de deux like I can't wait for the scene to be over; I'm too fast for the music, even I notice that. Everett curses in my ear, but I can't help it.

Out of the corner of my eye, I see Fabienne sit up straight and reach into her purse. To my shock, she takes her phone out and answers the call. I almost miss a beat and collide with Everett.

"What's wrong with you?" he hisses.

Fabienne rushes out of the auditorium. I somehow manage to get through the rest of the pas de deux. Then we bow to the two remaining people and leave the stage.

Walter joins us within seconds. "Terrible," he says with a shrug. "Terrible. But then again, Naomi, you haven't given me any reason to think it would be different. Have low expectations, they say, and you'll never be disappointed."

"I'm so sorry, I—" I start to stammer, but he holds up his hand.

"You still have a chance to wow me with the death scene. So let's focus on that, shall we? Gamzatti! Where the hell is Gamzatti? Sarah!"

She steps forward.

"This is your act. Are you warmed up?"

She continues to look at him blankly. "Don't just stand there," he grouses. "Are you ready? Places! Places in two!"

There are hurried steps, and Fabienne bursts into the backstage area. She no longer looks bored, no longer purses her lips. I take one look at her face and know that a disaster is looming.

"Everyone," she exclaims, breathless, "stop everything. Stop the rehearsal."

"This is the run-through," Walter says. "We're not stopping anything unless someone died."

Fabienne doesn't seem to notice he's spoken. "It's Anna," she blurts. "Anna's gone missing."

Everyone stops in their tracks, reality suspended in that one moment, like a bomb a millisecond before the explosion.

"What do you mean, gone missing?" Walter sounds genuinely confused. The smug expression is gone from his face.

"I just spoke to Georgina. Anna has vanished from their apartment. Georgina called the police, and they're on their way here. They want to question us. They want to question everyone."

It feels like every single person backstage gives me that same evil look.

"Where's Anna, huh, Naomi?" one girl says. The one next

to her shakes her head. "You shove her down the stairs, and now she's gone. Funny how that worked out."

"Everyone shut the fuck up," Walter barks. He paces the backstage area, his hands sunk into his hair. His expression is wild, almost demonic. He finally zeroes in on me, grabbing me by the arm so hard I think it might bruise, and pulls me aside.

"Was it you? Just be fucking honest, Naomi."

"No," I said. "I didn't do anything."

To my surprise, he chuckles. "Even if that was the case, who do you think is going to believe you?"

"Then you better convince them," I say in a low whisper. "Or you'll be going down with this ship."

"Oh God. You're fucked. We're all fucked." His laugh cracks, more like a sob. "How did I get myself into this shithole? Someone fucking tell me how."

"It must be sad," I say, surprising myself. "You used to dance. You used to be so famous."

And while he glares at me, stunned, fury plain on his gaunt face, I turn on my heel and walk away. Right to the barre. Where I start to warm up, like nothing happened.

Everyone stares at me like I'm crazy, their gazes scorching my skin.

Well, you know what? Fuck you. Fuck all of you. You can't stop me. Better people than you have tried.

Tears fill my eyes, and the lights overhead refract and flood my whole vision with iridescent bokeh until it's all I can see.

Plié, tendu, port de bras, cambré, and again, and again. One, two, three, four, and again.

The next thing I know, Everett comes over, swoops in, and picks me up unceremoniously. I still cling to the barre, grabbing on for dear life. I try to kick him, then scratch him. "Let go of me!"

"Stop it, Naomi. Stop it. You look like a nutjob."

"I'm warming up! Let go of me!"

"There's no need to warm up. The show's not happening."

"I don't care. I'm going to dance."

"No, you're not."

"I'm Nikiya. I'm fucking Nikiya and you're all just jealous!"

"Naomi, look around you. Everyone is gone."

He puts me down so abruptly that my teeth clack together. The tears spill down my cheeks, taking my makeup with them, and I find myself staring at the empty backstage space. He's right. Everyone has left.

Who cares. Who fucking cares. I'm dancing.

I know the music by heart, it's all in my head, engraved forever on my brain, just like the moves. Start in fourth position. Lunge, piqué, plunge.

And look sorrowful, Naomi. Sorrow.

You're dancing at the wedding of the love of your life.

19

February
NAOMI

As I make my way to Alexandra's office for my final fare-well, it's as if everyone can tell it's best to stay the hell out of my way. They part, letting me through, and it could be my imagination, but they seem to be avoiding even looking in my direction.

Until—

"Hey! *Hey!*"

I don't turn around even as Anna's steps thunder down the hall behind me. She hasn't removed her pointe shoes. If I turn around, I'll probably see her still wearing her Nikiya act two costume and makeup.

"Naomi, what are you doing?"

She grabs my arm from behind, and I throw her off violently.

"Mind your own business, for once."

"No, I won't. You're my best friend. Why did you storm off like that?"

Tears burn in my eyes. I turn around and find myself face-to-face with her, a look of incomprehension in her blue gaze. Of course. How could Anna ever understand what I'm feeling right now?

"You did great. You were this close to nailing the fouettés. At this rate, you'll be doing them with your eyes closed by the final performance. Walter was so impressed. Did you even see his face?"

"Wait. You're not mad at me?"

"No. Why would I be mad?"

I suppose she's right—there's no reason to be mad. She danced a perfect Nikiya from the entrance to the apotheosis. I'm the one who fell on my face.

We walk to the other end of the school, to the staircase that leads nowhere. As soon as we're out of sight, a pack of cigarettes appears in Anna's hand as if by magic. Gingerly, I take one.

"You should be happy," I say as she lights it, our faces so close our foreheads almost touch. Like in the old days when we were friends, really friends, and told each other everything. "You were amazing today. Even Walter won't be able to get to you now."

"Fuck Walter," she says. "Walter's been trying to pit us all against each other since the year started. How stupid does he think we are?"

"He sure seemed to be getting under your skin," I point out carefully.

"Nah. You think I ever danced badly because of *Walter*? Seriously, Naomi. He might think so because he's an egomaniac and an asshole, but you—you know me better than that."

"You didn't dance badly. Well—badly for you, maybe. The rest of us can only aspire to your bad."

"I'm so sick of everything, Naomi, I swear to God." She takes a long drag on her cigarette. "Sometimes I just want to throw myself down these fucking stairs and let that be the end of it."

"Don't," I say on autopilot. "You definitely shouldn't do that."

She measures me with a look. "Why not?"

"Because then who the fuck is going to dance Nikiya? Not me, that's for fucking sure."

Anna giggles. The silvery peals of her laughter echo through the empty staircase, and I can't help but join her. For a few minutes, all we do is laugh until my cheeks hurt and my abs cramp up.

"It's just, sometimes it feels like everything around me is fake," she says once the hilarity subsides. "I feel like I'm not living in the real world but on a ballet stage. My whole life is made up of fake cardboard castles and sky made of dyed fabric, and all around me are not real people but *characters* with fake smiles on their faces. Fake fake fake. Everything is a fucking lie."

She leans in closer. She smells like her expensive shampoo and designer perfume, all of it lurking under a thick veil of cigarette smoke and sweat.

"Remember how I lost my gold medal because of a stumble in the last half second of my act?" She chuckles. "And for what? Because my dad said he'd come to the competition and didn't. Big fucking surprise."

I gulp. "Your—dad?"

"Yeah. I really should have seen it coming, I guess. I kept looking for him in the audience, and that's why my balance was so poor." She shrugs. "And you know what? It turned out..." She pauses, and her face becomes soft, her eyes almost dreamy. "I later found out someone else came to see me, someone so much more important. He was there in the audience all along, and he thought I did great. That's what matters to me, and not some medal."

"You're talking about your older man," I say in a low voice. "The creepy guy you've been sneaking off to see, the one you talk to on your secret phone?"

Anna blinks. "Huh?"

"Your boyfriend in Boston," I say. "I kept your secret—when I didn't have to, I might add."

Anna laughs. "What boyfriend? I don't have a boyfriend in Boston. Are you out of your mind?"

"Don't tell me I'm out of my mind," I say. "I didn't imagine all that."

"You think he's my boyfriend." Anna shakes her head. "Wow, Naomi. You know what? You think everyone's as rotten as you are. That's your big problem. And not your dancing."

She says this in a light tone, like she's joking, or teasing. Except it doesn't sound like a joke to me. I gulp.

"I should go," I say, my mouth dry.

"You're not going to try to drop out and leave me in the lurch, are you?"

"No."

"Good."

I leave with a heavy feeling, like the last curtain has already started to descend, somewhere in the dark above my head, and I just can't see it yet.

20

February

PERCHED AT THE top of the old staircase, Anna watches her best friend go. She told her she was staying behind to make a phone call, but in truth, she just wants to be alone.

She's overcome with a sense of anticlimax. The run-through was a huge success, but she doesn't feel triumph. She very rarely does. Whenever she fails, however, or underperforms, or even dares to get a silver medal instead of the gold—now that's another story. The triumphs have become the norm, what everyone expects from her to begin with. It never occurred to Georgina to congratulate her when she did well, so Anna grew not to expect it from anyone.

But here she is, having just danced Nikiya to perfection. Next stop, the end-of-year show, and then Georgina will drag her out in yet another too-expensive dress to meet the recruiters. And then they'll go to wherever Anna gets hired, and life will continue like it is right now. Up at dawn, rehearsal, rehearsal, cigarettes, coffee, diet Coke, until she collapses into bed exhausted to do it all over again the next day.

She thinks of the application to the modern dance program of that one prestigious school sitting on her computer. The deadline is fast approaching, and Anna already knows she won't go through with it. Maybe Georgina is right, she should be dancing while she's young and flexible and her articulations are solid. A career is so quickly over, even without an injury like the one that ended Georgina's. Then again, wasn't it her own fault? Why did she keep dancing when she knew she had a hairline fracture? Had she taken one season off, she could have gone back onstage the following year and danced for another decade.

She never dared ask that simple question. Anna wonders if her mother ever asked it herself. If she did, would she like the answer? Anna has always suspected that Georgina's ambitions outmatched her natural talent. A simple truth with such explosive implications: *I'm a better dancer than you ever were, Mama.*

This should bring her joy, but it doesn't. She wonders how she'll endure it all, the future Georgina has in mind for her, all this time by her mother's side, all the smiling and doing what she's told—especially now that she knows the truth.

She hears steps echoing closer and closer. Too heavy to be Naomi's—these steps don't sound like a dancer's at all. Even the teachers don't walk so heavily, their former dancer habits too firmly ingrained. Anna quickly stubs out the remains of her cigarette and shoots to her feet.

"Anna?" calls a voice. "I know you're here. Please don't be afraid, I just want to talk to you."

The voice is so familiar, but here, in this context, she just can't place it. Luckily, a moment later, the woman steps into Anna's line of sight. She too has a cigarette between her lips, unlit.

"Got a light?"

The situation is a little surreal. The woman comes up the stairs to join her, and Anna wordlessly hands her a lighter.

"Ms. Thompson," she says colorlessly.

"Please. We've known each other for so long. Call me Dawn."

21

Now

THE STAGE WITH all its props is still there, bathed in the bright lights of projectors someone forgot to turn off, except the lush set is empty. Officer Tayler focuses on the task at hand. There is, after all, a girl who's gone missing, and with every new thing that comes to light, she becomes more and more concerned. At first she was sure this would be nothing, a routine case that would take a couple of hours, that Anna Prescott would turn up someplace predictable and be returned to her mother. Then she became convinced the girl had left of her own free will, but Tayler couldn't blame her. With that woman for a mother, it seemed understandable. She does her best not to judge anyone. In her line of work, being judgmental doesn't serve. On the contrary, it obscures clues that otherwise would be obvious, and she's seen too many in her profession make that critical mistake. As it stands, Anna is missing, and something terrible could have happened, and so it's Tayler's job to bring her home safely.

And now her phone buzzes with a text from one of the subordinates she called up to help her track Anna's last movements. Tayler reads the text and can only shake her head. This just gets better and better, doesn't it?

"So let me recap," she says. "This girl fell and broke her foot while on school property, correct?"

The teachers are gathered in a row, seated in the audience chairs covered in red velour. Tayler might tower over them, but somehow, she doesn't feel superior or authoritative, far from it. Truth is, she's still trying to wrap her head around everything she's just learned.

One of the teachers gets up. A former ballerina, Tayler recognizes at once. Sure, just like Georgina, she has the posture, and, Tayler supposes, a sort of timeless grace, but what gives it away is the style, the hair pulled back in an unflattering bun, the clothes and shoes, and, most of all, the air of arrogance. This blond woman is the principal, Alexandra something. "I'm sure Ms. Prescott told you all kinds of things," the woman says defiantly. "You must take it all with healthy skepticism. She hasn't been herself lately, and this—this probably pushed the poor woman over the edge."

"Nevertheless...," Tayler says. She hates to admit it, but a part of her enjoys lording it over them. "She has a point. When this happened, I assumed there would have been an internal investigation. A thorough internal investigation."

"This is ballet," pipes up another teacher, the brunette with the red lipstick. Tayler doesn't have their names fully memorized yet, but she's already figured out who they are and where they fit on the social strata. "We can't do an investigation every time someone gets injured."

"No, actually," Tayler says. "It's not ballet. This is a school. You're responsible for the well-being of your students."

"Well, as much as we'd have liked to have an investigation, Anna wouldn't cooperate," says the principal. "As I'm sure you already know."

"So I'm told."

"So how were we supposed to conduct an investigation when the main interested party just shrugs and says it was an accident? Did you expect me to torture her with pliers?"

"I just find it interesting. Just a while ago, I learned about the incident at the Christmas gala…"

Tayler knows she hit the target. The principal pales; her nostrils flare.

"That should have been investigated as well. Especially seeing how those involved were minors. And yet, once again, Anna Prescott shrugs and says she doesn't know anything, and then the whole situation is swept under the rug."

"We expelled the other student," Alexandra says dryly. "I don't see what more you expect us to have done. Besides, his parents—"

"You didn't want legal action," Tayler says. "That's hardly an excuse."

"Come on now," says the brunette. Fiona? Fabienne. That's right, that's her name. "As you just said yourself, this is a school. A boarding school! Do you expect us to mediate every little spat between teenagers? That's insane!"

The principal gives the poor woman such a glare that she cuts herself off and slumps in her seat. Tayler almost feels bad for her.

"I think everyone here will agree," Tayler says, "that there's a highly unhealthy environment among the students in this school, and that the teachers not only do nothing about it—they encourage it."

"The job of a school," Alexandra says, "is to prepare our students for the real world. In our case, the ballet world."

"Which plays by different rules," Tayler says, nodding. "I get it. I've heard it a dozen times by now. Tell me about this ballet you're staging for the end-of-year performance. The one where Anna was supposed to dance the lead."

"There's not much to tell," Alexandra says. She's going from pale to a bright red flush of fury, her cheeks mottled. "Anna was supposed to dance the lead because she's the best student in the graduating class, if not the whole academy. I don't see who else would be dancing the lead. And no matter what you insinuate, we've always loved Anna and protected her. Nobody in this school would ever—"

Tayler stops her with a gesture. "I don't think you speak for everybody when you say that. Somebody was determined that

Anna not dance the role. At least, the choreographer you hired as artistic director seemed to do everything he could to make things difficult for Anna."

"That's not true!" Alexandra exclaims. But Tayler has already turned her attention elsewhere.

The choreographer in question, with the receding hairline and beady eyes, twitches in his seat.

"I understand you're a new addition to this school," Tayler says.

"I heard all kinds of great things about Anna before I started teaching here," Walter says, "but unfortunately, I haven't *seen* many great things. Anna hasn't exactly lived up to her reputation."

"And could the toxic climate at this school have something to do with it?" Tayler asks. "Or is that just another part of preparing students for the real world?"

"Whether you like it or not, it's the case," Walter snaps.

"Walter," Alexandra mutters under her breath, but it's too late.

"The truth is," he says, "no one at a dance company gives a shit that you're having a bad day. If these girls can't take the pressure, they have no business being here!"

"So the new girl who dances Anna's part, she can take the pressure, I suppose? I guess we'll find out. As I understand, there was some upheaval around this girl, Naomi Thompson. After Anna's accident, assuming it was an accident, there was quite a hate campaign against her on social media. For no reason other than rumors. Was there any truth to those rumors?"

"You're the investigator. You tell us."

Tayler ignores him. "And once again, nothing was done about this campaign of harassment against one of your students. Is that also meant to prepare them for the real world?"

"Those were baseless accusations," Alexandra fumes. "We ignored them as such accusations should be ignored and told the students to do the same."

"Your choreographer spent the entire year pitting the students against one another," Tayler says.

Walter leaps from the seat. "I did absolutely nothing of the sort!"

"Sit, please. I have to ask myself why he would do that. And as my colleagues and I looked into it, I only had more and more questions. For one, it took us fifteen minutes and two phone calls to find out why exactly he was let go from his previous place of work. Should I show you the text I just got, or just summarize it?"

"We know about the rehab," Alexandra says levelly, but Tayler can tell how nervous she is. For all her tremendous self-control, she fails to contain her fidgeting.

"I'm not talking about that," Tayler says. "Allegedly, Mr. Graf had an affair with a seventeen-year-old apprentice. Which wouldn't be illegal exactly, except he was in a position of authority. Now, how did this not come to light when he was hired to teach teen girls?"

"It was Edith," Alexandra stammers. "She found him, hired him, brought him in. We didn't question anything because Edith would never—"

"But Georgina Prescott says otherwise."

"Georgina Prescott is delusional!"

"We've already reached out to Ms. Spencer," Tayler says. "And she confirmed that you were the one who suggested Mr. Graf. I don't know what's going on between the two of you, but I'll find out. In the meantime, I'd like you all to proceed to the police station, where my colleague will take your individual statements. I'm going to get to the bottom of whatever happened in this school of yours, no matter how ugly it gets."

The girls from Anna's class stand in a disorderly row by the barre in one of the classrooms. They all have an identical look to them, those slicked-back buns and those costumes with the giant fake rhinestones. They fix Tayler with their eyes like saucers, made even bigger and rounder with copious amounts of stage makeup. What she should do is separate them, have them taken to the station, leave them to stew for a bit, and then have them give their statements. But she suspects the moment the parents get wind of this, there will be lawyers involved, and then she won't get anything out of them. So at first she wants to try another approach. Of course, all of the other students were here when Anna went missing—bright and early at warm-up, ready for the final rehearsal or whatever the teachers called it. But that doesn't mean none of them had anything to do with Anna's disappearance.

"I won't talk without a lawyer," one of the girls immediately pipes up, as if on cue.

"We're not there yet," Tayler says, smiling warmly. They keep eyeing her with mistrust and suspicion. She's aware of their gazes, shrewd as any teenage girl's, inspecting her every bit as stringently as she inspects the evidence in her cases, missing nothing. Teenage girls do that, and these are no ordinary teenage girls.

When she was about their age, Amy Tayler played hockey. She remembers the dynamic, the camaraderie, sure, but also the rivalries, and not just between opposing teams. She remembers how some of the parents took it all so very seriously—seriously enough to start fights in the bleachers. And she remembers the figure-skating girls who trained in the same arena, the girls with their elegant white skates who looked down on the hockey girls and didn't try to hide it. These young would-be ballerinas remind her of them. She remembers feeling sorry for them back then—the stakes seemed so high that it had to take all the fun out of their sport. Now she wonders how many of the students in this school will grow up to hate dancing. It's a pity, really.

But this bit of insider knowledge, small though it is, has given her an idea. She'll try something on these girls before they can get their bearings and decide to lawyer up.

"I'm not here to accuse you of anything," she says in the nicest, most conspiratorial tone she can muster. "On the contrary. I spoke to your teachers, and if anything, I think you're the victims in all this."

They sneak furtive glances at one another even as Tayler observes them. They look identical at first glance, but just like with the teachers, she figures out the hierarchy almost at once. The girl on the far left, the one in a gaudy, rhinestoned costume that's little more than a bra, with a stricken, wide-eyed look on her face, is Naomi Thompson. Tayler recognizes her from her Instagram account. Well, Naomi will have to wait.

"There are strange things happening at your school," Tayler says, "and I hope you can help me make sense of them. From what I gather, Anna isn't quite the angel everyone says she is, is she?"

Some of the girls begin to fidget.

"We love Anna," says one of the girls. "She's never done a single bad thing to anyone."

"But it must be tough, to always be in her shadow," Tayler says. "When I know all of you work just as hard. It doesn't seem fair."

"This is ballet," pipes up another girl. This one is Sarah, if Tayler remembers correctly. "It's not meant to be fair."

She sounds just like their teachers. Tayler is tempted to shake her head, but instead, she continues smiling at them blandly.

"I hear there was quite a bit of bullying," she tries again. "After the Christmas gala incident."

Now nobody will meet her eye.

"Everyone knows James did it," mutters the first girl who spoke—Gemma. "And they kicked him out, as they should have. A lot of girls have stories about James. A lot."

"Oh, we'll get to James," Tayler assures her. "We're contacting his parents as we speak. Right now, it's Anna who interests me. It was a bad situation for her. Embarrassing. And she's such a perfectionist too."

"Anna didn't do anything wrong."

"Well, this fall sure turned out to be well timed," Tayler says, observing the girls keenly. "It really turned the tide for her. Suddenly, all everyone has is sympathy."

A loud snort interrupts her. Tayler looks up—it came from Naomi. This is the first sign of life Naomi has given since the whole thing started. Now she's staring at Tayler with a death glare that clashes with her white, sparkly costume.

"Really? You just figured it out?" Naomi asks.

"What do you mean?"

"Ever since she fell, all her wrongs are forgiven. And of course, whoever took her place was going to get all the hate. Isn't it convenient? For Anna, I mean."

"Naomi, shut the hell up," Gemma mutters.

"Oh, Anna is no angel all right," Naomi says louder, her voice cracking. "You're wondering where she went? I have a guess.

She had a boyfriend in Boston. That's right. She goes there every summer to stay with her dad. Well, last summer she met some guy there. An older man. That's why she wouldn't tell me who it was. Because it's some perv her dad's age. There you have it."

"Wait," Tayler says. Jackpot. "How do you know this?"

"She told me. No details, of course. Our Anna looks out for herself."

"You're a liar!" Sarah gets to her feet. "She's lying. She's just making it up on the spot. She's always hated Anna. She's always been jealous, and the worst part is, she pretends to be her friend! We all wondered why Anna keeps this snake around. And now look what happened—she paid the price."

"Hang on," Tayler says. Just as she finally seems to be getting somewhere, she's losing control of the situation, and she must get it back, fast. "If what Naomi is saying is true—"

"It's not. She's making it up, probably to draw suspicion away from herself. I bet she did push her. Come on, Naomi. Everybody knows you had something to do with it."

Naomi gets to her feet, her fists clenching at her sides. "You shut the fuck up, you fucking druggie."

"Girls," Officer Tayler says.

Naomi lunges at Sarah, but before she can reach her, something happens. Sarah sways and grabs on to the barre to regain her balance, but it doesn't work. She collapses like a dropped doll, the sparkly yellow tutu of her costume crushed underneath her.

The other girls shriek. Naomi freezes midmotion, her eyes like pools of darkness in her face.

"Ambulance!" somebody yells out. "Call an ambulance!"

At the far end of the auditorium, the doors bang open, and the principal and Fabienne come rushing into the room. Tayler reaches for her phone and calls backup, at last.

22

Now

NAOMI

EVERYTHING HAS FALLEN apart.

Sarah woke up, finally, and didn't wait another minute to spill the beans. I was the one who gave her the pills on which she OD'd.

At least that's what the woman, Officer Tayler, is saying. I don't have many reasons to doubt it. Sarah would sell out her own mother to cover her ass.

It's the word choice that gets me. *Gave.* I didn't give anyone shit. She's the one who came to me and pleaded and offered me her entire giant bloated allowance that her rich daddy sent her from Washington. *You have to get me through this show, Naomi. I'll give you anything you want.*

And I held up my part of the bargain, didn't I? So far, she got through it all right. Better than I did. She pulled off the variation and the pas de deux, bad ankle or not. And she would've gotten through the final show just as well. Except now, there won't be a final show. Except now, I'm the one getting screwed.

"I want to help you, Naomi," Tayler is saying, like I'm an idiot. "If you tell me everything, I can find a way to help you." There's something grotesque about her, her height and her bulk. She hates girls like me, and she doesn't hide it. I overheard her saying to one of the other cops, *Who knew such a beautiful art could be so ugly?*

I decide it's time to say something because I can't keep weathering her condescending, pitying looks. Who does she think she is, with her meaningless, mundane existence with its pathetic little joys, rewarding herself with a pedicure and soothing herself with McDonald's after a bad day—who is she to judge me? Has she ever had a dream, a real one worth pursuing? Has she ever done anything but go with the flow in her entire life? Does she know what effort is?

She has no idea how much pointe shoes cost. She never had to lie to her mom—and not have Dawn realize a thing because she doesn't even care enough about what I do to google the simplest basics of ballet. Yup, Dawn still thinks that I can make a pair last a week, sometimes two. Ignorance, they say, is bliss. If she'd had to pay for everything herself, I'd have been out of the academy years ago.

The first time I pocketed one of Dawn's scrip pads, I had

just turned thirteen. It's not that I never realized the potential of having a mom who's a nurse or that I was unaware of the market value of a good painkiller that could get you through a recital on a sprained ankle. But it was only after my own injury that delayed my introduction to pointe work that I became truly aware of what I had within reach.

I had only just come back to class when a girl approached me in the locker room. "What are you on?" she asked me in a furtive whisper once we were alone.

"I'm sorry?"

"What are you *on*?" she repeated, and rolled her eyes like I was slow in the head. She wasn't from our class. She was a ninth grader, already well into her pointe classes—and oh, how I envied her and the other older girls who looked so effortless on pointe when it felt like I'd never be able to do anything more than hobble around. That she spoke to me at all was shocking.

She nodded at my foot, her long neck craning. "Your injury. What did they give you? What medication? Don't tell me you're back in class already without something to take the edge off."

I was taking some medication. Despite much grumbling from Dawn, they'd prescribed me a mild painkiller that I took twice a day with food. But by now, I had already mastered the trick of sneaking an extra pill between classes to get me through recitals. This meant the supply would dwindle faster, and Dawn watched the little pill bottle like a hawk, so I'd saw a single pill into two, into four, anything to make it last longer.

I told her the name on the bottle, having little idea if it was good or bad. She scoffed. "Ugh. Anyway. I'll give you fifty dollars per pill because it's weak shit."

I looked at her, stunned.

"I can't sell them to you," I said. Because if Dawn saw pills missing, she'd have a fit. Already she'd given me a whole speech about the dangers of painkillers as well as an embarrassing pamphlet from the hospital about the opioid epidemic.

The girl only laughed. "Come on, Thompson. I know you need money. Isn't your family, like, on food stamps?"

We weren't rich—everyone at school knew, for sure, but I'd never realized they thought we were *that* poor. I suppose, to this golden child, living on a nurse's salary and being poor was the same thing.

"My mom's an NP," I said, to shut her up. And it had the intended effect. Her eyes became huge, and she whistled through her perfect teeth.

"You're sitting on a gold mine, Thompson. If you can steal me a scrip, I'll give you five hundred dollars."

"I'm sorry?"

"Five hundred bucks. I don't want the whole pad, just one page. Your mom won't notice. Come on, be a sport!"

I couldn't tell her that she could pay me five hundred bucks or five thousand, it made no difference because my mom didn't keep the scrip pad at home. But that's when I first realized the full potential I had at my fingertips. Next time I was at the hospital, I took advantage of a moment alone to sneak a scrip pad into my pocket.

I didn't sell it to the ninth-grade girl. By then I realized there was more to be made than her stupid five hundred bucks.

I could have enough money to not have to make my pointe shoes last and to have nice, high-quality gear. I could save up enough for my new start once school was over and I was out there auditioning in Boston or New York.

For the first time, I had options. And the sick irony is that all these rich spoiled brats whose parents came to see them in Maseratis—for once, they all wanted what *I* had. I was their motherfucking fairy godmother. Everett, Sarah, Madison— everyone. James too. A guy like him doesn't need money. I was the one who supplied him with Percocet after he injured his back that year. In exchange, he dumped Anna the day of her competition.

Now, you're probably wondering if I sold to Anna too. The answer is no. Anna knew, without ever explicitly bringing it up. But she never asked me for painkillers, not even once. Anna just pushed through the pain.

But there's no way I'll tell any of that to this cow.

"Just tell me the names," she's saying. "Everyone you sold to. Then I might be able to do something for you."

But I know there's no point. They all have rich parents who will summon their lawyers and rescue their offspring. I'll get thrown to the wolves, and they'll resume their lives.

I mean to sound confident, but I don't. I have been meaning to say *I want a lawyer*, but what comes out is, "I want my mom."

Dawn races down the hall of the station, her heart in her throat. Being a nurse for almost twenty years, some of those years in the ER, has taught her a certain amount of sangfroid. She actually prides herself on this, although, every once in a while, she lets her mind wander in frightening directions. Would she be able to keep her cool, she wondered, if it were Naomi brought in after a crash or hit-and-run?

Well, she figures she has the answer now.

"You do realize," Dawn finds herself saying, "that this girl could have told you literally anything? There's a lot of...competition at that school. And Naomi—" She glances at her daughter, who sits with her legs pulled up, her chin propped up on her knees, and won't meet her gaze. She's wearing an oversize sweatshirt that's slipping from one shoulder. In the unflattering halogen lights overhead, it's so immediately obvious how undernourished Naomi is, how her bones jut from under her skin. Dawn can only imagine what they must think of her as a mother. In this new light, she can finally see herself and her daughter from a new angle that she has willfully ignored.

But they don't understand, she finds herself thinking with increasing desperation. It's not what it looks like. They have no idea what's really happening. In her urgent need to explain, she stumbles over her words. "Naomi is dancing the principal role. In the end-of-year performance. It's—*La Bayadère*. It's a very famous ballet. There will be recruiters…"

The woman, Officer Tayler, puts her hand on Dawn's forearm. The woman is a head taller, and she can be intimidating if she wants, but the gesture is sympathetic. And, with a sinking feeling, Dawn just knows. But she continues anyway because she can't admit defeat like this.

"Naomi is innocent," she says, aware of how lame she sounds. "She had nothing to do with this. She's not some juvenile delinquent, she's a ballerina. She's dedicated, hardworking, and full of determination. Do you have any idea what it takes to make it this far at the academy?"

"Ms. Thompson, it's not your fault," Officer Tayler assures her. "Most parents have no clue what really goes on at this school. You can't have known either. You're a busy single mother, aren't you?"

"What?" Dawn's ears are ringing. "What does that have to do with anything? And I don't care what goes on at that school. Naomi had nothing to do with it. She's worked her ass off since she was ten years old. Do you think she'd jeopardize it all like—"

"You're a nurse, working night shifts, doing your best to keep your head above water," Tayler narrates smoothly. Dawn's face flares. Just like that, her whole life, and Naomi's, and all their struggles have been reduced to a cliché. The worst cliché there is. Does this woman realize she sounds just like the snobby moms at the academy? Yes, those snooty bitches with their designer bags, who've perfected the art of making her feel out of place with a seemingly benign comment. Dawn always told herself she skipped all the recitals because she was overworked, but in truth, every time she couldn't go because of her schedule, she felt secretly relieved. Sitting next to them made her feel inferior.

Tayler, oblivious to her distress—or maybe spurred on by it—goes on. "You just want what's best for Naomi. Every child deserves a chance to follow her dreams, doesn't she?"

"*Dreams*," Dawn snaps. "These aren't just dreams. Naomi is extremely talented. Ballet is her calling."

"Of course, of course. And tuition is expensive, and all those pointe shoes and the costumes. You come home from work exhausted. No one blames you for not seeing the red flags...Do you have any idea how long she's been stealing your prescription pads?"

Dawn's head throbs like she's been sucker punched.

"That's not—I don't bring them home," she retorts. "That would be—"

"Yet she somehow managed. Did she drop by to see you at work? Think."

Dawn tries, she really tries. Her mind is blank.

"You can't just keep her here," she blurts. "What are the charges? Where is the proof? You—"

"There will be proof, all right. As soon as we investigate and track down all the scrips from the town drugstores, we'll have plenty of proof."

"And then what happens?"

"That depends on Naomi. But one thing is for sure, she won't be dancing the lead in anything. So she might as well change out of this belly dancer getup."

But Dawn's mind snags on one word. *Investigate.* She pictures it as vividly as an HD film: them showing up at the hospital, inspecting all the records, sniffing out any inconsistencies. Again, she starts to feel queasy.

She has to grab Naomi and get out of here. Somehow.

"And then there's the matter of Naomi's missing friend," Tayler is saying, but her voice sounds far away. "Her mother has been notified, and she's on her way to the station. I don't know what's going on, or whether there's a connection, but if you can think of anything that might help me figure it out—I'll make it count in Naomi's favor."

Dawn looks up and meets the woman's gaze. Tayler must see the blank look in her eyes, because she shakes her head. "Ms. Thompson..."

"Naomi had nothing to do with Anna's fall," Dawn says, her voice smooth. "Not a thing."

She isn't sure who gets her a chair and who helps her sit down. She wouldn't have been able to stay on her feet anyway, and if not for the chair, she would have collapsed right onto the floor.

That's what I get for trying to help, she thinks. But then again, that's not the case, is it? Sure, she was only trying to help—to help her own daughter and her friend in one fell swoop. She wanted to be the go-to person, the trustworthy adult, the cool mom. Was that what it was all about?

And the more she thinks about it, the more she's forced to admit that no, that's not all. The undeniable truth from deep within her soul is that she wanted Naomi to succeed. Maybe, in her heart, she's as bad as Georgina. Worse than Georgina, because at least Georgina kept her meddling mostly legal.

It's just—it's so unfair, she wants to scream. All these interminable years of scrimping and saving and sacrificing time with her own daughter to pay for that same daughter's one-in-a-million dreams. Yes, she supposes she should have nipped it in the bud, said no to the beginners' ballet class at the strip mall studio, but she didn't do that. It's too late, and she must assume the consequences.

Naomi deserves to have this chance. If she doesn't get it, it's all been for nothing. And that is the thing that Dawn really can't accept.

23

February

"Dawn," Anna says. She realizes now how long it's been since she saw her last—this woman who she used to think was practically family. If not for Naomi and her mom, she never would have survived those long, lonely years when she lived at the boarding school. "What are you doing here?"

"I thought I'd surprise Naomi, pick her up after class and take her out to dinner or something. It's a big day, right?"

"Yeah," Anna says. "It was the general run-through."

"How did you do?"

"Shouldn't you be asking how Naomi did?"

The woman's mouth twitches, but just as soon, the genteel smile returns. "I know Naomi always does well," she says proudly. The thing a mom is supposed to say. Unless your mom is Georgina. Still, Anna wrestles with the temptation to tell her that Naomi didn't do so well after all. Fouettés were never Naomi's strong suit.

"You must be proud of her," Anna says.

"I am. She's dancing—what is she called? The second role."

"Gamzatti."

"Such a silly name. I looked up *La Bayadère*, and it's so strange. These pseudo-Hindi costumes and the generic classical music. Then again, I guess I just don't get ballet."

Anna chuckles softly. Dawn probably thinks this is such a quirky, clever thing to say, but Anna grew up surrounded by people who *just didn't get ballet*. In elementary school, she got teased and had no friends because instead of playing in the schoolyard after class she was picked up by Georgina in her husband's Porsche and whisked off to ballet class. Then she came to the academy, and things changed. She was suddenly the height of everyone's aspirations and hopes. She thought she'd like it, but it only made her more miserable.

"It's a universal story," she finds herself saying.

"Yes, yes. I suppose. Love triangle, rivalry, et cetera. It seems like all these ballets have a woman dying over some guy."

You're right, Anna thinks. You *don't* get it. "Dawn, what is it? Why are you really here?"

The friendly look on her face falters for a second. "Naomi told me," she says. "You want to go to college to study modern dance, but Georgina wants you to start dancing at a company right away."

"Naomi told you that?" Anna asks, wary.

"She's my daughter. She tells me things," Dawn says, a touch defensive.

Things, maybe, but not everything, Anna thinks.

"And what does it have to do with you?"

In the face of such directness, Dawn seems to hesitate. "Anna, you know I've always been there for you girls. Any problem you have, you can come to me—I think I made that clear. I helped you out last year, didn't I?"

Anna gives a nod. "I'm sorry about my mom," she says. "I'm sorry she made such a scene. I tried to get her to simmer down."

"Don't mention it," Dawn says. "I did what I thought was right. I'm not sorry. And maybe I can help you with this too."

Anna examines her, searching her face. Dawn is the polar opposite of her own mother: She has a generous, round face and short, frizzy hair that escapes from the stubby ponytail she always pulls it into, and she dresses like she just reached into a drawer in the morning at random and wore whatever she pulled out. Anna remembers the spaghetti dinners at Dawn's house back when she first started at the academy, before her parents divorced and Georgina came to town and moved the two of them into that condo apartment. Dawn was—and, Anna supposes, still is—a terrible cook, but it didn't matter: Those pasta dishes were the tastiest Anna had ever had. She'd never had pasta sauce from a can before, and she stuffed her face like she'd never get another chance.

As if sensing her hesitation, Dawn goes in for the kill. "These are crucial years, Anna. This is when you decide your destiny. You can't turn your back on it because your mother doesn't approve."

"For all I know, I won't even get in," Anna huffs, even though she knows she'll get in.

"Well, do you want to try?"

"Who's going to let me? She already has everything planned out. I dance in the end-of-year performance, and then off I go to apprentice in the corps de ballet of whatever company will have me. No discussion."

Dawn sighs. Anna watches her carefully, noting every shift in her expression.

"Unless, of course," Dawn says, "you couldn't dance."

24

Now

WHEN GEORGINA BURSTS through the doors of the police station, Fabienne is already there. "Thank God!" she exclaims, and encases Georgina in a hug. But right now, Georgina doesn't want a hug. She stands there stiffly and waits for the other woman to pull away. The smell of her perfume makes Georgina queasy.

She's always known Fabienne had a crush on her, and she never saw anything wrong with nourishing that crush—nourishing it just enough to keep it from fizzling out. As it stood, she held Anna's fate in her manicured hands. Besides, once Edith retired, Fabienne was primed to take her place—except then they brought in that tattooed freak and upset all of Georgina's plans. She knows Fabienne had nothing to do with it. If anything, she had every reason to be just as furious as Georgina about such a backstabbing move by Alexandra. But she can't lie, she feels bitterness toward Fabienne, bitterness she struggles to get past.

If only, if only. Everything would be different. Anna would be dancing Aurora, and everything would be perfect.

"Have they arrested her?" Georgina asks when Fabienne's bear hug finally loosens.

"Naomi?"

"Who else?"

"I—I don't know. I guess they're still gathering evidence—"

"Evidence? What evidence? It's obvious. She did something to Anna. Oh God, oh God..."

"It's not about Anna," Fabienne says carefully. Blood drains from Georgina's face.

"Then what on earth is it about?"

"Some kind of sordid business. Apparently, she sold painkillers at school—a girl passed out, and it all came out. I'm sorry, I would have told you—"

"Painkillers? This is about painkillers? They're investigating petty drug dealing when my daughter's life could be in danger?"

"Georgina, please." Fabienne places her hand on Georgina's forearm, but Georgina recoils.

"I need to talk to that officer. What's her name? Tyler?"

"Georgina, please, wait."

"I swear," she says through her teeth. "I'll wrap my hands around Naomi's stumpy little neck and squeeze until the little bitch tells me what she did to my daughter."

Farther down the hall, a door opens. The officer is the first one to exit; Georgina recognizes her at once, that height and build. A short, plump woman follows, and at first, Georgina can't place her. The frizzy hair, the scrubs peeking out from under the acrylic sweater—it's the nurse. Dawn Thompson.

Her face looks drawn, ashen, like she's aged fifteen years since the last time Georgina confronted her. For a fraction of a moment, Georgina feels bad for her. Only for a fraction of a moment. Then a third person emerges, head down, sweatshirt hoodie pulled low over her face, but the tattered pointe shoes and the chiffon costume give her away. The fabric hangs like a rag off her scrawny figure. Naomi.

Ignoring Fabienne's pleas for her to stop, she rushes toward them. "What did you do?" she bellows, her voice a broken howl that shocks even her with its hoarseness. "What did you do to Anna, you criminal?"

"Ms. Prescott," says Officer Tayler, "I know you're in a very emotional state. But I'm glad you're here because I just got some news I'd like to discuss with you."

Georgina thinks her legs might go out from under her, betraying her for the third time in her life. "She's dead," she whispers. Her lips feel numb as she forms the words. "Anna's dead?"

"Nothing of the sort," Officer Tayler says. She must notice Georgina is about to collapse because she crosses the distance between them and offers Georgina her arm to hold on to. For once, Georgina couldn't be more thankful. She grabs on to her blue sleeve like she's drowning. "We're still investigating Anna's possible whereabouts. But I do have some news. My colleague just called me from the hospital—"

"She's in the hospital?" Georgina mumbles.

"No, no," says Officer Tayler. "But there's been an interesting development. It appears there's no evidence of your daughter being there in the last few months at all."

Georgina blinks. The meaning of the woman's words eludes her, slipping through her fingers like sand. Just like when she was young and stayed up half the night after recitals, poring over a big, musty English grammar book, cramming the unfamiliar words and turns of phrase into her tired brain. *Hello, how do you do? My name is Mary. Which way is the library, please?* She hardly notices how Fabienne creeps up by her side and squeezes her hand.

"What exactly do you mean by this?" Fabienne comes to Georgina's rescue. "No record? Anna was there only a couple of weeks ago—"

"Apparently not," says Tayler. "Or, if she was, there's no record. No X-ray, no diagnosis, nothing."

"I don't understand," Fabienne says.

"To be honest, neither do we," says the woman. "My colleague has spoken to the doctor who was on duty that day, and he'll call me as soon as he can. But it appears that Anna's injury may never have happened."

25

February

"IF THERE'S NO end-of-year performance," Dawn is saying, "then there are no recruiters, no offers. The coast is clear for you to make a case to your mother about going to college. After all, without the end-of-year ballet, it's your best bet for a career. Even Georgina can understand that."

The truth is that Dawn isn't so sure. From what she knows of Georgina, she's hardly a shining example of rationality.

But that's what Naomi said, didn't she? She'd rather have her for a mother than Dawn. For a moment, Dawn lets herself imagine it: a daughter swap, kind of like reality TV but minus the confession cams. Would Naomi have accomplished more with someone like Georgina to push her every hour of every day? Probably. And what would it be like for Dawn to have sweet, docile Anna for a daughter instead?

She doesn't let herself dwell on the thought. Sure, she's not a former ballerina with a fancy last name and a collection of spike heels she can actually walk in. She doesn't have connections all over the ballet world. She's only a nurse who works nights to afford tuition and pointe shoes for her talented ballerina daughter.

But being a nurse can have its perks too. And she may not be able to give Naomi the ballet world on a silver platter, but she can give her this.

She can give her the starring role in *La Bayadère*.

"What are you saying?" Anna asks with an uncertain half smile. "You're asking me to throw myself down the stairs, like in some bad soap opera?"

"Good God, of course not!" Dawn lets out a nervous laugh. "What am I, crazy? There's no need for that. I work at a hospital, remember?"

Anna looks at her, her stare once again blank. Dawn wonders what Anna might be doing if not for Georgina, who pushed her into ballet. She feels bad for Anna, she really does. On one hand, one look at her and it's impossible to deny that she was made for this. Her build, her arms, her feet—even when she's just standing around, she has that perfect posture, the swan neck, the long legs. And who knows, she may have had a real interest in ballet once upon a time. But Georgina crushed it out of her a long time ago. Dawn can see it in Anna's indifferent china-blue eyes. Dawn can keep making her case, but Anna has already made her decision.

"Let's go," Dawn says softly. "Before someone sees us."

"Wait," the girl says. Dawn is assailed by doubt. Is she going to say no?

But Anna reaches into her bag and takes out a tablet, which she holds out to Dawn. "This is the application," she says. "I have to submit it by the end of the week. It's ready, but I need to pay a fee. And I can't put it on Georgina's credit card, so..."

You sly little minx, Dawn thinks, shaking her head. She takes the tablet from Anna's hand. "Not a problem," she says. "What is it, like two hundred dollars?"

"Seven hundred and fifty dollars."

Dawn groans under her breath. Her credit card is perpetually maxed out—she isn't even sure the payment will go through. But she paid down the balance recently, so she crosses her fingers as she enters the information and then waits. Finally a green check mark appears on the screen. Payment accepted.

"There you go," she says, and gives Anna the tablet back. "Application sent. Now you know I mean it—that was like three months' groceries."

Anna chuckles. She picks up her duffel bag and slings it over her fragile shoulder. "Let's go."

Bradley—Dr. Huang—is reluctant at first. "Is this some kind of insurance scam?" he asks Dawn sotto voce as Anna waits on the examination table. "You know I could get in a shit ton of trouble."

"You won't." Anna speaks up, surprising them both. "We have no insurance anyway."

And she resumes staring at a blank wall, her face indifferent. Weird, Dawn thinks. She always assumed they were provided for by Papa Prescott because Georgina has no job that anyone knows of, and yet someone pays for that condo, and for the tuition, and for Anna's top-quality ballet gear. She figured the insurance came from him as well.

Dawn always thought it was nice—she'd never seen a red cent from Naomi's dad. But perhaps she was wrong.

"So you want me to put a brace on her healthy foot," Bradley is saying.

"Only for a little while. So that she can get out of a dance recital."

He only shakes his head. "Dawn...why are you doing this? Why put your job on the line...and mine, potentially...to help out one of your daughter's friends? Unless there's something I'm not grasping?"

"There is," she says levelly, all too aware of Anna's proximity. Her face flushes, and for the first time since she conceived of this whole crazy idea, on a whim, she realizes how transparent it is. Surely Anna understands that she's not doing this out of the goodness of her heart. That with her gone, it'll be Naomi dancing her role.

If she does, she must have one hell of a good reason for going along with it. And it's not just the modern dance program that she claims to be so obsessed with. The modern dance program will still be there either way, especially for someone like

Anna. But no one would willingly give away the principal role. Not even her.

But it's too late to second-guess. She can't back out. If she does, then Anna can go around telling everyone about Naomi's crazy mom who tried to bribe her into faking an injury. If they go through with it, though, Anna will be complicit, and she too will have something to hide. Imagine the scandal...

"Are you ready, Anna?" Bradley asks.

She turns to them like she just remembered they were there. She measures Dawn with that watery blue gaze. Dawn's skin crawls.

"Yes," Anna says. "I am."

26

Now

SINCE THEN, DAWN has had ample time to think about it. To recognize the full extent of her folly, the disastrous stupidity of her plan. Even with her foot in a brace, Anna had everything to gain and Naomi everything to lose.

What the hell have I done?

But the more she thinks about it, the more she finds herself confronted with a fact she can no longer deny. She's spent all these years secretly wishing Naomi were *normal*, a typical teenager with typical, vapid teenage problems. Wishing the ballet phase would just pass already so her daughter could move on to more serious aspirations. It was only when Naomi yelled those words into her face, *I wish Georgina was my mother*, only then she realized how wrong she'd been. What if Naomi isn't obsessed? What if she's exceptional? What if it's not a phase but Naomi's destiny? Dawn always patted herself on the back for paying the tuition and buying the pointe shoes, but this didn't make her a martyr; it made her a hypocrite.

And before she knew it, it was too late. School would be over in a few months, and Naomi would be out there in the world. She'd missed her chance to be supportive, so now was her last opportunity to make up for it.

At least that's what she thought she was doing.

Maybe she has more in common with Georgina than she ever thought. After all, how far would a mother go for her daughter? How far would she go to protect years of hard work, years of hopes that threatened to turn out futile? She couldn't let that happen to Naomi. So she did what she had to do. What Georgina would have done.

"Mom?" Naomi's eyes are like saucers, caked in stage makeup. And in them, Dawn doesn't exactly read gratitude. No, it's something more akin to revulsion. Dawn wants to grab her by the shoulders and give her a shake. *After all, you're the one who stole my scrip pad—and what's worse, you got caught like an idiot.*

But she knows she has her share of responsibility too. She's the one who set this thing in motion and toppled their lives.

"Anna asked me," Dawn says dryly. She's not sure whom she's speaking to: Officer Tayler, who maintains an impassive front, or Naomi, or Georgina, who looks like she's about to strangle her. "Because she wanted to get away from the academy. She wanted to get away from her mother." Yes, you, she thinks, glancing at Georgina's livid face.

"Mom, how could you?" Naomi shrieks.

Georgina rubs her eyes. This is the first time Dawn has seen her without makeup, but to her disappointment, she doesn't look horrible or like a ghoul. She looks roughly the same, maybe a little closer to her real age than usual.

"I don't believe," Georgina says. Her accent comes through stronger than usual. "If this is true, then where is she right now? Where is Anna?"

"I'm not lying. I paid the fee on her application to the modern dance program at the university. It's on my credit card statement."

Georgina's nostrils flare. "Why couldn't you just mind your own business?" she hisses.

"Please," Officer Tayler interferes. "Everyone, stay calm. Our priority right now is locating Anna."

"Exactly." Georgina raises her chin. "And let's not forget that the reason Anna is missing in the first place is because this woman"—she glares at Dawn with pure, undisguised hatred—"this woman tricked her and dragged her into this nonsense, all to aid and abet her juvenile delinquent of a daughter. Who wanted Anna's role from the start. So don't tell me to stay calm. The way I see it, Anna and I are the only victims here."

"Ms. Prescott, I understand your concern," Officer Tayler bleats.

"If not for these two, Anna would be dancing Nikiya at the

costume rehearsal right now. Dancing flawlessly," she adds with a razor-sharp glance at Naomi.

"Excuse me," says another voice. Georgina turns instinctively, and so does Officer Tayler.

"Ms. Prescott." The younger police officer in front of her looks from Georgina to Tayler and back.

"Mironoff," she snaps, out of sheer reflex.

"I think we need to have a word," he says.

Georgina draws a deep breath. "Unless you found Anna—"

"We were able to reach your ex-husband," the officer says.

A silence lingers as Georgina's mind begins to reel again. "Is Anna with Colter? At his place in Boston?"

"No. But I think you should speak with him."

"We have nothing to say to each other."

"He says he left you a voicemail," the officer says. "Please come with me."

27

One day earlier

Anna slams the bathroom door and backs away, hobbling on her foot in its brace. She makes her way down the hall, past the half-open door of her room. The door swings in the breeze that tears in through the broken window. Anna goes to sit down on the living room couch—at least there isn't glass everywhere. She buries her head in her hands.

She knew it was a stupid idea the moment she crossed the threshold of that hospital room. She never should have gone along with it. Should have told that crazy woman to fuck off, and then gone home and gone back to dancing the next day. She should have known it would escalate, that Georgina would never accept it without questioning and that things would inevitably spiral way the fuck out of control.

There has been more than enough time to kick herself for her own stupidity, but not once did she imagine it would all lead to this. Georgina, determined to press charges against Naomi? Had anyone told her this a couple of weeks ago, she would have told them they were insane.

Anna has every reason to dislike Naomi. To hate her, even. But she could never bring herself to hate her. She never wanted the rivalries, the struggles for roles. If she had gotten cast as the third Shade from the right, last row, she would have shrugged. If nothing else, she thinks she might have gone along with the whole crazy plan simply because it meant a couple of weeks off school. Except Georgina made every minute of these two magical weeks unlivable.

She should have known.

But for the first time, when she looked ahead into the future, she glimpsed, faintly, things she might actually look forward to. Her whole life wouldn't be just an extension of the present, the confined ballet life made of 6:00 a.m. rehearsals and of Georgina breathing down her neck to make sure she didn't dare eat an extra calorie. For the first time, she glimpsed a path of her own.

Except now, with every minute this madness goes on, that future grows murkier and more uncertain. Georgina will still find a way to ruin it, Anna thinks with stunning clarity. She'll still figure out how to worm her way in and poison everything.

She gets up. No need to pretend to hobble. She tiptoes to the bathroom door, but all she hears is the rush of running water. Georgina always takes long, silent baths whenever she's angry or upset over something trivial.

"Mom?" Anna calls out softly. But even if she hears her, Georgina gives no indication.

Anna's gaze turns toward the dark doorway of her room, the door still swinging on its hinges. That future she was looking forward to sharpens into a single narrow image, a thin stripe of light in the darkness.

Anna goes to her room, careful to avoid the glass shards on the floor. She retrieves her duffel from the closet, throws in only the most essential things, slings the bag over her shoulder, and exits the room. In the hallway, she puts on her light jacket even though it might not be warm enough—but she hates her coat, the off-white wool thing better suited for a fortyish divorcee. She forgets about Dawn's note she found under the door and stuffed into the pocket. She does think to grab the crutches that wait by the door, but since she doesn't really need them, she just tucks them under her arm.

And she leaves the apartment, shutting the door quietly behind her and letting it lock.

It's not the impulsive decision it looks like. As she makes her way outside, she becomes aware that it's been a long time coming. She just didn't think it would happen like this, in the middle of the night, and so soon.

But now that the opportunity has presented itself, Anna has gone and taken it, like she did that evening when Dawn came to see her on the old staircase.

As soon as she's far enough from home, she sits down on a

nearby bench and wrenches the brace off her foot. It's only been a couple of weeks, but already the foot feels weaker than the other, which throws her into a panic at first. She rolls her ankle and points, flexes, curls and uncurls her toes until she's certain she can walk without limping.

Then she throws the brace into a trash can. She leaves the crutches carefully leaning against the back of the bench.

The bus station is uncrowded at this hour, welcoming her with its smell of fumes and burnt rubber. To Anna's luck, the next bus to Boston leaves in fifteen minutes. She buys a ticket with cash. She's been saving for a while; a little here, a little there, she'd ask Georgina for a few bucks for makeup or hair products or simply nick a handful of twenties from her purse. The irony isn't lost on her that it was always Naomi who had the cash, a seemingly endless supply. But it's so difficult to trick the ever-vigilant Georgina, who orders all of Anna's pointe shoes and costumes herself, of course, and lunch money is out of the question. She and Naomi never talked about it, and Anna thinks her best friend still assumes she has no idea where the cash comes from.

The sleepy woman behind the counter doesn't care about the origin of the carefully folded bills. She counts them, plunks the change down onto the counter under the Plexiglas with a clink, and then slides the bus ticket over to Anna. Minutes later, the bus pulls up, hissing and shuddering like a giant, grimy beast. With one lazy glance at her ticket, the conductor lets her onto the bus. She takes a seat by the window and waits for the boarding to end, for the doors to hiss closed and for the bus to lurch away from the terminal, out onto the dark road.

There. She left home.

Has it always been that easy, and she just didn't know?

28

EVERYTHING DIDN'T START to fall apart with that phone call from the hospital, telling Georgina her daughter had broken her metatarsal. It had been falling apart for a lot longer than that. Maybe it went all the way back to before Anna was born, all the way to Georgina's last ballet.

She was supposed to be on top of the world. She had every reason to be. She finally had everything she ever wanted, and the world was supposed to be at her feet.

The truth was that she'd struggled through ballet school. Almost nobody knew about it, and at this point, she had practically forgotten about it herself. It didn't correspond to her own idea of this new, reinvented Zoya Mironova, with a better name and a biography to match. But she'd spent long years in the dreaded classroom spot by the piano, literally watching from the sidelines as the real stars did their battements and tendus in the center spot in front of the big mirror.

Gradually she moved up, gravitating toward the center of

the classroom and, eventually, to the back, to the corps de ballet of a renowned company. It was nerve-racking, awaiting the decision about which corps dancers would go on tour to America; she still remembered the feeling, the all-consuming anxiety that undermined her balance, her confidence, her appetite and sleep. Her hair started to fall out from stress. But at the last moment, one of the chosen girls twisted her ankle, and so Georgina took her place.

She swore that never again would she find herself in this situation, her fate at the mercy of random chance and the clemency of others. But to be a ballerina was to be exactly that, even though she, low ranking at her old company, suddenly found herself a soloist at the new place, where she was hired on the spot. It was the eighties, the USSR's evil-empire patina had dulled somewhat, but still, it all made such an impressive and romantic story: a leap of faith into nothingness.

She was made principal dancer when she was twenty-seven. That was the year that the hairline fracture made its first appearance. That summer, after many furtive doctor visits, the last X-ray before the new season showed that the fracture was on the mend. Which would have to be good enough. That year she danced Myrtha, a short but punishing principal role in *Giselle*, and fucking it up wasn't an option. Finally she pushed through and got rewarded for her efforts with the role of Raymonda in the premiere.

That's when Georgina Mironoff, prima ballerina, was officially born.

But even as she stepped into the very spotlight she'd spent her whole life coveting, the darkness that lurks at the edges of every triumph began to creep up.

The fall she danced the lead in *Swan Lake*, the hairline fracture appeared again. Georgina made it through the season on painkillers and a prayer. Her doctor was unequivocal: She had to spend the summer resting, or else.

Easier said than done, especially when no one at the company could know.

Colter came along just in time. She got off the stage after dancing Juliet to be surprised with a bouquet of white roses. A card hidden among the exquisite blooms spelled out a name that sounded ridiculous to her: Colter Prescott. She was this close to throwing the card in the trash when the AD burst into the dressing room and practically dragged her out to meet the company's esteemed patrons, who turned out to be Colter and his elderly mother.

She still remembers his words to her, clear as day: *No matter what, no one dances like the Russians.* Then he kissed her hand. *I didn't know Georgina was a Russian name.*

She told him it was a flower in Russian. The next day she got another bouquet: pink dahlias, each one as big as her head.

She spent the summer with Colter on his yacht in Majorca, and in the fall, she came back with a (seemingly) healthy foot and a giant rock on her ring finger. If she were composing and choreographing her own life like a ballet, she couldn't have done better.

All the girls at the company hated her. Has there ever been a more certain marker of success?

She had it all for one season, almost one whole season from September to June. Not quite a year. But those few months—no one could take them away from her. Most people wish they could live for fifteen minutes the way she lived for ten whole months.

It was just before Christmas, during one performance of the obligatory *Nutcracker*, that the metatarsal hairline fracture returned. That whole performance was unlucky from the start: In the first act, a ribbon came off her pointe shoe, and to this day, she thinks it was sabotage, even though it would have been difficult to pull off. Nearly impossible, even, but what hadn't ill-wishers tried over the years? She'd been upset. Because of that, and because of other things.

And God knows that if there could have been some way to blame what happened next on the other dancers, she would have. But, sadly, no one had control over her metatarsal except her. Not even her. In the final pas de deux, familiar pain lanced her foot and shot all the way up, traveling along her nerves like electricity to explode in her chest. After the show, Dex, her dance partner, found her in the dressing room, sweat running down her forehead and streaking her thick stage makeup as she frantically pressed an ice pack into the top of her foot, which had turned blue.

She felt so raw in that moment, so exposed. Vulnerability

had never been her strong suit, but now she found it absolutely intolerable.

Maybe that was the moment she could have changed things. Turned her destiny around. But she didn't see the opportunity, and she still isn't sure it would have made a difference. As it happened, she only looked up at him. Their gazes met, locked, tension sizzling in the air like a violin string pulled tighter and tighter until it snapped.

Shut the fucking door, she hissed. *I never want to see you again.*

The last ballet of the season was *La Bayadère*. The AD hinted to her that if she didn't feel like tackling the main role, she could take the time off, but that was out of the question. She never once so much as hiccupped about her injury and could only guess how he figured out something was wrong. Of course, that meant that she had to deny it—to prove him wrong, no matter the cost.

She hadn't even wanted to dance the role in the first place. She had never liked *La Bayadère*. She no longer even remembered why, but it must have been some exam where she didn't do a variation to her teacher's liking. But she found it distasteful from start to finish, the costumes that didn't fit with the dance itself, the derivative story, Minkus's banal pseudo-baroque score whose simple little melodies got stuck in her head and refused to be dislodged. It lacked the raw emotion of *Swan Lake* or the ethereal beauty of *Giselle* or the simple perfection of *Romeo and*

Juliet. Besides, Gamzatti was the other principal dancer, who had been there longer than Georgina and saw her as an intruder on her territory.

It all boded poorly.

Worse yet, that's when Colter, who was all too aware of her metatarsal problems since he was the one to pay the medical bills, began to gently but firmly press her that perhaps she could take a year off. Or even two. If they wanted to have children, it would be better to do it before she was too old. Why not kill two birds with one stone?

But only Georgina knew, on a deep, almost genetic level, that if she took a year off, hell, if she took even a fucking minute off, she would never come back to the place it had taken her her entire life to conquer.

And so she swore to herself that she would defend it to the last.

When she said that, she probably didn't mean it so literally. Because at the second performance, her bone split apart. Her dance partner all but carried her from the stage, and the B-cast lead had to dance the last act.

There was, effectively, no way back. Or so she thought, because now Colter's voice, distorted slightly by the static of the phone, drags her right back into the past—the past that has decided to come back to haunt her.

"I know everything. I should have seen it sooner, and it's not like I haven't suspected it for a long time. I just didn't think you were this treacherous. I'll put Anna back on my health insurance plan only for her sake, Georgina, because none of this is her fault. But I've cut you off financially, and it's staying this way—and you don't really want to go through the court. Anna told me everything, and we got the paternity tests done. But I want absolutely nothing more to do with you, so don't contact me again."

Just as well, Georgina thinks. It will be her pleasure.

29

Anna didn't let Dex know she was coming. She was afraid that he'd talk her out of it, or, worse yet, call her mother, and such a betrayal would splinter their budding relationship. As soon as she got on the bus, she took the regular SIM card out of her phone and replaced it with the other one, the one Georgina didn't know about. She used it for everything she didn't want her hypervigilant mother to be aware of. Georgina wasn't above snooping, reading texts, and scanning the monthly phone bill.

Anna supposed that she could easily be traced to the bus stop by her phone, but it didn't matter. She wasn't really hiding from anyone, not even Georgina any longer. She just didn't want to be bothered.

At the bus terminal in Boston, she clambers out of her narrow seat and exits with a little nod of thanks to the driver. The terminal slowly begins to wake up; people wait at the curbside, pace semi-energetically back and forth, line up in front of the coffee and doughnut shop. It's very late, or very early, depending on your perspective.

She wouldn't mind a coffee and something to eat—the siren song of the greasy treats Georgina would never allow her to have is strong. But she decides not to delay any further. She hails a taxi, and within twenty minutes of weaving in and out of thin traffic, she's at the door of his building.

She's never been here before. After she initially looked him up and then contacted him, they met in other places at first, in public, until she was sure he could be trusted. Anna never really thought of herself as spoiled, not with the army discipline of Georgina's household and then the ballet school. But she feels intimidated. Unprepared for what she's seeing around her. The building is covered in graffiti almost to the second floor, and the windows have bars. The lock on the front door is broken, and it creaks open without resistance. Anna climbs a claustrophobia-inducing staircase to the fourth floor and finds herself facing his front door.

She can still turn back. All she has to do is turn around, make her way down, switch the SIM cards in her phone again, and call Georgina. Or just wait for one of the million calls Georgina is no doubt making right now to come through.

But that would mean conceding defeat forever. Georgina will sweep in triumphantly on a cloud of I-told-you-so's and drag Anna back home, back to the academy and to the stage and to Nikiya's rhinestone-studded bra. And then her life will resume exactly as before. She can't allow that to happen, not only because of all the craziness she unwittingly unleashed, but also because earlier that evening, she got an email. The dean of admissions wanted to meet her.

She can't throw that away.

So she raises her hand and presses her fingertip down on the doorbell. The sound resonates hoarsely behind the door, and for a moment, she fears that no one's there. There are no steps, nothing at all that she can make out, right until she hears the click of the lock and the door creaks open.

And when she looks at him, she knows that she's in the right place.

30

"I'M GOING," GEORGINA says.

"There's no need." Officer Tayler, she swears, looks amused as hell. Not every day she gets to witness such a showdown. "I've contacted the Boston Police Department. They'll drop by Dex Carey's address to check."

"Check?" Georgina demands. "You need to get her away from him."

The woman is unflappable. "Do you believe he poses a danger to Anna?"

Georgina opens her mouth and closes it. All the manic energy leaves her at once, and she feels like she might implode any second. Does he pose a danger to Anna?

No, probably not. He's her father, for God's sake.

Georgina still wonders how things could have been different. She thinks of every turning point, every decision made, and her mind goes straight to the alternate paths and all the ghostly possible outcomes that shimmer in the distance. A part of her knows that these outcomes are like the Shades in *La Bayadère*: enticing but no longer possible, tempting but not real. And does she really want them in the first place? It may feel like another life to her, but it still happened; she was once a little girl in a small Siberian town, surrounded by ruin and bleakness. She didn't want to return to it. She knows there's nothing noble about poverty, obscurity, and misery. She made the right choices. No one could argue with that.

But what if, instead of *shut the fucking door*, she'd said something else?

You can't go through life guided by whims and emotions. Not if you want to amount to anything. At least ballet has taught her that. This is how she always rationalized it. No one who let their emotions rule their life came to a good end.

And what if she had? Her life would be different indeed. So would Anna's. For all she knows, there might not have been an Anna, and would she want that?

No, she thinks with sudden clarity and a feeling of profound peace that fills her soul. I *have* done everything right. No one may ever thank her for it, least of all her own daughter, but Georgina doesn't regret any of it.

"I'm still going," she says, and raises her chin haughtily. She's still Georgina Mironoff, and no one can take that away. "I'll drive there myself if I have to."

31

"It's a small place," Dex says apologetically as he nods at the chair by the kitchen table. Anna gives a polite nod. *As if I can't see that.* There is no kitchen proper, or living or dining room—all three are the same cramped, overcrowded space. The small TV on the wall is right above the table, and an armchair in the corner serves as a sofa.

She pulls out the chair and sits. Dex is putting the kettle on the prehistoric gas stove. He's doing it to cover the awkward silence, but she won't lie, she could go for a coffee.

"It's cozy," she says. On the wall are ballet posters and framed photographs. Her gaze slides along them: One captures Dex midjump, his body one taut, perfect line. He used to be famous for his jumps. This is where Anna gets hers from, she now understands. The athleticism that Anna possesses, despite her delicate looks, was never Georgina's thing.

There's a newer photo of Dex, a little heavier and without such a nice head of hair, with a group of his students at the ballet school where he teaches. It's not a dedicated ballet academy like De Vere, but a little studio at a strip mall that also offers tap dancing and Zumba on the weekends.

Why didn't he parlay his long ballet career into something more prestigious? She wonders but knows she won't work up the courage to ask. And at the same time, she understands that, in the words of Fabienne, to ask a question is to answer it. That photo holds the answers: This is without a doubt what awaited Georgina after she retired from the stage. It wasn't enough. It never would have been enough.

As irony would have it, Anna finally spots the photo hanging right next to the one at the dance studio. She first found it online when she looked up her mother in her dancing days, which prompted the whole search that ultimately led her here. In person, the photo looks even more impressive. She recognizes Dex, whom she's only met a handful of times, before she recognizes her own mother. Dex looks similar, only younger, but Georgina...there's something about her face that makes her look like a completely different person. The two of them are in the middle of the pas de deux in *Swan Lake*, frozen in a perfect pose. Georgina, in her Swan Queen costume, looks angelic, and it's not just the feathery headdress and the makeup. Her face is different, not just because she's younger but also because of something else, some kind of glow that comes not from the flattering stage lights but from within. It makes Anna struggle to remember the last time she saw her mother dance, and eventually come to the realization that she's never seen it.

The sadness that fills Anna comes as a surprise. Georgina looks so different. She transcends. This is what made her a great ballerina, and not the height of her jumps or the flexibility of her ankles. You can see that it's not the spotlight or the stage or the attention that she loves, but the act of dancing itself. It's a fragile magic you can only see in person, but this photo captured it.

What is it like, Anna finds herself wondering. To be deprived of the thing you love the most, for years and years and years? To be unceremoniously left behind and forgotten by the art to which you gave your all?

"That's the famous *Swan Lake*," Dex is saying. She gives a start because she didn't hear him come up behind her, lost in her thoughts. "We got a standing ovation for that performance. There was an article in the *Globe*."

"Were you already—"

"Together?" He smiles. "Yes. We were together. We'd been together since she was a first soloist."

He makes it sound like they never broke up, Anna thinks.

"She was such a beautiful Myrtha," Dex is saying. "She worked tirelessly on that role. Never has a promotion been more deserved. And she proved them right with *Swan Lake*. She was a force of nature."

That, Anna can't disagree with.

"If only I'd known about the injury, maybe I would have done things differently," Dex says. "Maybe she wouldn't have left."

"I doubt it," Anna replies. She's not trying to hurt his feelings, on the contrary, but she sees him wince and regrets her words.

"It was so—out of nowhere. I had no idea. She suddenly got sneaky, secretive. And then...One day we're madly in love, and the next she's going to Europe with some rich asshole for the whole summer." He glances sideways at Anna. "Sorry."

"I went to boarding school," Anna says. "I've heard worse."

"I didn't understand it. I was hurt, and jealous, and I made things worse. Or at least I thought so. Then she came back with that ring on her finger, and that was that. She was married, and we were done. I'd lost her before I even realized it. She refused to talk to me and made the AD give her a different dance partner. Everyone said it was her best season ever. So maybe I'm the one who doesn't get it."

"But it was you, though," Anna says. "You danced Solor in *La Bayadère* that time."

"It's true." He lowers his chin.

"How did you make that happen?"

"I didn't. The other guy refused to partner with her because he said she was being difficult. The AD went nuts and almost fired him. Georgina went nuts and almost refused to dance at all. I kind of wish she had."

"But in the end, she did dance," Anna says. "And the rest is history."

Dex is silent for a long moment.

"I never understood why she didn't go back," he says. "Once her foot had healed."

"She was thirty-five," Anna says with a shrug. "She never explicitly said so, but she insinuated it. She was too old to go back. That's why she was pressing me to go audition instead of going to college. Because the dancing years, she said, are short. Before you know it, it's over."

"But she was Georgina Mironoff," he says. "A big name. A star. She could have gone back. There had to be another reason…"

Anna says nothing because she suspects that the other reason is sitting in front of her. She's hit with the oddest kind of cognitive dissonance: not simply pity for Georgina but sympathy. Georgina once danced, and loved, and hoped. And when ballet was taken from her, only a bitter shell of a woman remained. She'll never again have that look on her face like in the Swan Queen photo, that glow that's almost holy.

"But that wasn't it," Anna says. It's not really a question because she can do basic math. "She came back. Not to the stage but to you."

"She did." Her father—how strange is that?—lowers his head.

Except Georgina couldn't do it in the end, couldn't give up all her material comforts and status and the promise of a well-off future—for what? Love. It's such an odd concept. Georgina in love.

"Does she know where you are?" Dex asks, and Anna winces. She pulls her gaze away from the photo with some difficulty.

"She probably does by now."

"So you'll have to dance in the end-of-year show after all," Dex says softly. "You shouldn't have done that, the stunt with the fake injury. That was cruel."

"There's no other way to stand up to her. For as long as I'm physically able, she'll find a way. She'll drag me onto that stage herself if she has to."

"Maybe you should cut her some slack. You really are an exceptional dancer. I was at the competition, remember? I saw your grand pas classique."

She feels herself blush. "I fucked it up," she says. "I stumbled—"

"Didn't fool me," he says. "Or the judges. You did get silver."

"I don't even know if I like ballet!" Anna explodes. "Before I ever got a chance to decide for myself, I was already balancing in pointe shoes. And by then, I'd come too far to turn back. Maybe I want to be—I don't know, a veterinarian? An architect?"

"Is that why you applied to the modern dance program?"

Anna's face grows warmer still.

"You've had a sheltered life, Anna," he continues. "You think you can turn your back on all this any moment and never regret it. You don't know the real value of being the best at something. You were chosen—by luck, or a mysterious concordance of luck and genes and possibility. It doesn't matter how or why. You were chosen. You can't just ignore that."

"So I was *chosen*," she grumbles. "So what? I'll be great for five years, ten, and after? I'll end up like Georgina." *Or like you.*

"Or maybe you end up making history. You have no idea how many people would kill to have the choice that you have before you."

Anna thinks of Naomi. "I know," she says darkly. "They literally would."

The doorbell trills insistently, once, twice, three times, and refuses to stop.

"I think," Dex says, "they're here for you."

32

ANNA IS COMING back, and she's going to dance Nikiya, and everything will be back to the status quo like nothing happened, like Dawn's own life and her daughter's isn't lying broken in its wake.

Naomi is in big trouble. Despair creeps into Dawn's soul, dark and thick as tar. Sinister words with their sinister meanings swirl in her head: words like *bail* and *lawyer* and *juvenile detention*. She's going to need money, more money she doesn't have because it all went to pointe shoes and tuition and pointless little costumes because apparently every sequin on those is worth thirty dollars. No money, and now, probably, no job, because she doubts the hospital will take kindly to the fake-injury thing. Naomi thought that she didn't care—that she never cared—but proving her wrong has cost Dawn everything.

And the worst thing about it isn't even the risk of prison or the possibility of a criminal record that will hobble Naomi for life. By the time all these troubles are over, after they deal with the accusations and possibility of a trial and everything that entails, it'll already be too late. Even in the best-case scenario, Naomi will have missed her chance.

Because people like them only have one chance to begin with. Even if Anna's broken metatarsal had been real, once the bone healed, she would have picked up seamlessly where she left off with the help of all the gold threads of her security net. But Naomi—Naomi always was one accident, one misfortune, one stroke of bad luck away from losing her dream forever. That has been the thought that has kept Dawn up at night ever since Naomi's first beginners' class at the mall studio. That was the thought she could never bring herself to articulate.

Naomi only ever had one chance, and now it has disintegrated before her eyes.

The house is deathly quiet. All the lights are out. Dawn sits alone in the kitchen, facing the counter piled high with dishes from a week ago, and she can't summon the will to get up and switch on the ceiling light. She turns her phone over and over in her hands, its screen the only source of light. Finally she selects a number and dials it.

"Officer Tayler, please." Her voice is hoarse and too loud in the empty kitchen. She clears her throat. She owes this—owes it to Naomi. "Yes, this is Dawn Thompson. Naomi's mother," she specifies unnecessarily. "There's something I need to tell you. To confess."

33

CODA

IT'S BEEN A week since everything unraveled. The longest week of my life. I used to be the only one to think that time flew in ballet class, but now it no longer flies—it drags. It's like dancing with weights around my ankles. Even my jumps, so good once upon a time, are now weak. When I see myself in the mirrored wall, it's like I'm looking at someone else, and when I finally land with that dreadful, heavy thud, the look on my face is that of bewilderment. Surprise that I landed at all.

On Friday I enter the building a little later than everyone else. It's a strategy to avoid all those looks of pity: *Here's the girl whose mom is going to jail.* I don't know why Dawn did that. I'm lying. Of course I know why she did that, but it doesn't matter. What was she thinking?

This time, I'm really *really* late. Class has already started. I'm alone in the hall, my steps echoing eerily along those walls covered with photographs of other ballerinas, other girls with a dream. I pass the photo of Anna, and just like always, I don't want to look but I can't avoid it. She has that ballet smile plastered on her face even though her performance has ended. Nothing genuine about it, but it's expected, and that's Anna for you—she never disappoints. Even when she wobbles or falls or fails and fakes a goddamn broken metatarsal, she never lets anybody down. They take her back with open arms, every single time. Her whole life is a performance, even the ugly parts.

That's okay. I'm not going to class anyway.

I head straight to Alexandra's office. The door is closed, but just as I raise my hand to knock, it flies open in my face. Walter storms out. That's too mild a word, and I brace myself to be yelled at, but he hardly seems aware I'm there. He just thunders past me and disappears around the corner.

I go in. Alexandra is at her desk, and she doesn't look up. "I thought you had more pride than that," she says quietly. I freeze in my tracks, blood rushing to my face, but then realize she thinks I'm Walter who came back to grovel.

"Hi," I say. She looks up at last, but her expression doesn't shift.

"Naomi," she says in an almost bored voice. "What brings you here?"

I draw a breath. "I would like to drop out, effective immediately."

She looks at me motionlessly for a few seconds. I'm starting to get unnerved when she speaks at last.

"Drop out? Well, isn't that interesting. Graduation is in two weeks. Why?"

"I think you know why."

She gives a thin-lipped smile. "You can drop out if you want to, but if you ask me, you're making a big mistake."

"I'm not asking you."

Her gaze darts, lightning fast, over my shoulder. "Close the door," she says, lowering her voice. I obey. When I shut the door and turn back to face her, the look on her face is completely different. I see naked hostility in it. "Your mother made a big sacrifice, you know," Alexandra says. "She took the fall for something *you* did. Something very, very serious. She's probably going to jail, all so that you could finish your year and graduate. And, not the least of it, dance in the final performance."

"Well, I don't want to do any of that," I say. "Not anymore."

Alexandra laughs. I don't think I've ever heard Alexandra laugh. I don't think anyone has. It's a little unsettling. Even her laughter has a stiff quality to it. "Then you're an idiot," she says with shocking bluntness, the laughter cutting off as abruptly as it started. "Do you think I don't know what's been going on with you? I know. Everybody knows, all the teachers and students. This doesn't exactly reflect well on the school, does it?"

"Then why not throw me out?" I snarl. "Why not just expel me? Why continue with the charade? Not because my mom made a sacrifice, as you say. You don't give a shit about my mom, Alexandra. You don't give a shit about anyone but yourself. That's why you brought Walter in. So you could have a shot."

She doesn't even flinch at my words. "The only reason we didn't throw you out on your ass a long time ago," she says, "is because, like it or not, we have no one to dance Gamzatti in case Sarah doesn't make it out of rehab. There. It's a shame, but it is what it is. Do whatever you want, Naomi, but I hope you stay on. Who knows, maybe out there in the audience there will be some recruiter who doesn't happen to have an internet connection."

I leave the office without another word. Out in the hall, a big clock tells me there's still more than a half hour until the end of class. I have nowhere to be. So I just slide down the wall and sit on the floor, stretching my legs out in front of me, reflexively pointing and flexing my feet and rolling my ankles like it still fucking matters. Before I know it, tears are rolling down my face. I wipe them away with my sleeve, but more come. The cuff of my sweatshirt is black from my runny mascara.

"It'll be okay," comes a familiar voice from above. I shudder, my head snaps up, and I find myself looking at Anna, all in white like a ghostly apparition from the second act of *La Bayadère*. She looks beautiful, her foundation dewy after her morning stretch, her waist tiny and wrists thin. My gaze drops to her foot, which is now free of the plastic boot, matching its twin in a freshly broken-in, cream-colored pointe shoe with satin ribbons. Perfection restored.

"What do you want?" I snarl. "And why aren't you in class? Don't you have a principal role to dance in two weeks?"

"Don't you?" she asks. Those fabulous, lean, sinewy legs fold as she comes to sit next to me on the floor. "I didn't feel like going. Walter will forgive me."

Of course Walter will forgive you. Everyone always forgives you. The strangeness of the situation doesn't escape me. It's thick in the air, hovering over the two of us like a fog. We're alone in an empty hallway, snuggled up against the wall, sharing our deepest secrets, BFFs again.

"I just wanted to make sure you were okay," Anna says.

"Why do you care if I'm okay? I threw a rock through your window."

"Look, I didn't mean for it all to happen the way it did."

I look at her, that sweet face and earnest eyes, Ballet Barbie in a $500 leotard. And gradually it all becomes clear to me. "That's such bullshit, Anna."

"We're best friends," she says, a non sequitur if I ever heard one. "We've been best friends since we were little. I never wanted to harm you. Even though you're a giant bitch."

I expected this, and still it feels like a slap.

"I could never bring myself to be mad at you," she's saying, "because I've always felt a little sorry for you."

"*Sorry,*" I echo. "Yeah, poor little Naomi, always second best."

"I never felt threatened by you," Anna says pensively, tilting her head. "Maybe that's why I let all your schemes slide. You really think I knew nothing? James told me what you did *months* ago. That you bribed him with painkillers to sleep with me and then dump me before the competition. And I'm betting that's what happened with that recording too."

I'm struck speechless. She knew this whole time?

"Oh God, if you could only imagine the things I know," Anna says with a laugh. She sounds like her normal self—like my best friend. Like she's about to share some juicy gossip. "I'm so sick of you all. If only my talent was something I could just give away. Here! Take it if you want it so much. But you know what? Someone recently told me that being the best at something is the greatest gift one can imagine." She gets to her feet with such lightness and ease you'd think her narrow, taut body was full of feathers. "Anyway, I have to go. You keep practicing those fouettés!" She starts down the hall before looking over her shoulder and adding, "You've got to keep your core pulled in! That's been the secret all along. Aren't you lucky I'm your friend?"

Her steps are so light that the moment she turns the corner, I can't hear them anymore. Like she vanished into thin air.

It's not hard to hate Anna Prescott.

But right now, I can't bring myself to do even that.

34

APOTHEOSIS

IT'S A DREAM come true.

Tonight's the night of the final performance, and Georgina still can't believe her luck. She's thanking her lucky stars, counting her blessings, embracing all these American clichés. Clad in a somewhat aged but still perfectly fitted designer shift dress, her face made up and shaded and blended, wearing her biggest diamonds to emphasize her ballerina neck—the one thing that hasn't changed over the years even as her face and figure became an uphill battle to maintain—she idles in the reception hall with a glass of champagne in hand. She takes the tiniest sip, fighting the temptation to drown her nervousness in the bittersweet, fizzy drink.

Not that there's any real reason to be nervous. Anna is back where she belongs. When Georgina saw her off, she had changed into her act one costume and was stretching backstage. Released from the plastic boot, her leg got back into shape remarkably quickly—Georgina had to remind herself that there never was anything wrong with it. She wanted to stay until curtain call to run Anna through the warm-up herself, then to help her with the stage makeup and hair, but Fabienne joyfully booted her out. *Anna's a big girl*, she said with a grin. Georgina knows she's right and that she meant well, yet somehow that comment rubbed her the wrong way. A big girl, indeed. About to dance Nikiya in *La Bayadère*. About to graduate from the De Vere Ballet Academy. About to fend off recruiters falling all over themselves to sign her. Anna is all grown up.

Georgina is alarmed by the stinging she feels behind her eyes. Her makeup is not waterproof. She takes another tiny sip of champagne.

Everything is for the best, she tells herself, playing with the diamonds in the hollow of her throat. A present from Anna's father. Well—no, she won't dwell on that. She left her mistakes in the past, where mistakes belong.

Alexandra knows all about that. It still makes Georgina smile when she thinks about it. Last week, she had a discreet meeting with her in her office after school hours. No one knew, not even Anna, although Georgina supposes she'll find out soon. But by then Anna will be dancing with some prestigious company all the way across the country, and Georgina will stay here, in this little town where fate once led her.

Alexandra was cold and formal. "Is this about Anna?" she

asked. Everything is about Anna, Georgina thought. Everything was always about Anna. Until now. Now she was there for herself.

"Because otherwise, you shouldn't be here," Alexandra said.

"You never used to mind," Georgina pointed out. "Especially when you needed my help, or my contact list. I'm here with a proposition. I want you to hire me."

Alexandra measured her with a look but said nothing.

"Think about it. You—and the school—have everything to gain."

"You're thinking of teaching?" Alexandra asked carefully. "But—"

"Not teaching, no. I was thinking—something along the lines of official event coordinator. I'll take care of all the galas and fundraisers and you name it. To the best of my considerable abilities."

"We don't have such a position," Alexandra said.

"Then create one," Georgina replied with a shrug. "I think you'll manage to convince the owners. You know why?"

"Georgina, if this is about the money again…" Alexandra dropped her voice, unnecessarily. There was no one to overhear them—Georgina had made sure the door was shut and that no one lurked outside.

"I bet there's something you don't know," she said. "That police officer…Tyler…Taylor…whatever. It doesn't matter anymore. Back when I first called her in a panic when Anna went missing, when she was asking me questions about where Anna might be, she asked me if there was anything else I had to report. Any other suspicious goings-on that could have something to do with Anna disappearing. And you know what I told her?"

"Georgina..." Alexandra lowered her voice even further, to a whisper.

"You look like you've seen a ghost," Georgina told her with a laugh. "Relax. I had my wits about me. I told her there was absolutely nothing else going on at the school that needed the attention of law enforcement."

She watched the other woman slowly exhale.

"That's right, Alexandra. I lied to the police for you. Surely you have some kind of sense of gratitude for that."

Alexandra pretended to think about it. "But how would we pay you? The budget..."

"With all the negative publicity you've had lately, you're hemorrhaging donors. The way I see it, my salary will pay for itself. If anything, you can't afford *not* to hire me."

And so it has just been made final. Georgina works at the De Vere Ballet Academy, officially on the payroll. It'll be announced at the staff meeting before the next year starts.

The good news didn't end there. Just a couple of days ago, Walter announced that, to his great regret, he would not be staying on as artistic director and head choreographer. He was headed to the UK to pursue other projects. That was the announcement, at least. The truth was that several parents had expressed concern about Walter working alone with teenage girls for such long hours. And in our current climate...blah, blah, blah.

Things are looking up, indeed. Georgina glances around at all the other parents schmoozing and swigging overpriced champagne as they wait to watch their children perform their final ballet at the academy. There's probably a few million dollars' worth of jewelry in this room right now, she thinks. But she has something none of them have: She has Anna. For all their privileges in life, their own daughters will be identical Shades, hopping and bourrée-ing in the corps de ballet while Anna gets to be the star. As she deserves.

This is where her life has brought her, finally. When she made the leap of faith during her last fateful tour, this may not have been what she envisioned, but now that she looks around, she can't help but feel a certain happiness.

And isn't happiness, after all, the foundation of that strange thing they call the American dream?

The first bell chimes, the melody rolling above everyone's heads. Georgina puts down her glass, forty dollars' worth of Veuve untouched, and heads toward the entrance to the auditorium.

Anna checks the time on her phone. Still twenty minutes left until curtain call. It takes about five to walk back to the auditorium, so that leaves her fifteen minutes alone. It's long enough. She dials the number that she no longer has to hide. No need for a second phone, for subterfuge or sneaking around. Georgina knows that Anna is in touch with her father, her real father. She just has to deal with it. And she has been dealing with it surprisingly well. Anna thinks she might be just pretending it's not happening.

Anna perches at the very top of the staircase that leads to nowhere while the phone rings. She flexes and points her feet in her performance pointe shoes that match her costume to an exact degree. Dex picks up after only a couple of rings.

"What's up?" he asks. "Isn't your show about to start?"

"It is," she confesses.

"I really wish I could be there."

"It's fine," she says, and means it. The last thing she wants on the day of the final show is a meltdown from Georgina because Dex dared show his face. She might be okay with the idea of Anna hypothetically talking to him on the phone a couple of times a week, but Anna decided not to push her luck.

"I know you'll be amazing," he says.

"I didn't call for a pep talk," she says, and almost adds *Dad*. It's still weird for both of them, and she's glad she caught herself. "I have some news."

"Oh?"

"I just got my offer of admission to the modern dance program," she says. She's smiling, and she wonders if he can hear it in her voice. "I haven't told anyone yet. Not even Georgina. Especially not Georgina."

"Congratulations. Not that I doubted you. So what do you want to do?"

"Do?" she blinks.

"Do you want to accept, or would you rather go audition at companies? Maybe I can put a word in."

"No," she says. "No need to put a word in."

"You want to make it on your own. Got it. Anyway, after the show, they'll be lining up to sign you. You won't need me."

Anna bites her lip. She's silent for a beat too long, and he picks up on it. "Anna, is something the matter?"

She sighs. "I ... I don't know if I should go dance."

Now it's his turn to be silent, and she wonders if he's judging her. *Not this again! We've been over this. Make up your mind, girl!*

"Why don't you want to dance?" he asks instead, his voice gentle.

"It's not even that I don't want to. I just don't know how. Everyone is acting like nothing happened. Like everything just went back to normal and I'm expected to pick up where I left off. Put on my pointe shoes, slap the shit-eating grin on my face, and go do my pirouettes. And I don't know if I can. Not with everything I now know about everyone. James, Naomi, my mom, everyone. How full of shit they all are. I'm supposed to go out there and act like everything is so fucking beautiful, you know?"

He chuckles softly in the phone. "Oh, don't I know it."

She feels a rush of relief. "I knew you'd understand."

"And if you decide not to dance, know that I'll support your decision. I've got your back, no matter what."

Anna's eyes sting. Good thing the stage makeup is tornado-proof. "Thank you," she says. "Dad."

She hangs up the phone and looks at the screen, at the background image of a ballerina caught midleap into nothing. Funny how it is, she thinks. You don't see the before, all the hard work that had to be done to make this perfect moment happen; and you don't see the after. You just have to trust that the landing will be as spectacular as the jump itself. Do your best every single time, they say, and you'll stick the landing, but the truth is, it's not always on you. Sometimes you can do your best and still lose control for one fateful second, sending everything crashing down. In the end, you can never be sure there will be a safe spot to land on, and yet you have to leap, over and over and over again. Just trust yourself, trust your every muscle to hold you, trust your feet not to wobble.

Trust fate to catch you.

Out in the auditorium, Georgina takes her place. The final bell chimes, and the conversations all around her die down as softly and gradually as the lights overhead dim. The only light is now on the heavy velvet curtain. The music starts, a gentle river of beautiful sound, and the crowd holds its collective breath. The energy in the air in that moment—it's incomparable, unlike anything else Georgina has ever experienced. She takes a discreet glance sideways, at the faces of the others, and sees that they're feeling the same. Their expressions are soft, almost holy, their eyes on the curtain even though nothing is happening yet. For the next ninety minutes, nothing exists except what's on that stage.

The music swells, the velvet curtain floats aside, and everything dissolves into light.

ACKNOWLEDGMENTS

Writing a novel may be a solitary process, but turning that novel into a book sure isn't one! I'd like to thank all the people who helped me bring this story to life. A special thank-you to my editor, Alex Logan, and everyone else who helped me navigate the complexities of publishing.

To my friends and family, your unwavering support and encouragement kept me grounded and inspired throughout this process. Your belief in me made all the difference.

Finally, to the readers, bloggers, reviewers, and Bookstagrammers: Thank you for being there for me and my books. Your support means more than words can say, and I hope this story finds a place in your hearts.

ABOUT THE AUTHOR

NINA LAURIN studied creative writing at Concordia University in Montreal, where she currently lives. She arrived there when she was just twelve years old, and she speaks and reads Russian, French, and English but writes her novels in English. She wrote her first novel while getting her writing degree, and *Girl Last Seen* was a bestseller a year later in 2017.

Nina is fascinated by the darker side of mundane things, and she's always on the lookout for her next twisted book idea. Learn more at NinaLaurin.com.